SERPENTS OF THE DUST

ISBN: 978-1-964660-04-2

"They shall be burnt with hunger, and devoured with burning heat, and with bitter destruction: I will also send the teeth of beasts upon them, with the poison of serpents of the dust."
(Deuteronomy, 32:24)

One

The mouth had a slight smile, as if contemplating a truth that escaped others. The lips open, whispering of promises more than fulfilled. The eyes were a distant, mystic green as if looking at far-away places. The arms were long, toned and tanned. The legs were the same, with just a hint of fleshiness at the top. Her hair was shoulder length, deep brown, lush. Breasts full, firm yet gently soft. *Every young man's dream*, Detective-Sergeant Cassius Toledo thought. He frowned because this increased the list of possible suspects exponentially. *Every young man's dream can become his nightmare.* In the strange hierarchy of vengeance murder, the best victim is a very unattractive, overweight individual of about fifty, with few friends, and a dysfunctional family.

If one of them has a violent criminal history so much the better, Toledo mused, as he peered closely at the breasts. No sign of trauma on either of them. *Odd.* Vengeance killings, especially those stemming from sexual jealousy, tend toward disfigurement, as if the murderer wants to obliterate the humanity of his victim. The breasts are an obvious target, often being removed or mutilated. But outside of the obvious – the knife stuck through her panties into one or other orifice, *wait for forensics to determine which* – no evidence of frenzy or hatred.

Toledo glanced out of the bedroom window. In the growing morning light, familiar faces from the Berkeley Police Department were gathering. *Berkeley PD an institution as out of place as a Catholic nun in a brothel.* Toledo frowned. *Or was that a brothel in a Catholic*

4

nunnery? Someone had cracked the joke at a party a few weeks ago, but its details evaded him. The gathering had been a bore, but the wine was great - *Californian for a Californian retirement.*

A small BMW convertible edged through the blue uniforms and dour, mostly middle-aged plain-clothes officers. The detective smiled as some of the newer and/or younger officers did a double take at the figure who glided out of the vehicle.

He looked back at the girl on the bed, then up a couple of feet.

The writing on the closet mirrored door was strange – THIS IS WHAT HAPPENS TO CHEATERS? PIGS?!– presumably using the girl's blood as improvised ink. The question marks were ambiguous. Toledo would not attempt to fathom such mysteries at this early stage, outside of identifying them. but it was promising to see the fluid handwriting. Whoever had written that question had done so quickly and made no attempt to disguise their writing.

Toledo stood up, took a step back toward the door. He wanted to take in the whole scene before forensics arrived, when it would be dissected and fragmented. What had the killer been trying to communicate? What effect? If he had been trying to communicate anything at all. *Or she.* Instinctively, the detective thought that it must be a man – the whole knife thing spoke of male sexual gratification, or frustration, or vengeance – or a mixture of all three. And anyway, only a tiny minority of murderers – around five percent – are women, and an even smaller proportion commit this kind of savagery.

The door opened slightly, and a familiar face peeked through.

"Toledo," the woman said. "Great to see you!"

"You too Amanda, but we must try for more romantic settings."

5

"Oh, this is romantic in its way."

"It is?" Toledo replied.

"Well, obviously there is a love angle to this," Amanda said, kneeling by the corpse. It always fascinated Toledo to watch the young medical examiner at work. So precise, so detail oriented, yet always so respectful. She peered at where the knife stuck out from the girl's panties. They were soaked with blood and a pool had congealed on the bed just below them.

"New car?" Toledo asked as Amanda crouched even lower, her nose just a few inches from the girl.

"Yes…I thought it was time for a change." She looked up and smiled. "Do you like it?"

"The important thing is whether you like it."

"Well, I do."

Then she turned back to the corpse, pointed at the knife, and shook her head.

"Kind of weird, no? It's stuck in neither her vagina nor anus, but into the perineum – that little area between the two. Must have been incredibly careful."

"Strange," Toledo said. "But how can you tell that?"

"There's something quite deliberate. The insertion. And it is so precise – neither vaginal nor anal, exactly between. There's only really a thin membrane separating them, but somehow, he got it … exactly right."

She almost seems impressed.

"A surgeon is about the only person I know who could do that. I doubt whether she was struggling that much when it happened. If at all."

"You mean she was already dead?"

The medical examiner paused for a second.

"Probably not. Too much blood flow to be already dead. Maybe near to it, perhaps unconscious. She can't have been moving."

6

Her face was now just a few inches from the panties again.

"This was done with great care."

Amanda stood up, started to whisper into her voice-recorder. Toledo knew not to disturb her when she was dictating, and he looked at the writing bloodily scrawled on the wall again. THIS IS WHAT HAPPENS TO CHEATERS? PIGS?! Without the question marks it would be simple, too simple perhaps. The pretty girl lying on the bed had been caught cheating, and this was her punishment. A knife sticking out of her panties. Why had the killer written the question? Toledo frowned. *Something like – 'this girl was murdered for the insignificant act of cheating!' If this is the case, then the murderer is pre-emptively answering the consternation at the lack of proportion between the crime (cheating) and the punishment (knife in panties).* Toledo sighed deeply. *I am getting ahead of myself.* He frowned. *And, of course, he reminds us that we are pigs. Strange word for the twenty-first century. Older killer perhaps?*

"Do you know who she is? Or was?" Amanda asked, closely examining the girl's face, or to be more precise, her lips.

"Caroline Ramirez," Toledo said, reading from his notebook. "She's lived here the last two years. Kept to herself apparently. Roommates say she used to go to Cal but dropped out about a year ago."

"Dropped out?" Amanda said. "No-one drops out anymore. They just take a break."

"Well – she did."

A knock on the door, and a young, uniformed police officer entered. He looked down at the corpse, cleared his throat nervously, smiled sheepishly and stood to attention for Toledo.

"Yes?" Toledo said with soft sarcasm.

7

"The roommate says she had a steady boyfriend – Mark Shaffer. They had been arguing recently. Something to do with Ms. Ramirez seeing other men."

The young uniform was obviously pleased with himself. Equally obvious, he had not seen too many corpses before.

"Officer …" Toledo looked for his nametag. "Officer Carlisle."

"Yes, sir!" the young man replied.

"Officer – you are not in the army – stand easy, please. And call me Toledo, everyone else does. Well … everyone other than the good doctor here. Could you find Mark Shaffer's cell number perhaps? Even an address?"

"Yes, sir! I mean … Yes, Toledo!"

This sounded even stranger than the "sir", but Toledo just waved him out of the room. Amanda started laughing as soon as the door closed.

"You are mean, Cassius," she said.

"Me? Mean?"

"The poor guy was nervous. Couldn't you see that? He wasn't talking with just any detective. He was talking with *the* detective, Cassius Toledo. A living legend! And – there was the body of a young girl on the bed."

"All I asked for was some info on her boyfriend. Not too much."

"Just remember you were as young as him once."

"I was?" the detective said wearily. "It seems so long ago – I was never as young as him."

"Well, are you done here?" Amanda asked.

"For now, yes." Toledo said.

"So, I can …?"

"Yes, you can call them in."

And within seconds several crime lab techs entered the room, essentially pushing Toledo out into the corridor. Amanda soon joined him.

"Apparently, my legendary status doesn't stretch to a polite request to vacate the room," Toledo said.

"Ah, poor Cassius!" Amanda replied.

Toledo glanced down at his watch.

"I think it is time for a coffee. Milano?" he asked, slipping his arm through Amanda's.

"Too early for me, but I'll see you out."

They walked down the stairs, passing Officer Carlisle, who nearly saluted Toledo, but managed to stop himself just in time.

"Jesus!" Toledo said as they walked into the foggy cold of a Berkeley morning.

"Oh, come on Cassius, you love it," Amanda said.

Toledo just smiled and opened the car door with an exaggerated chivalry. Then he paused, flipped out his phone and texted someone.

"A McMannis case? You do know what time it is?" Amanda said, surprised.

"Eight on a Sunday morning. Just the right time to get hold of him. Didn't you know? McMannis never sleeps."

Two

In a house perched in the Berkeley Hills, only a few miles distant from the apartment Toledo had been in, but a whole world of experience and privilege removed, Ian McMannis, Assistant-Professor of Folklore, looked down at his gently snoring wife. He had been at Berkeley five years now. He was entering the nervous years when the job-for-life represented by receiving tenure moved from a prize to be captured to something ominous, even frightening. The gap between Assistant and Associate had seemed just a little jump from a distance, but now assumed massive proportions. The fact that he was the whole Folklore department did not make things any easier for McMannis. *In reality*, he thought gloomily as he padded the couple of steps from bed to bathroom, *it makes it more difficult.* Despite assurances to the contrary, he was always worried that the university might decide to close his whole program, thus making the tenure decision moot.

He looked in the mirror. His eyes were tired and vaguely bloodshot. Brown hair thinning a little, a few specks of grey appearing around the temples. He didn't care much about signs of aging as a certain gravitas in his profession was an advantage. But it was the gaunt gaze, the harrowed look of the haunted that got to him. Tenure, tenure – the word hangs around an Assistant-Professor like some demonically smiling snake.

Or maybe – he thought as the stream of pee started to weaken – *like an alligator looking up at you from a toilet.*

Alligators in toilets. Urban legends. The stuff of 21st century folklore.

As he was shaking off, his cellphone rang. The Girl from Ipanema swayed into his ears again and he looked down at the screen.

It simply said TOLEDO.

"Jesus!" McMannis whispered loudly. "It's a bit early!"

But he knew he was protesting too much. A phone call from Detective-Sergeant Cassius Toledo at 8 a.m. on Sunday morning could mean only one thing.

Murder.

A few seconds later the phone rang.

"McMannis?"

"Yes."

"Milano in an hour. Want to hear all you know about cults and possible mutilation," Toledo said.

McMannis heard a female voice say, "where do cults come into it?"

"Is someone with you?" McMannis asked. "A woman at eight on a Sunday morning, Toledo?"

"Yeah … yeah … nice try. It's Amanda, she arrived just as I was leaving.

"Hi Byrnes!" McMannis shouted. "I'll see y'all at Milano."

He pressed END on his phone and smiled. Louisiana born, the medical examiner had been a sorority girl at LSU before going to medical school. Occasionally, McMannis gently made fun of her accent, as it seemed so incongruous for her profession. Joking, Amanda argued this perceived incongruity was both "sexist" and "Southist". But they were on last-name terms – the most genuine friendship possible in a Bay Area full of instant intimacy and trust based on first names. McMannis, who had Majored in English at Stanford all those years ago – well, actually twenty – always liked to think that he, Toledo and Amanda were living out Shakespeare's old dictum "those friends thou hast, and their adoption tried, grapple them to thy soul with hoops of steel - but do not dull thy palm with entertainment of each new-hatch'd, unfledged comrade" – or, as Toledo once translated for a bemused colleague after McMannis drunkenly pronounced this wisdom – "don't piss out of a window until you know which way the wind is blowing."

Toledo defended his version by arguing "that's something you could write on a bumper sticker - nearly."

Ten murder cases in and counting – didn't they know which way the wind was blowing? *Maybe*, thought McMannis, as he watched his wife's breasts slowly move up and down with her breathing. *But it is always good to keep an eye on the marine layer in case it rolls in at a minute's notice.* The Bay Area marine layer of fog is a natural air conditioner that never allows more than two or three ninety-degree plus days before returning.

As if in reply, a glint of sunlight passed through the window before being hidden by the fog again. But sunlight so early could mean only one thing. A hot day ahead. McMannis had discovered early in his first case with Toledo that heat and murder were unfortunate partners. A corpse goes through rigor mortis to bloating and then decomposition with eerie speed. Coming near it meant clothes permanently stinking of the experience.

McMannis remembered the look of surprise on his wife Cathy's face, one that soon changed into disgust as her instincts, if not her conscious mind, recognized the smell.

"That smell's a bitch all right," Toledo said with grim satisfaction when McMannis had told him about Cathy's reaction.

Despite trying to put his clothes on as quietly as possible Cathy stirred and murmured his name. She opened her eyes as another stream of sunlight poured into the room. It lasted a little longer than the previous one, showing the eternal Bay Area battle between fog and sun was running its predictable morning timetable. No matter, thought McMannis, the fog will get its vengeance once again this evening.

Cathy shaded her eyes.

"What time is it?" she asked, quietly beckoning to him.

"A little after eight."

"And you're getting up already?"

Her head was now up on one hand.

"Yes. Toledo called."

"Toledo?"

"Yes," McMannis said, not knowing why he felt guilty.

"Well, I suppose it's been a little quiet. Where are you meeting him?"

"Milano."

"Could you bring me one of their croissants and a latte?" she asked, getting out of bed before changing her mind and relaxing back.

"Sure, I don't know how long I'll be though."

"Okay, okay ... I'll still be here."

A hint of come-on in her voice with those last words. Eight years ago, it would have been enough for him to be back in bed. But the passion wasn't like that anymore. It was, McMannis had rationalized, more like a fine wine to be slowly savored rather than a cold beer to be guzzled.

Or perhaps, he thought as he kissed her by the mouth, but not quite on it, *the beer just went flat long ago and all we are left with is the aftertaste.*

As she settled back on the pillow, he looked at her. Still slim with tussled, blond hair on her shoulders. Blue eyes with a hint of crows-feet in the morning and last thing at night. A pretty, if not a beautiful face. *One to grow old with*, McMannis thought, with an ambivalent pleasure.

Their house was perched on one of the impossibly steep, angular hills that rise above the Berkeley campus. Roads that can barely fit one car wind in crazy switchbacks from sea-level to near one thousand feet. The sun broke through again as McMannis got into his car and, looking up, noticed the fog visibly evaporating in the strength of the light. Soon all trace of it would be gone overhead. But a glance out towards the ocean revealed it sulkily hanging around near the Golden Gate, patiently waiting for its evening reprieve.

McMannis drove deftly down toward the campus, veering quickly left onto Spruce Street, the road marking the northern boundary of the massive university, before passing by the peculiarly ornate International House and then down a virtually empty Bancroft Avenue to Café Milano.

Three

McMannis walked into the café and saw Toledo sitting
at his usual table by the stairs. The detective was dressed in
gray shorts, a black T-shirt, sandals, and a baseball cap.
McMannis smiled at his friend. *He looks like an aging grad
student.* The detective stretched his 5'10", 190-pound
frame as if he had just woken up, but the gray stubble and
slightly bloodshot eyes suggested he might not have gone
to bed at all.

"No riots today, I see!" Toledo said.

"No," answered McMannis, "and no Byrnes either."

"She had to get back to office. Important bodies to see
to."

McMannis smiled, wondering why Toledo always
brought up the subject of the Berkeley riots, even though
they were now more than forty years distant. Both men had
barely been out of diapers when they occurred, but Toledo
obviously enjoyed the romantic notion that he had once
attended the infamous UC Berkeley – mother of the free
speech movement and curse of Conservative America.

In a reflective moment, Toledo once noted that there
are more homeless people *and* more Nobel Laureates in
Berkeley than any other city in the world. McMannis had
pointed out that this was almost certainly not true, but
Toledo insisted that it almost certainly *was* if you looked at
the numbers "proportionally". McMannis bowed to the
detective's wisdom on the matter as they both enjoyed the
notoriety that exuded from their alma mater.

Several years ago, a mixture of co-incidence and
arcane knowledge led to him becoming Toledo's unofficial

partner. It was after a meeting in the very café they were now in. The co-incidence was buying coffee at the same time as Toledo, while the knowledge involved the intricacies of 1980's Goth culture, and how they might explain a particularly bizarre teenage murder-suicide. While waiting in line, Toledo had been reading the case file, and a bored McMannis looked over his shoulder and started reading it too. That random coincidence had, one way or another, changed their lives. Casually, McMannis started to help solve the case with his knowledge of teen culture, and then used his role as a young professor on campus to gain the trust of one of the suspects. The info thus gained helped Toledo get the student behind bars quicker than he would have done without McMannis. Thus, the investigative relationship had been born.

Soon after the case was over, Toledo suggested taking advantage of an obscure California law from the Nineteenth Century that enabled McMannis to become the "County Constable" of Alameda. While still officially on the books, in practice the position had gone the way of the gold rush and gunfighters, and it entailed no duties beyond ensuring "the general peace." Sensibly, McMannis decided that the general peace was already adequately preserved by traditional police, so he only joined Toledo when needed. He had access to any case that Toledo was working on, but had no other responsibilities, or powers. The professor was a county officer but could not arrest anyone. He could carry a gun, but chose not to, arguing that if he had one "more good guys would be harmed than bad guys stopped".

Since then, McMannis had helped with many cases, and while they joked about it, his sworn position did make moments like this far easier as it enabled seamlessly sharing evidence.

"So, what made you get me out so early?"

"This..." Toledo said and showed McMannis a photograph of the murder scene writing on the wall. The detective watched the professor carefully. His eyes were ice blue, displaying an ironic intelligence that implied lying to him would be useless, insulting his intelligence worse.

"I assume there was a body ... nearby?"

"Yes. You can look at it if you want ..."

"No. No need ..."

McMannis was still a bit squeamish about murder scenes, even though he had popped the cherry on one more than five years before.

"It was a female, teenage student, who had a knife inserted in her perineum."

"Her peri...?"

"It's that little area between ..."

"I know what it is – just didn't know women had them. Not much room."

Both men considered this for a moment before Toledo moved on.

"The only reason you are here is the question mark."

"The question mark?"

"It makes the murder ... strange. More than the everyday jealous lover."

"And the PIGS – is that what made you call me too?"

"Well...obviously."

"I know PIGS was written at the Manson Family murders, in Sharon Tate's blood I think."

"It was her unborn baby's."

"Pleasant ...," McMannis continued. "But at least there was some rationale for it there, however twisted. Manson hated the police, saw them as supporting a corrupt society that should be destroyed in a race war. This? This is more like an afterthought."

The professor looked more closely at the photograph on Toledo's phone.

17

"It is more hurried or angrier."

"Or both."

"I'll look into it, Cassius. And now, I promised Cathy a latte and a croissant."

Toledo watched as his friend went to the counter and purchased them. Such a mundane task, he knew that, but somehow melancholy to a man like himself. *No need to buy a latte and a croissant for my wife*, he thought. *I haven't got a wife.* He frowned at his maudlin thoughts, then raised his hand slightly as McMannis sauntered out of the café, wife's requests diligently in hand.

The detective left the café and wandered the mile to his own house. His habit of walking was seen as eccentric at best and suspicious at worst by both colleagues and friends.

"Why don't you just drive?"

If they needed to ask the question, they would never understand the answer, so Toledo just smiled pleasantly and shrugged at the inquiries. First, he simply enjoyed walking. Second, it helped to keep him fit. Third, you can tell a lot about a town, and its people, by simply walking around it. Fourth, it gave him time to mull over cases, while adhering to his creed:

A car isolates, walking immerses.

He was the first to admit that Berkeley, as a small city with many sidewalks, leant itself easily to the walking lifestyle. He would not attempt it in Los Angeles, where movement without a car was akin to a certifiable offense. But in his hometown if he could walk, he did.

Four

Mark Shaffer sat in the interview room, leaning back in a chair while attempting, and failing, to look nonchalant. Detective Toledo studied him through the two-way mirror. *Early thirties. Educated but currently a slacker. Average looks. Oddly well-developed upper chest as though he works out, but no evidence of it elsewhere. John Lennon glasses give a studious, philosophical look.* Shaffer was now leaning back in his chair even more, precariously close to tipping over completely. Toledo watched as this nearly occurred and smiled as the young man looked up toward the glass, embarrassed at being so clumsy.

Shaffer now sat upright, hands under his chin.

But is he a murderer? Instinct told Toledo that he was not, but the detective was equally sure that he did know something about the killing. *To what extent?*

Toledo cleared his throat, straightened his tie, and opened the interview-room door. Mark Shaffer looked up and smiled at him.

"Detective ... Toledo?"

Toledo sat down at the table.

"Am I right?" Shaffer continued.

"Yes, I am Detective Toledo."

"I read all about that case with the eyes, and the heads. How did you ever solve that?"

"Luck and intuition, with a bit of chaos thrown in," Toledo replied truthfully.

This had not started the way he wanted. Somehow the suspect had taken the initiative and was interviewing him. But the self-confidence that this revealed could be easily turned. It was mixed with the arrogance of the wealthy; an overestimation of what money could do. Sometimes the rich got away with murder, but most of the time they did not.

"You are being too modest," Shaffer continued. "I never understood exactly how you went from ritualistic murders in Berkeley to ..."

But here Toledo stopped him. *Allow him enough rope to feel safe, to hang himself even, but not so much to let him escape.*

"Several books were written about it, I believe. You should try them."

"OK."

Toledo smiled, stopping the conversation mid-track. Time to reverse positions.

"Tell me about your relationship with Ms. Ramirez."

"With Caroline? I don't know – what do want to know about us?"

"How long have you been seeing her?"

Shaffer paused momentarily, as if placing the girl on a long continuum of conquests.

"Just over a year."

"How did you meet?"

"Mutual friends – drinks."

"How would you characterize your relationship?"

A slight pause.

"Boyfriend and girlfriend."

Another pause.

"Lovers, I suppose," Shaffer continued.

"You loved one another?"

Shaffer laughed slightly, nervous and buying time.

"I guess you could say we loved one another."

"But you come from very ... diverse backgrounds, am I right?"

"In what sense?"

"You are the son of one of the Bay Area's leading cardiologists – Ms. Ramirez was not. You live in your family's home in rich Hillsborough. Ms. Ramirez came from one of the poorest parts of Oakland. You graduated from Berkeley; Ms. Ramirez dropped out of ..."

"She is taking some time off, that's all."

Toledo looked at him closely. By accident, *well, with a little design*, he had hit a sore point. Shaffer was maintaining his own status as much as he was defending his girlfriend. The lower Ramirez went, the more Shaffer needed to buffer her for his own ego.

"You came from different places though. That would be fair?"

"I guess."

"And you are also twelve years older than her."

"About that."

Toledo looked down at the folder he was carrying, opened it in a way that Shaffer could not see the contents. He pretended to read.

"Detective Toledo, I came here voluntarily – well, kind of voluntarily – but no-one has told me why I am here."

"Kind of voluntary?"

"The officer made it clear that I needed to come, and if I didn't volunteer it would be required. Had a way of talking to me like I'm in the military, or some shit like that."

Carlisle, Toledo thought with an inward smile. He continued reading for a second.

"But you did come voluntarily?"

"Yes."

The detective closed the binder, put it down on the table. He leaned forward slightly, looking straight into the young man's eyes.

"You are really claiming you don't know why you are here?"

21

"Yes."

"Caroline was found dead last night at about four am. She was murdered."

"Dead?" Shaffer laughed for a second, as if discovering he was the brunt of some sick but not too subtle joke. "Murdered?"

"Is that really what happens to cheaters?" Toledo said, his blue eyes never straying from Shaffer's.

"Is what ...?"

"Is that really what happens to cheaters?" the detective repeated, more slowly.

Shaffer laughed again, started to look around the room.

"Am I being punked? Is that it? I can't see any cameras in here other than those two." He said, pointing at the clearly visible surveillance cameras.

"Well, if I am, it's over. You can come out now."

The young man looked around the room expectantly, then his eyes settled again on Toledo.

"You are not being punked," the detective said quietly. "This is deadly serious." He paused.

"Excuse the pun."

Shaffer smiled, rubbed his eyes, then slammed his hands down quite forcefully on the table. The move was casual, but assured Toledo of the very real physical strength of the man sitting opposite him. *One-on-one I wouldn't stand a chance.* As Shaffer stood up, Toledo laughed at himself, *not that I have had to use physical force in ...,* but he could not remember how long.

"Caroline ... is dead?"

"Yes."

The man looked shocked, then confused, and finally slightly panicked. He looked around, as if seeing the room for the first time. Then he closed his eyes and was completely still. Toledo looked at him quizzically. *This is no normal attempt at relaxation. This is something he is trained to do.* When his eyes opened, Shaffer looked composed and calm.

"So - am I free to go?" Shaffer asked.

Toledo stood.

"Yes. You always have been."

The young man went to the door, gripped the handle, and pushed down. The door was locked, and he turned quickly with an accusatory look at the detective. After a second's delay, Toledo nodded slightly, and a barely perceptible click came from the door. It was opened from the outside.

"Officer Carlisle will escort you outside. There is one thing though." Toledo said.

"And what is that?"

"You never asked how she was killed."

After a pause, Shaffer said,

"It seemed … impolite … to ask."

Arcane, but genuine. High School back east probably.

Shaffer turned toward Officer Carlisle and smiled wryly.

"Isn't this the time when I am meant to say that I know my own way out?" And with a fluid, patrician movement of his hand, Shaffer asked the officer to lead the way.

Carlisle looked toward Toledo again, and the detective nodded slightly.

"This way, sir."

And they were gone.

Toledo sighed. He was normally pretty expert at knowing if someone was telling the truth, and the young man seemed completely genuine. If it was insincere, parrying the accusation with an assertion of being punked was clever. Suggesting it would be impolite to ask how she was killed. That was genius.

Five

"As a sworn police officer, I expect you to offer a little more input to the case," Toledo said, looking at the professor opposite with him with mock exasperation.

"I am sworn only in name, Cassius, as you well know. I don't see what help I can be," McMannis said, leaning back and rubbing his eyes.

They were sitting on the small porch outside Toledo's diminutive house.

"After all, there are no heads, or eyes, or dams to be blown up. No sign of obscure Goth music leading to murder, or even or a girl murdered in broad daylight in a well-travelled university building."

"I know that."

Toledo liked McMannis a lot, but his tendency to go over the greatest hits of their cases together grated a little.

"Perhaps it is precisely what it seems – Mark Shaffer became pissed off one time too many at his cheating girlfriend."

Toledo frowned at him.

"OK – what makes you think that this is *not* just a case of a jealous boyfriend?"

"Just a feeling."

"And the reason for that feeling?"

"The brutality of the murder – and the message written on the wall," the detective replied quietly. "It seems too clear to me. It's as if he is saying – I killed her in an overtly sexual way, then used her blood to tell the world that this is what happens to cheating women. It all is too … neat. Presented to us in a little package, like one of those baggies that they sell weed in. "

"I'll take you word for that." McMannis said.

"For what?"

"That they sell weed in little baggies."

"Very funny."

"Sometimes, Toledo," McMannis said, closing the binder, "you just have to accept that things are exactly as they seem. No more complicated, no more simple."

Toledo pulled the binder over and opened it. He looked at the two driver's license pictures, trying to glean something from the flat, vaguely impatient smiles. *Nothing, absolutely nothing. Just must wait till the evidence of Shaffer being there comes in. And it will.*

"I'm off then," said McMannis, and in a moment was in his car and away.

Toledo looked out at the park right across the street from his little post-war bungalow. Toledo lived in what had become the wrong part of Berkeley, or at least that was how it was put by some of his colleagues. The wrong part of Berkeley becomes increasingly "wronger" (A McMannis invention) the further toward the Bay that you get. Roughly west of Shattuck Avenue. To the east lies richer country as the University sprawls into the hills like some ever expanding, but casual monster, unaware of its own strength.

Shattuck leads to Sacramento, and then further West to San Pablo Avenue, after which some of the real slums start. These end quite suddenly in the dense hedgerow by I-80 – the constantly busy road that runs all the way from San Francisco to the East Coast. Three thousand miles. One day he would drive the whole way. *One day.*

The houses are small in Toledo's part of Berkeley, designed for young couples with perhaps one baby. They were now populated by single people like himself, and by larger families – mainly ethnic – who somehow squash several generations into the tiny spaces. Toledo liked this neighborhood. The neighborhood liked him. Having a police detective living among them made people feel safer, as they assumed he would intervene if trouble came their way. After a couple of beers, Toledo always said that when his front door was closed, it was closed, and the world outside could go to hell for all he cared. At least in theory. But if one night the shouts that occasionally echoed turned into something more urgent, a scream or gunfire for instance, then Toledo conceded he would go outside and see what was going down. So far, those screams had never occurred, but the drug dealers of Oakland and the extremes of West Berkeley were starting to move ever closer. Gunfire could not be far behind.

Toledo looked outside again, seeing one of those young couples running past at a strange speed with a child in a jogging stroller. In Berkeley you did not take your child out for a walk – it had to become aerobic exercise.

He had never had children, never even a serious wife. An early marriage to a fellow grad-student soon fell apart when he left the Psychology Ph.D. program. He had lost interest in knowing more and more about less and less, and she had lost interest in him. Since then, only some strictly uncommitted affairs with similarly career-minded women who gave and received pleasure without expectation of attachment. The relationships ended with a series of phone calls at that weekend late afternoon hour when no-one was ever in. Since landlines had disappeared it was difficult to call someone at the convenient moment when you knew they would not answer, but a little knowledge of work schedules made the task easier, especially with women who regularly put in twelve-hour days.

Toledo sat back in his chair. He took it all in. A few children running with a joyful aimlessness, a homeless man sitting on a bench and a couple who had just moved in a few doors down.

The thing is, thought the detective, *I need McMannis to be involved with this. My instinct tells me.* He went inside the house and put Stan Getz on his stereo. A Stan Getz record. Toledo liked the physical presence of a record, enjoyed its substance and fragility, appreciated the odd scratch that made the music more real.
When something else turns up, he'll see the light.

The record ended. Toledo closed his eyes, lost in the familiar click click cachung, and then opened them again twenty-seven minutes, thirty-two seconds later as the record slowed quickly to a stop. The ceremonies of music now lost to digital precision.

Six

There's something very humbling about a body on the slab, Amanda thought as she looked down at the pale corpse of Caroline Ramirez. A young person's death presents questions, even when it is a violent end with clear suspects. *The body is trying to tell me something,* she thought. *I just need to be in exactly the right place to hear it. And the right state of mind to listen to the words.* She looked down to the girl's feet, noticed the nail polish starting to flake. *And I also need to be listening for the right language.* Sometimes a body screamed its message in an obvious way – the stab wounds to the girl's genitalia were an example of this. But if Amanda left it there, if she allowed the obvious sounds to drown out subtler whispers that might be more vital to solving the case – then she would fail both the girl and the legal system.

And whoever did this needs to be off the streets fast.

The medical examiner bent down and carefully picked up a fragment of the nail polish with her tweezers. She reached up, and smoothed the girl's hair away from her forehead, where a strand had fallen out of place.

"You are so beautiful. I am so sorry. So sorry."

Her words echoed in the room strangely, and Amanda felt self-conscious, as though she had committed an obscure social sin.

Just as she was about to cover the body, she noticed a few grains of sand under the nail where she had removed the polish. She always carefully examined both finger and toenails in a murder case, as they often offer a wealth of evidence, but somehow this one toe had been missed. Amanda's deft fingers pulled the nail up slightly. She winced as she felt it give a little, then she picked the sand out one grain at a time.

Once again, what she always called *the last look* had yielded results.

Amanda covered Caroline's body, patted her shoulder lightly as she passed by, then left the room. Within a few minutes, she was in her civilian clothes, and frowned slightly at her reflection in the mirror. Despite her lovely face, body, and mind, she would be alone once again this evening. She looked toward her tapering, elegant fingers. *My hands, however beautiful they are, always remind men of my profession.*

With a shrug, she turned off the light, and went out into the night.

Seven

Piedmont Cemetery is massive, with acres upon acres of monuments reflecting the history of the Bay Area. Toledo often went there to escape from the madness and mayhem of being a homicide detective. The most visible monuments belong to the richest families. The so-called millionaire's row, featuring luminaries like the chocolate-magnate Ghirardelli family, stretches down street-length paths in the middle of the grounds. The Ghiradellis – of chocolate fame - are protected by four eerie figures on the corners of their monument, and Toledo liked to sit beside them, staring out toward the Bay just as they did. *Perhaps*, he had often thought, *I might learn something from their patient, everlasting vigil.*

Caroline Ramirez was being buried in one of the newest sections of the cemetery. Here the dead are commemorated by simple stone slabs laid flat to the ground. From a distance, this area might just be another grassy open space, parched brown by the Californian drought and sun. *Somehow it all seems anticlimactic,* Toledo thought as he saw the long procession enter the cemetery and wind its way slowly toward the plot. It passed by the absurd Pyramid monument, a homage to late nineteenth century hubris. *Some mad industrialist,* Toledo thought.

Earlier, he had visited his favorite grave – Elizabeth Scott, better known to the world as the Black Dahlia. She was the victim of one of California's most notorious unsolved murders. It reminded Toledo how every detail and nuance must be absorbed before the evidence becomes muddy, the trail cold, and the investigation dead. He enjoyed the myth that he had a one hundred percent closure rate. It was true that every case with a "newly dead body" had been closed with a convicted suspect, and yes, even the cold cases he reopened were all solved, but that was because many other files had remained shut after a glance at the first page. For many murders there was simply no evidence to follow.

"They aren't cold, they are cryogenically frozen," he had once said to McMannis.

"In cryogenics, they wake up once thawed," the professor answered.

"Perhaps these cases are just ... waiting for you."

"Waiting for *us*, don't you mean?"

McMannis had just smiled, knowingly.

Toledo surveyed the cemetery again, his gaze lingering momentarily on the grave where the teenage boy and old woman first met in the cult movie *Harold and Maude*, before embarking on their unlikely love affair. They liked to attend the funerals of total strangers. Toledo himself occasionally indulged in the same strange hobby, attempting to glean the relationships among the other attendees from looks alone. The loves, the hatreds, the indifference, the resentments, the hopes ... how did they intermingle and play off one another at a moment of supposed solidarity in grief?

The hearse stopped by the plot, and the line of cars slowed to a snail's pace before resting in a serpentine line stretching toward the entrance of the cemetery. Toledo wondered how many of them knew the girl in any meaningful sense; surely not the several hundred who were now congregating on the grave site, like slow-motion ants.

He always felt a little awkward coming to these funerals, but it was standard procedure in an unsolved case. A surprising number of murderers attend the funerals of

31

their victims, even when they might escape detection completely without their presence. In the perverse world of the random killer, anonymously going to a victim's funeral is a little added pleasure. It gives the murderer a sense of power; after all he is the reason for the whole ceremony – yet also the risk of being identified. But the danger merely adds to the seductive pull of the event as it provokes an adrenaline rush.

At the very back of the funeral procession Toledo saw a familiar vehicle. It was an old Volvo, and it made him smile. *McMannis. I knew it!* The professor's appearance was a silent nod to his respect for Toledo's instincts. If McMannis was as convinced of the simplicity of this case as he claimed, he would not have come. Waiting for his friend to arrive, the detective glanced down toward the mourners as he slowly walked down the hill toward the ceremony. *Someone in this group probably killed her.* His heart rate increased slightly at the thought, and he looked intently at the people as he approached.

Mark Shaffer accompanied Caroline's immediate family. He was dressed in a perfectly fitting black suit. *So well-fitting that it must be tailored*, Toledo thought. He scanned the mourners, finding several others that were just as well dressed. An elderly man, morbidly obese with a shock of white hair, and a professorial goatee. His wife, a little less fat and about a foot shorter. They had exited a brand-new BMW. *Six figures.* Then a woman of about thirty. Her clothes were tailored, but a little worn, and she had obviously grown somewhat fatter since they were made. She was acutely aware of how awkward she looked. Oddly, she was with a man a few years older who was dressed in filthy black jeans and a crusty black leather jacket. Toledo looked more closely and saw they must be siblings.

He frowned.

McMannis stopped at a respectful distance from the back of the group surrounding the coffin. Far enough away to acknowledge he did not know the girl, but close enough to gauge reactions. The coffin was simply adorned but made from an expensive type of wood. *Mahogany?* Toledo thought, then moved toward McMannis, feeling sure that the professor would know. *He is after all a store of useless information that often becomes anything but useless.*

"What is that made of?" Toledo whispered.

"Mahogany," McMannis whispered back. "It's expensive, and I doubt Caroline's family could afford it."

McMannis was already doing what Toledo constantly advised against – personalizing the murder victim by using her first name. *It clouds the judgment*, Toledo thought, but he was glad to see the professor taking more interest. He had come to rely on the professor more than he cared to admit, especially in these eccentric cases that grew with organic chaos, rather than logical precision.

The ceremony was starting. A priest intoning something in Latin. The biological family crying. Caroline's mother was inconsolable, and Toledo worried that she might fall into the grave along with her daughter. *If emotional agony has a face*, he thought, *it is in the expression of a murder victim's mother. Even when the mother is the murderer*, he mused bitterly.

As the prayers began, Toledo and McMannis bowed their heads in respect, even though they were both confirmed agnostics. About halfway through, Toledo looked up, searching for faces that appeared to be pretending, or at least were struggling with the need to keep their eyes shut.

Caroline's biological family had grown from the beginning of the ceremony. They were genuinely praying. They possessed the easy stances of those accustomed to prayer, retreating into habit as a small break from the pain

33

of this moment. A few other mourners were simply standing with their eyes open, making no pretense. Then, and these were most interesting, those in the middle. Enjoying a starring role among the Ambivalent was Mark Shaffer, boyfriend of the deceased and, by default, the prime suspect.

Shaffer looked at the coffin, then up to the crowd surrounding him. He seemed both distant and intrigued, as though experiencing something new that he did not quite understand, but which was nevertheless interesting. As Toledo watched Shaffer, he realized that the young man was looking for someone. A someone that he did not find, as he sighed slightly and then looked straight into Toledo's eyes.

Shaffer was implacable. He nodded slightly, politely, and Toledo returned the gesture. Shaffer's eyes next turned to McMannis, and here his gaze was more uncomfortable. There was something about McMannis that made Shaffer uneasy, or maybe it was about the ambiguous role that he played. *Must remember that for the future*, Toledo thought.

As the priest finished his Latin prayer, and the ceremony moved into new regions, just as baffling to Toledo, he surveyed the other well-dressed people. The startling facial resemblance left little doubt that the awkward woman, and her leather-attired brother, were Shaffer's siblings, while the older couple must be his parents. *Why is this young man's family attending his girlfriend's funeral? Surely, they hardly knew her.* More to the point, they must know that their son is a suspect, if from nothing else than the several police interviews that he had been "invited" to. *A show of solidarity?* Toledo wondered. *But if so – to who? Their son? The girl? Her family?*

The detective looked at the older man. His hair and neatly trimmed beard were startlingly white, with just a tinge of grey remaining around the temples. About fifty pounds overweight he stood at an imposing six foot. As a younger man he must have been impressive, even intimidating, but now he was paunchy and loose skinned. While his eyes still shone with intelligence, his hands were shaking slightly, and an uncertainty lurked in his facial muscles. Toledo wondered whether he still performed cardiac surgery. *For his patients' sake – I hope not.* But he had known people whose hands became as precise as a machine when performing the skills of their profession who were clumsy and frail in everyday life. If you exchanged hands for emotions, it might fit Toledo himself. As the detective looked at the old man, he glanced over and, in a mirror image of his son, slightly nodded with a polite smile.

Miss Manners would love this funeral, Toledo thought.

And then, with a quiet immediacy, the coffin was lowered into the ground.

The girl's family threw dirt, an extensive line of agonized faces that became a little more controlled near the end, as more distant relatives, who barely knew her, took their turn. *They normally don't do that*, thought Toledo. *In fact, I can't remember the last time I saw a coffin being lowered into the ground during an actual ceremony.*

As the mourners started to scatter slowly toward their cars, Toledo looked down into the grave. The coffin looked out of place, shiny and new with a layer of dirt on the lid. It was soon to be completely covered, and the detective thought of the darkness inside the coffin. He could see murder-scenes that would make the average person vomit with the cold, analytical eyes of an experienced investigator, but the idea of a coffin in the ground still gave him shivers.

"You always do this," McMannis said.

The professor had joined him by the open grave.

"Why does it always affect me so much?" asked Toledo, looking carefully into his friend's eyes as if the answer lay there.

"Because it is something that you can neither control nor understand. It simply is. Nothing to be investigated."

Toledo considered this for a moment, then felt his cellphone vibrate in his pocket. He looked at it, and his eyes turned toward Shaffer, standing about twenty yards away. He was reading the inscription on another memorial, although he occasionally glanced in Toledo's direction.

As if he knew this was coming, Toledo thought.

The detective's hand reached inside his coat toward his handcuffs, passing by the shoulder holster on the way.

"Not here," said McMannis.

Toledo showed him the cellphone.

SHAFFER'S HAIR FOUND AT NUMEROUS PLACES IN THE ROOM. SHAFFER'S SEMEN IN CAROLINE'S ANAL REGION.

"Amanda is never one to understate things," McMannis said.

"Still think it is the wrong place to arrest him?" asked Toledo.

As if in answer, Shaffer walked toward them. At first, his hands were casually thrust into his suit pants pockets, but then he took them out and placed them just outside his hips as he walked, like some virgin criminal who has been asked to raise his hands for the first time. It looked oddly comical.

"Detective Toledo?" Shaffer asked when he was about twelve feet from them.

"Yes?"

"I understand you want to talk to me again, but must you arrest me now? I can even drive my car to the police department if you want."

Toledo paused for a few seconds, as if this was a difficult decision.

McMannis smiled inwardly, knowing that Shaffer's offer to come to the department not under arrest was the ideal situation. Miranda Rights did not count before a person was arrested. Shaffer was playing into their hands.

"Let's compromise," Toledo said.

McMannis raised his eyebrows in surprise.

"I won't arrest you, but I will drive you to the police department.

Shaffer stood silently, looking at him carefully.

"Can someone from your family pick up your car?"

A quick glance to their right showed that Shaffer's family was still milling about their vehicles, watching the scene unfold from a distance.

"Yes," Shaffer said, gesturing with his hand toward them. "I am sure one of them will take it."

"Good," Toledo said. "That settles it then. Professor McMannis can take your keys if that's all right."

Shaffer paused for a moment, then shrugged, took a step forward and handed over the keys.

"Make sure that you don't let my sister drive it home – she is a terrible driver."

McMannis looked over to the family.

"She's the well-endowed one," Shaffer said, then stood silently by Toledo as if waiting to be told what to do.

That is a strange way to talk about your sister, thought McMannis, as he walked over to the family. *Even if true.* They parted slightly to let him pass, and he found himself facing the old doctor. He was the apparently unchallenged patriarch of the clan if their deferential attitude toward him was genuine.

"Your son, Mark. He asked me to give you these," McMannis said, feeling more awkward with each word.

"Thank you."

The voice was soft yet resonant. A bass used to being heard due to authority rather than volume.

"My name is Jerry – Dr. Jerry Shaffer."

He extended his hand to McMannis, who shook it quickly.

McMannis looked over toward the young woman as the doctor threw the keys to her

"Ophelia will drive the car home."

Am I being tested? Is it some family joke that Ophelia is never allowed to drive another person's car?

Ophelia – who was indeed well-endowed, McMannis noticed almost despite himself – was looking at him with a mixture of vague amusement and open hostility. She had a pretty, but not lovely face. Blue, or green eyes – McMannis could not decide. A small, delicate mouth and careless hair that occasionally drifted across her face.

None of my damn business who drives the car, McMannis thought, and turned away from the silent group.

"Professor McMannis?" Dr. Shaffer said.

"Yes?"

"I hope we shall meet again. I have heard about you. Most interesting. Most interesting."

"Thank you," McMannis said. "And I am sure we shall meet again."

As he walked away, McMannis tried to identify the doctor's accent. Upper class New England, with summers in Europe, winters in Aspen. *Close to half a million dollars in cars*, he thought as he passed by their vehicles.

Toledo and Shaffer were already in the car, and the detective just waved goodbye slightly as the professor walked up. Strangely, Shaffer was sitting in the passenger seat rather than in the back. They were talking energetically

38

as the car pulled away. Toledo obviously made a joke, as McMannis saw them burst out laughing.

This young man, thought McMannis, *is nowhere near as intelligent as he thinks he is.* The professor watched as Toledo's car moved away, then stopped near the entrance to the cemetery in the cremation garden, where urns stood silently. In the far corner was a simple but elegant marble wall, with the names of dead people whose bodies had never been found. Not war dead unless you count the casualties of the internal strife of mental illness as war victims. The wall was a simple homage to suspected suicides at the Golden Gate Bridge.

The passenger door opened, and Shaffer half exited the car as Toledo crouched and put his hand on one of the names. Then he took a couple of steps to the right, bent down, and repeated the homage. The young suspect obviously was at a loss at this strange diversion, uncertain whether to join the detective or not. But in a moment Toledo had turned and walked quickly back to the car. In a few seconds it was gone.

He always needs to stop at them, McMannis thought a little sadly.

By the time the professor had reached his own car, nearly all the mourners had left the cemetery. He noticed a small backhoe making its careful way down toward Caroline's grave. At the entrance another hearse entered, and like some somber pied piper, it led a short line of cars toward the newest part of the cemetery.

Just as McMannis was about to get into his car, he noticed that one of the Shaffer cars was still parked. Ophelia was standing by it, looking over at McMannis intently, as if wanting to say something, but unable to. She shifted her weight as she realized he had noticed her. She raised her hand a little in greeting, then quickly got into the car and sped away. Driving so quickly that she nearly drove into the second car in the new funeral procession. It was only sheer luck that made her miss. McMannis winced a little at this sight, wondering why she had been in such a hurry to leave. *But then, cemeteries are not places to linger*, he thought.

With that he got into his own car and drove, with suitable care and respect, down to the exit, and out onto the road.

Eight

"So, you admit to having sex with her, but nothing else?"

"Precisely."

Toledo looked across at the young man. He possessed an unusual self-confidence for his age, and even now, when the questions had moved from the general to the specific, he had yet to ask for a lawyer. Mark Shaffer was too intelligent to be unaware of the risk in answering questions without a lawyer present, but here he was, doing precisely that. *Perhaps there is more to this after all.*

An innocent man just might have the confidence to take on a full police interrogation without legal representation.

"What kind of sex was that?"

Shaffer rubbed his chin, glanced downward, as if a little embarrassed. Then he looked straight into Toledo's eyes, confidence returned.

"You name it."

Toledo's phone buzzed. He looked at it. A message from Amanda.

SEMEN FROM TWO DIFFERENT MEN

His eyes moved back to Shaffer.

"It is getting more complicated by the moment," Shaffer said, as if he knew the content of the text.

"Detective Toledo, do you mind if I ask you a, question?

"Fire away."

"How did you get your name?"

"My father was from Mexico."

"I meant ... your first name."

Toledo smiled. He did not mind indulging in small talk with suspects. Such conversations might lead anywhere, and it was when talking about apparently insignificant subjects that a man's guard was down. He was vulnerable to accidental revelations.

"Well, my father was a boxing fan. He watched the 1960 Olympics and became a fan of a young boxer called Cassius Clay. He easily won the gold medal even though he was only eighteen. My dad became such a fan that when Clay was due to fight the Heavyweight Champion a few years later – the supposedly invincible Sonny Liston – he placed a bet on him beating Liston. How much do you know about betting?"

"Not much."

"There's something called an accumulator. That's when you bet on more than one outcome occurring, and the more specific...the higher the odds – so my dad bet one thousand dollars – a lot of money in those days - that Clay would win his first fight with Liston by a stoppage at the beginning of the seventh round ... and then, as part of the accumulator, that he would knock Liston out in the first round of the return fight."

Toledo was silent for a moment, letting all this sink in.

"The odds against this were pretty astronomical – so high that many casinos wouldn't take the bet. But one did. And the rest is history ..."

Shaffer smiled.

"Amazing."

"My dad bought his house with cash from that bet. Bought it outright. And I was born nine months later. So, he thought it only fair to name me after his hero – who had provided security for his family. Now Cassius Clay had

42

been reborn as Muhammad Ali after the first fight ... but he decided on the original ... incarnation."

"I see."

"Hence, Cassius Toledo."

"That's one hell of a story."

"And totally true."

"He did you a favor." Shaffer said after a slight pause.

"How?"

"By going with the original name – Muhammad Toledo wouldn't have sounded right."

Toledo smiled. He couldn't help liking the young man.

There was more to the story. In the end, his father's romance with betting led to co-dependency, and eventually ... *but don't think about that. Keep your mind on the man opposite, not the father who has gone.*

"The strange thing is that the second fight ended with what was called the phantom punch – one that seemed so light and insignificant that it could not knock out anyone, let alone a giant like Liston. My dad won so much money that he was investigated as potentially part of a Mob fix. But nothing came of it – and the nearest my father ever came to the Mafia was watching *The Godfather.*"

"That's funny."

"But it wasn't a phantom punch, anyway. It was short, apparently light – but fast, lightning fast, and ... most importantly – Liston never saw it coming. Those are the punches that get you. The ones you never see coming."

Toledo saw the young man was off guard for a moment. More importantly, he saw that their liking was mutual. He could pursue it, but instinct told him to hold back, deciding to let the suspect stew for a little. *Let him go or arrest him?* They had enough evidence for the latter, more than enough in fact, but instinct told him that the case was more complex than simply a jealous boyfriend murdering a cheating young woman. Shaffer was not a threat to others and would reveal far more out in the open than behind bars.

"Thank you, Mr. Shaffer. That will be all for now."

Shaffer looked nonplussed. Toledo was pleased to see that he expected to be arrested, rather than released. But behind the smile that sprung to his face as he stood up, Toledo saw that perhaps he *wanted* to be arrested. Shaffer paused by the table.

"You can stay if you want to," Toledo said.

"No. I just…" Suddenly the young man was at a loss for words, and he looked around, absorbing the dank coldness and sterility of the interrogation room for the first time. Superficially, the confidence was still there, but something else as well.

He sniffs the future. And it is a future he does not like.

Toledo escorted Shaffer out of the department, even though he said a couple of times that he knew the way and could go alone. The detective wanted to see who would pick him up, and how close to the department they were already waiting. There was bright sunshine outside, and both men squinted a little as cars sped past. The breeze blew the last Fall leaves around on the street.

He called with his back to Toledo, and within a few minutes a BMW slid serenely up to the sidewalk. Without a word, Shaffer got into the car. Toledo dipped a little and saw a brief glimpse of Jerry Shaffer. He was surprised that someone else was not performing such a mundane task. But then, maybe he wanted to debrief his son as soon as possible. Just as the car moved away, Shaffer looked out at Toledo with a little, sardonic smile, then his father pressed down on the accelerator, and the luxury car disappeared with deceptive speed.

Toledo sighed and walked slowly back up the stairs into the police department.

"You let him go?" It was the Police Chief, in all her splendor – uniform buttons shining as if brand new.

"Yes, I let him go," Toledo replied.

"Well, it's your call Toledo, but don't you think, with the evidence …?"

"Logic – and policy – suggest that you are right. But there's something else here. Out of sight right now, and I need Shaffer to lead me to it."

"You think this was a one off?"

"Pretty sure of it."

"Fine. Just keep me posted."

"Don't I always?" said Toledo sardonically, and with a little groan the Chief went past him, back into her office.

Toledo knew that a few years ago it would not have been anything as easy as this. But as the number of solved cases stacked up, a lot had changed. He was given freer rein, *or that might be more rope to hang myself with.* He had even become known on the media, at first local news stations but eventually some of the cable news outlets where he was drawn upon as an expert to comment on cases. Normally, police detectives like to stay out of the limelight, as anonymity is a key component to their effectiveness, but Toledo came to realize that his persona, almost akin to a star, made suspects more vulnerable. They assumed he would reveal them instantly, as if he possessed Columbo-like perception that made lying to him a non-starter.

If Shaffer was not a repeat murderer – and that was a huge assumption that the detective might come to regret – there was no harm in keeping him out a little longer. Of course, a suspect with access to money was always a flight risk, but Toledo felt the young man would not take that route. Obscurely, he was enjoying the attention. After all, he was being investigated by Detective Cassius Toledo.

Toledo's cellphone rang. It was McMannis.

45

"What did he say?"

"Not much – he admitted to having sex with her – no more."

"Oh, I assume he is still there?"

"No," the detective said. "I released him.

"Really?"

McMannis was the amateur, and Toledo the professional, so the professor did not openly challenge the decision. One key feature of their successful partnership was that both accepted their roles, but McMannis's doubtful tone was unmistakable.

"Busy tonight?" McMannis asked.

"Well, let me check my social calendar," Toledo joked. He paused for an impressive amount of time, then replied.

"Yes, I think I am free."

"My wife has invited you over for dinner."

Toledo was distracted, looking over at a homeless man picking through the garbage in a trash can. *He is so methodical*, the detective thought.

"What was that?" Toledo asked. He thought McMannis had just said that his wife had invited him over for dinner, but that could not possibly be the case.

"I said – my wife has invited you over for dinner."

"Tonight?"

"Yes, tonight."

Rotting corpses, sexual assault victims with knives sticking out of unmentionable places, decapitated heads mysteriously absent their bodies, international incidents with worldwide implications – few of them fazed Cassius Toledo – but dinner with McMannis *and his wife* … well that was enough to put fear into any man. This might seem strange to an outside observer. Cathy McMannis was a charming, welcoming woman whose dinner conversation was unchallenging and comforting. McMannis cooked

46

superbly, his wife socialized, and their guests nearly always left satisfied.

But Toledo knew things that made any dinner in the McMannis house uncomfortable. For a start, the professor's ambiguous relationship with two of his students, Ginny and Selena. Ginny, still alive, was the daughter of a well-known Berkeley professor. She had recently graduated and joined the police academy. Selena was Ginny's lover and had died in the last stages of a case. Their emotional entanglement with McMannis possessed an intensity that made most illicit affairs pale in comparison. Exactly what the attraction McMannis held for young, beautiful women was beyond Toledo, but its existence had been proven time and again.

Cathy McMannis had heard rumors about the girls, and she suspected that Toledo knew more about it than she did. She accepted that her husband entered the mysterious world of police detection with increasing regularity and duration, and that young women like Ginny apparently always came with the territory. Cathy didn't like it but had come to an uneasy tolerance. *She also*, Toledo thought, as he watched the homeless man move down the street toward another garbage can, *relishes some of the fame and/or notoriety now enjoyed by her husband*. Slowly but surely, Ian McMannis was becoming something more than an Assistant-Professor of Folklore at the University of California, Berkeley. Much more.

"Tell her that I would be delighted to come," the detective said.

"Eight?" McMannis asked, a hint of surprise in his tone.

"I will be ther

Nine

Heading into the Berkeley hills, Toledo felt increasingly nervous. It was not the increasingly perilous drops that presented themselves at every hairpin bend, although they did give him pause, but rather the prospect of negotiating the minefield of subjects to avoid at the coming dinner. Chief among them, Ginny and Selena. The latter's ghost haunted him still, even as the guilt created by that day at Lake Tahoe started to fade. *She made a choice, a very brave choice, and it was her own.* He knew all this, but her death still gently mocked him.

The McMannis home was surrounded by trees and an unruly mob of bushes that made walking up the path to their house a perilous undertaking. The professor had long ago given up attempting to tame the vegetation, and now it grew in tangled chaos. Toledo looked down at the steps as he walked, careful to place his feet on the least cracked stones. He hesitated for a second before ringing the doorbell, cursed his nervousness, and felt his phone buzz at the exact moment that the door opened.

"I'm sorry," he said, instinctively turning away to look at his phone, just as Cathy McMannis's smiling face greeted him.

It was a text from Amanda. As he read it, he marveled at how she always knew about local incidents before anyone else, often before many uniformed officers.

MARK SHAFFER IN SERIOUS ROAD ACCIDENT. PRESENTLY IN COMA AT SAN FRANCISCO GENERAL. UNOFFICIAL WORD IS THAT HE DROVE CAR OFF HAIRPIN BEND DELIBERATELY.

Toledo read the text again, and then remembered where he was standing and turned back toward the open door.

"I am so sorry Cathy, but …"

He stopped mid-sentence, as Cathy had transformed herself into her husband, who was looking with ill-disguised eagerness into the detective's wide eyes.

"I know that look!" the professor said. "Something has happened."

"Perhaps I should have arrested him after all," Toledo answered as he showed McMannis his phone screen. "Mark Shaffer might not make it through the night."

McMannis shook his head as he turned and called into the house.

"Cathy."

No answer.

"Cathy!"

She came out to them, dressed casually but stylishly.

"I'm sorry, but we have to go – something happened in the case."

"It's OK," she said, but her disappointment was obvious. They were silent for a second. The only sound was the breeze through the bushes framing the door.

"I will see you later then." McMannis said.

"It's all right. There'll be other nights. Other dinners." She kissed him on the cheek, then as he turned drew him back to kiss him on the lips. Toledo looked away shyly.

"Bye sweetie," McMannis said as they walked away.

"Be safe," she replied.

"I always am. You know that."

"If only I could believe it."

They shared a gentle laugh and Toledo felt the awkward sting of accidental eavesdropping on a couple's happy moments. He had seldom known such ease with a woman.

The two men turned and made their way down the steps. When they reached the bottom, Toledo turned to his friend.

"Are you sure we should go?"

"We must."

On the way to San Francisco, they said little, although McMannis glanced down toward his phone after he had sent a couple of messages, and audibly sighed.

"Perhaps I should call her," the professor said.

Toledo raised his hands in surrender.

"Don't ask me – marriages are a mystery to me, especially your marriage. Most of the time you seem so in love, or something like that. But then … there is distance."

"Just keep at least one hand on the wheel," McMannis said as the car started to drift a little.

Outside the ICU at San Francisco General Hospital several members of the Shaffer family were standing by the uncomfortable chairs that apparently met the vaguely sadistic leanings of hospital administrators. As Toledo and McMannis walked toward them, the detective realized that they looked the same as when they were lurking by the cars after the funeral. *As if they want to do something but are not quite sure what.* McMannis noticed the daughter, and her name echoed through his mind. *Ophelia. Ophelia.*

It is lucky she is as lovely as she is. McMannis thought. *What if you called your daughter Ophelia, and she turned out to be plain or ugly? Girls should always be given neutral names.* He shuddered at the reaction these thoughts would engender in politically correct colleagues.

"Detective Toledo," Dr. Shaffer said, extending his hand. "It is very kind of you to come."

Toledo shook his hand.

"And Professor McMannis," Dr. Shaffer continued. "Your wife must never see you."

50

It's like he is greeting us at a dinner party rather than the probable death of his son, thought Toledo.

"Oh, she understands the importance of what I do," McMannis said, accentuating the words just a little.

Dr. Shaffer smiled.

"I am afraid that you have had a wasted journey." He said this looking at the frosted glass of the door to the ICU as if he could see through it. "Mark is unconscious."

"And unlikely ever to be conscious again," his wife said, looking at Toledo.

"I am very sorry to hear that," Toledo replied, then glanced sideways as Ophelia made a sarcastic "uh-hugh", adding substance to the mother's accusation.

"Well, we should go," Toledo said.

"Why exactly did we go there in the first place?" asked McMannis as they sped south down Highway 101, toward where Mark Shaffer had crashed.

"I wanted to see their reaction when they saw me. They are a surly bunch."

"Wouldn't you be?" McMannis commented. "Son accused of murder, and now he's driven off a road. And he will probably die. I think I would be surly."

Toledo smiled at the professor's tendency to bring him back to reality. Death and murder were such normal, even mundane components of the detective's life, that he needed to be reminded how forbidding they were to others. *Still, I think they would be surly anyway – murder or not.*

Traffic was strangely light, and they soon passed the airport, slowing down as they approached the turnoff for Burlingame. A San Francisco suburb at the foot of the coastal hills, it provides respite for people who can afford to live in one of the most exclusive jurisdictions in America – Hillsborough. Bing Crosby once called it home, as did the Blues guitar great, Johnny Lee Hooker. The rich and the famous – and those who are both – own massive houses that are often invisible from the twisting roads that snake their way in a maze up into the hills.

"I heard a joke once," Toledo said as they slowed at a light in the middle of Burlingame.

"And what was that?" McMannis replied, but not with much enthusiasm.

"If you must ask what the price of a house in Hillsborough is, you cannot afford it."

McMannis delayed for a second, then looked over at the detective.

"And that is a joke?"

"What passes for one among the humorless people I call friends," Toledo said.

"I should be insulted," McMannis said. "I am one of your friends."

They were now moving up a gradual gradient, through some of the relatively modest parts of Hillsborough.

"So how much are these houses worth?" asked McMannis.

"Those? Low seven figures, but as we move further up into the hills, the prices get larger. Several of them are eight figures up there."

"Eight...?"

"Ten million plus." Toledo said, and McMannis whistled through his teeth.

Far up in the hills, the professor saw the tell-tale reds and blues of police activity.

"Is that it?" he asked.

Toledo nodded.

"Don't get too jealous though," the detective continued. "I've never met one of them who was really happy."

"One of who?"

"People who can own houses like these."

52

"I would take the risk though," McMannis said, and the two men laughed.

The accident site was at the outer edge of a hairpin bend. Toledo parked the car a few yards away and they walked slowly toward several uniformed officers. They were talking to a plain clothes detective who raised his eyebrows in greeting and nodded to them in turn.

"Toledo … McMannis."

"Detective Spander," Toledo replied. "It's been too long."

The San Francisco detective grunted. Thirtyish, average height, weight, hair, looks, clothes – Spander was the classic detective. He was instantly forgettable. Ideal for the job. But like many other plain clothes officers in the Bay Are, he resented Toledo's fame. Resented that he was the one the media always turned to when they wanted expert opinion on some famous case. Resented that Toledo was so at ease in the role.

"Obviously that opinion isn't shared," McMannis murmured as they walked toward the edge.

The car was still on its roof about a hundred feet down. It had torn a clear path through the bushes and small trees.

"How did he get out?" McMannis asked.

"Luck – driving a BMW – he didn't turn over too many times – some mixture of all those." Detective Toledo said as he looked closely at the ground. He turned and slowly stepped along the only course that the car could have taken.

"You notice anything strange, professor?" Spander said.

"Yes. No skid marks."

"Meaning he didn't break."

"Your student has learned well," Spander replied.

"Meaning," Toledo went on, ignoring this last comment, "either he was so distracted that he didn't notice this bend coming, or he deliberately drove off it. Is this the way back to their house?"

"Yes," Spander said. "It's about a half-mile further up the road."

"And he has lived here all his life, so he must know these roads so well he hardly needs to look." Toledo said.

"In this case, that may have been the problem," McMannis said.

"Sir! Look at this!"

It was one of the uniforms shouting out. Both Toledo and Spander turned to look at him.

"What is it?" Spander said, walking down to where the officer was standing.

"There are some tire marks here!" the uniform said, pointing down at the road as if they would need such directions to see what he had found.

Toledo arrived.

"And those are not brake marks," Toledo said.

"No," Spander agreed.

"Those are tires spinning as someone puts his foot on the accelerator and brake at the same time."

"You mean he stopped. Revved his engine then took off as quickly as possible?" McMannis asked.

"That's my boy," Spander said annoyingly.

"So, this was a suicide attempt?" McMannis continued.

"Perhaps." Toledo said, bending down to look at the tracks more closely. "Or maybe he wanted it to look like a suicide attempt. But it went wrong. He nearly completed it."

"Why…?" McMannis did not finish his question as Toledo interrupted.

"I have no idea, it's just what I see. And any person over the age of ten knows how to kill themselves one hundred percent for sure – I've never believed most 'suicide attempts' I've seen. They are more a message than an action. We just have to find out who the message was for."

"His family?" Spander offered.

"Or all of us," said Toledo.

"Or Caroline."

This last suggestion from McMannis, and the other two looked at him inquisitively. Spander studied the professor for a moment, as if finally understanding some annoyance that had bothered him for some time.

After exchanging facetious goodbyes with Spander, replete with promises to keep in touch more, Toledo and McMannis drove to where the Shaffer house was marked on the map. But all they could see was dense hedgerow along the twisting road.

"This can't be it," McMannis said.

"Well, it is," Toledo replied, and they wandered up the road a bit.

"What did you mean by saying that he drove off the road as a message to Caroline? I should think she was past receiving messages."

"In this world, at least," the professor replied.

"Here it is," Toledo said, deciding it was a McMannis eccentricity to be ignored.

The driveway to the house was almost invisible from the road. While most of the houses were far enough back, and thus hidden, the Shaffer home looked like it had been invaded by bushes and trees. Other residences enjoyed carefully manicured lawns leading down to architecturally structured plants on either side of impressive gates. The Shaffers had none of this. It was as if a house and its grounds had been dropped into the neighborhood from another, more primitive area. Or time.

Toledo started off down the steep driveway that led to the house.

"Toledo ... aren't we trespassing?" McMannis asked, still at the top of the drive.

"Just having a look," Toledo replied.

McMannis sighed, shrugged, and joined his friend. They walked carefully down the driveway, partly due to the dark, mainly because of the number of potholes and general collapse in the surface. When they reached the bottom, they found several cars parked haphazardly under overgrown trees. The house itself was oddly situated. The driveway led to what appeared to be a kitchen door. A path to the left ran to what passed for a front door, and to the right some very rickety steps sloped toward the yard. This area was completely overgrown, except for some small pockets of lawn, never more than about eight by eight in size. These were almost mockingly small, as if to show the sheer size of the overgrown mass.

"Not exactly house proud, are they?" Toledo said as he wandered down the path toward the front door. The windows were curtained, and nothing was visible through the frosted glass of the door. He went back to McMannis, who was loitering by the cars.

"Let's try this way."

Without waiting for the professor, Toledo set off down the steps. About halfway down he nearly lost his balance and grabbed hold of the railing – an inadvisable move, as it was even less secure than the steps. Toledo moved with the railing as it bent sideways, then swung at an odd angle. McMannis smiled, thinking the detective looked like some aging, drunk gymnast who had forgotten how to use a piece of equipment.

"Jesus!" Toledo said, trying unsuccessfully to stifle his voice. Finally, he regained his balance and went back up the steps, deciding to curtail his brief exploration. When he was nearly back to McMannis, the kitchen door opened and a very pale woman, about twenty years old, peered nervously at them.

"Can I help you?" she asked meekly, almost apologetically.

"We…" But Toledo did not finish the sentence as a much larger figure appeared behind the girl. It was a huge, surprisingly fast middle-aged woman who tore toward them shouting in what McMannis could swear was German. Incongruously, she was wearing a kimono that flapped around her like a tent caught in a gale. Just as she was getting within striking distance. Toledo pulled McMannis by the jacket and the two men ran back up the driveway to the road and then to their car. As Toledo turned the car around, their pursuer was briefly, dramatically illuminated in the headlights, still waving her arms, and still shouting something terrible at them.

Toledo drove at high speed around a few bends, then slowed to a safer speed. The two men looked at each other laughed nervously.

"Who the hell was that!?" McMannis asked.

"Don't you mean, *what* was that?" Toledo answered.

"She was going to attack us!"

Their exaggerated shudders caused more laughter, which was replaced eventually by a thoughtful silence. It was Toledo who spoke first.

"Would you think that the family that we met at the funeral was living in a place like that?"

"No," McMannis replied.

"And did you see that girl's face? The mouth and eyes – she looked – retarded somehow?"

McMannis shrugged.

"I am certain the woman was shouting German. Something about us being stinking dogs who should be shot."

"Well, it wasn't shooting she was after."

They drove quietly back to the lights of Burlingame, then on to the I-101 and back to San Francisco, the Bay Bridge – and home.

"It looks kind of unimpressive after Hillsborough," McMannis said, after looking up toward his house for a second.

"Maybe, but at least there is someone waiting for you."

McMannis raised his eyebrows, sighed, and got out of the car. He bent down and looked in at Toledo.

"Tomorrow, I think we should go back – but in daylight," Toledo said.

McMannis just nodded and slowly climbed the steps to his house.

Ten

"You were attacked by a kimono-wearing, middle-aged German woman, in the middle of the night?" Amanda asked, hardly disguising her laughter.

"That's right," Toledo answered, eyes downcast.

"And what exactly were you doing there in the middle of the night – without a search warrant?"

"We were 'just looking around' according to Toledo," McMannis intervened.

"You just chose that house at random?"

The two men looked at her across the café table.

"Are you done now?" Toledo asked.

"Yes, Cassius, I am done."

"And anyway, I *do* know who she is. Her name is Ruth Beringer – a native of Munich. Emigrated to the US twenty years ago. She's been working for the Shaffers since."

"Has she visited Japan?" Amanda asked, her face a mask of seriousness.

"Actually," Toledo went on, ignoring her sarcasm, "she has – she went on vacation there ten years ago. Stayed two weeks."

"Two weeks? On a nanny's salary?" McMannis said, toying with the foam on top of his latte.

"No, she went there with Ophelia."

"Ophelia?" Amanda asked. "Does she look like an Ophelia?"

Toledo and McMannis were silent.

"Oh God!" Amanda moaned. "Just so long as you do not end up in some … ambiguous relationship with her…"

Then she stopped, seeing the expressions on their faces. Frozen, distraught.

"I'm sorry. I just …"

McMannis sighed. An image of Selena, the girl who had fallen, passed across his mind's eye. Her quiet, appealing eyes and long hair framing a face of distant, exquisite beauty. And then, she was gone. He had not seen it himself, as only Ginny and a now-dead killer had been there, but the girl's description of her lover's fall had been so detailed, resonant, and evocative that he had created an image of it in his mind. An idealized vision perhaps, but all the more powerful in its intensity.

"The strange thing is that the two types of semen are from members of the same family," Amanda said, almost too loud.

People on the adjacent table stopped talking for a second. Amanda had fallen back to her profession, a field where her occasional emotional clumsiness mattered little.

"The same family?" Toledo said quietly.

"Yes."

"That's weird," McMannis said, noticing that those sitting at the other table had returned to their conversation.

"So, someone else in the Shaffer family?" Toledo murmured, staring down at his latte.

"No, I don't mean that," Amanda said.

"Then what do you mean?" Toledo asked, after a pause.

"The semen in her anal area is Shaffer's. Mark Shaffer's. There's another man's semen on her stomach and just outside her vagina. Too little of it to make any match really. But the weird thing is the semen inside her - that is from two different men entirely – although they belong to the same family."

"Jesus!" Toledo said, rubbing his eyes. "That makes four men? So, either she had one hell of a time during her last evening alive, or we are dealing with a gang rape."

Toledo's words left the other two quiet for a second. *Sometimes*, McMannis thought, *all those years in the police give Toledo a certain ruthlessness. So casual joking about a murder.* Of course, he knew it was a humor born from necessity – a pressure release for emotional tension without which the job would be impossible.

Still, sometimes it is jarring.

Amanda broke the silence.

"There's a problem with that theory - no actual evidence of rape – and the sex occurred pre-mortem rather than post."

"Or at the time of?" McMannis offered.

"I hadn't thought of that," Amanda said. "But I suppose it is a possibility."

"It means there are three other people we have to find," said Toledo. "But I still feel all roads lead to Mark Shaffer."

"Rather than Rome," McMannis murmured. "It is beautiful this time of year."

"Is the evidence of no forcible rape conclusive?" Toledo asked.

"Not exactly," the medical examiner replied. "But apart from the stab wound there is no sign of any violence. No bruising from being held. No defensive wounds. Nothing."

"Ms. Ramirez had voluntary sex with four men? Two of whom are related. One of whom does not produce much semen." Toledo was sardonically matter of fact.

"Yes, and I would guess that the one who does not produce much semen is older."

"How can you tell that?"

"As I said, it *is* just a guess, but his sperm count is lower. It varies naturally within men in general but tends toward low counts in the oldest."

They were silent for a few seconds.

"We need someone closer to the Shaffer family. The secret is there, I think. Something about that girl – the sister."

"You are showing your age, Cassius," Amanda said. "She is in her late twenties. "

Toledo sighed.

"That young woman then. We need someone who can get close to her."

Silence once again, but both Amanda and McMannis knew who Toledo was suggesting.

"Ginny Alridge," the detective eventually said, so quiet as to be almost inaudible.

"Cassius, we can't!" McMannis said loudly. The detective looked up sharply, knowing that the use of his first name meant that the professor was accentuating how serious he was.

"I'm not saying get her involved in the case ... not like last time. Just get her to talk a bit with Ophelia."

"Does she honestly seem like the type of girl ..." McMannis glanced at Amanda, "...woman, who would 'talk a bit' about a case that has led to her brother being suspected as a murderer?"

"She might."

"Cassius, we can't." This from Amanda, and here the use of his Christian name was gentle, appealing.

"OK! OK." The second time was much quieter. "I need to go and think about this. I'll see you both ... soon."

And with that, Toledo was gone. McMannis looked at Amanda, echoing the frown on her face. They both knew that thinking "about this" meant that the detective would convince himself that Ginny should be called upon if needed.

Eleven

An hour after leaving McMannis and Amanda, Toledo was sitting at the end of the pier at the Berkeley Marina. A well-worn, leather-bound report was in his hand. He knew it word for word, but had brought it along as … *well, for what? To remind myself how involving civilians in murder investigations can lead to tragedy?* Perhaps. Or perhaps to simply honor the girl who had died. *It is all within these pages*, Toledo thought. *And anyway, technically at least, Ginny is no longer a civilian.*

Years ago, this pier stuck out three and a half miles into the water, but after the ferry service ended, much of it was left to decay. Now half a mile was left, and Toledo often walked down to the very end - past the little fishing shelters smelling equally of old fish and urine – and looked through the barrier at the shambled, decrepit remains that jutted out into the blue water.

Toledo was born and raised not two miles from where he now sat, and as a child he often walked around this beach park with his family. But nearly always he had ended up here at the very end of the pier, wanting it to be repaired so he could carry on walking across the Bay. He imagined running faster and faster toward the end before diving into the water and swimming to Alcatraz. He had believed it could only be a few minutes' hard work away. Toledo now smiled at the thought. A child has such little sense of distance or, he thought as he glanced at the fog lurking just beyond the bridge, the cold.

The detective looked at the Golden Gate Bridge.

"Hi, Dad," he said, as he always did when sitting alone there. From this distance it appeared tranquil, almost ethereal in its still and graceful beauty. But he had walked across it many times and knew that its reality was metal, wire and concrete shuddering with a constant stream of traffic as it swayed slightly in the nearly constant ocean breezes from the Pacific. Occasionally the fog swept in with a surreal, almost time-lapse speed and the wires, three feet in diameter, howled in near gale-force winds. While some might see it as an homage to Man's ingenuity, for Toledo it spoke more of the immense and casual indifference that nature feels toward us. Yes, they were beautiful, but the sweeping orange arches were dictated by physics rather than aesthetics – essential for the bridge to remain standing.

And if the Golden Gate was a monumental example of human creativity, its ongoing history echoed with despair. Several times a month people traveled – often from the other side of the world – to jump to their deaths in the icy waters of the San Francisco Bay. The contrast between the bridge's beauty at a distance and its jarring reality in close-up reflected the often-deadly paradox of the city itself. Few people in the Bay Area were born there in Toledo's experience – they always came from another place. If you haven't made it anywhere else, or even if you have succeeded but dream of so much more, San Francisco has a seductive pull. In the Nineteenth Century it was the gold to be found in the mountains further inland, and now it is the vaster fortunes to be made in Silicon Valley. But for every person whose dreams are consummated in the city by the bay, there are a hundred who are impotent.

For at least some of those who fail, the Golden Gate Bridge offers an answer. Many have heard its siren call. You cannot go any further west, but you can still escape downward. In years past, when the ocean-facing side of the bridge had a walkway, most people jumped toward the Pacific, turning their backs literally and metaphorically on the city, and country, that had failed them. But in an attempt to limit the number of suicides the ocean-facing walkway was closed, and so jumpers now have a last view of the city before their few seconds fall into oblivion.

Does its beauty taunt them? Toledo wondered.

Suicide hotline telephones are regularly spaced along the walkway, and now – *helpfully* - even provide a text number so that the sad souls contemplating ending it all can receive a safely detached message to dissuade them.

After all, who uses their smartphone to talk to people?

It was not the local suicides that troubled Toledo so much. While tragic, he had seen enough of the dark side of life to know that despair could drive people to madness. His own personal isolation, albeit a deliberate choice as he was "married to the job", had given him hints of the loneliness that an empty house, and life, might bring. But those who traveled thousands of miles, sometimes on long-haul flights, were drawn by some fatal magnetism they only partially understood – *what of those people?* How dark and deep must their hopelessness be to plan weeks ahead, and then steadily make their way toward self-imposed doom?

Often the only sign of their passing, *of their falling*, was a rental car abandoned at the Marin end of the bridge.

Well, the agreements do say 'unlimited mileage'. Does that include heaven or hell … or oblivion?

Toledo sighed and looked away from the Golden Gate. He knew that the mystery of its deadly beauty had led him to his profession. He was still seeking an answer as to the "why?" of human destructiveness – both aimed at others and at ourselves.

Perhaps they are one and the same.
Why?

The question became branded on his psyche a few days after his twelfth birthday when his father, who had started losing bets after that glorious wager on a young Cassius Clay, jumped from the bridge early on a cold Spring morning. Or at least, they assumed he had. His body was never found. But the suicide note left in his car left little doubt, and a Coast Guard lookout "thought" that he had seen "something falling" into the water at "about 9.25 AM". *Curiously precise*, Toledo thought. This was before cameras were permanently placed to record ... something falling.

"Bye, Dad."

He looked away from the bridge, turning toward his much smaller paradox.

Should I call Ginny?

Toledo suspected anyone outside of the case would find his worry mystifying. Why, they might sensibly ask, would a twenty-one-year-old with minimal police training become involved in investigating a murder case? Especially after she had already worked on one with the same detective in which her lover died.

Well, he didn't just suspect they might ask such questions, as he was often assailed with jokes and near-insults by colleagues as some "civilian" helped in an investigation. In fact, McMannis had been the only one – or at least the only one he knew about – and he was now, albeit technically, no longer an outsider.

Some thought Toledo was uncertain of his own skills, maybe emotionally unstable or perhaps even outright "co-dependent" with the ever-present McMannis. One retiring uniformed sergeant, proudly old-school, suggested at a drunken party that perhaps Toledo and the professor were lovers. That accusation was met derisively by several openly gay police officers who assured the "old bigot" that

Toledo was no gayer than he was, using the detective's utter lack of style and dress-sense as proof.

Yet for all the teasing, doubt, and criticism, no one could argue with the results. Toledo solved apparently impossible cases, famously including those difficult cold file murders that took place several decades ago.

Toledo slowly stood up and took a final glance at the Golden Gate Bridge – which had turned a slightly different shade of orange in the constantly changing light.

"Goodbye."

And he walked back down the pier.

He smiled for a moment at those who questioned the legality of his civilian investigators. Most police investigation laws revolved around *unwanted* interference from the public – they were mainly silent when an officer openly invited it. As long as civilians did not pretend to be the police, or tried to use powers reserved to the police, they were quite free to be involved. McMannis becoming a County Constable had been one nod to a more formal position, but it was just that, a nod – in reality it meant very little to how he helped Toledo. It just meant he could look at confidential evidence.

I do need to decide about Ginny though.

He unlocked his car and sat in it.

Some light jazz via Sirius, and a shot of caffeine from his two-hour old triple latte.

He opened the report.

Twelve

For perhaps the twentieth time in the last year, he closed the report and sighed. The facts never changed. The conclusions never changed. In a quite ordinary way, two girls who were suspects in a murder case became witnesses. It happens regularly as those who know details of a murder are often socially closest to the victim, and thus the first to be investigated. But what happened next was far from ordinary. Ginny and Selena started to investigate the murder themselves, getting their information at least partially from McMannis, who had them both in one of his classes.

They helped solve the murder, and Selena died in the process.

Despite his vehement denials, Toledo was never quite believed. After all, he had one civilian investigating with him all the time. Why not another? Or another two?

Toledo's superiors made it clear that civilians, especially teenage girls who were the daughters of Berkeley professors, could never be included in future investigative teams. While they knew that banning Toledo from his unconventional associates was akin to attempting to make San Francisco summers fog-free, or Berkeley vote Republican, the underlying message was to avoid making these investigators too visible.

"Make them be a little more shadowy," one senior officer had murmured to Toledo after a few drinks at a benefit dinner.

Being shadowy, however, was not one of Ginny Alridge's strong points. *She has many of them,* Toledo thought, *but that most certainly is not one.*

68

But Ginny Alridge was not who she once was. No longer a Berkeley student, but a young woman about to graduate from the California police academy. One already marked as especially talented, being groomed for a few years in uniform before becoming a detective.

It was the fact that she was now on the verge of the police that decided it. The detective whisked out his cellphone, ran his finger down the list of contacts. He paused for a moment, then called her.

"Ginny. Would you like some coffee?"

"I thought you'd never ask … been waiting for this call. I knew you would see the light and realize you needed my help at some point."

"Just some brainstorming, just some brainstorming," Toledo said.

Twenty minutes later she flowed into Café Milano, where Toledo had just sat down. He was surprised to find Amanda and McMannis sitting in the same positions as when he had left more than an hour before.

Ginny always looks as though she has just got out of bed after sex, Toledo thought, *or is just about to go to bed for the same reason.* It was this casual but electrifying sensuality that drew eyes to her as much as her lithe yet subtly rounded body. Her green eyes reminded him of something. After small, pecked kisses on all three of their cheeks, Ginny sat down, and Toledo realized who it was. *She has the same eyes as Caroline. Caroline Ramirez.*

"Cassius?" the voice seemed to come from far away. "Cassius?!" And now Amanda was waving her hand in front of his face.

"You look like you saw a ghost," Amanda said.

"In a way, I did."

Ginny looked at the detective quizzically.

"So … I know the basic details of the case from the TV but tell me the rest."

"You've probably heard most of it," Toledo said, suddenly regretting that he had ever made the phone call. After all, the murdered girl was little older than Ginny. A sexual crime of the most brutal nature. She might be at risk.

As was her way, Ginny calculated the situation in an instant and turned away from the table.

"Well, I'll let you *adults* talk it through while I get my coffee. Let me know when I get back whether you really want me to be involved with this case."

"Cassius. What is the problem?" Amanda asked.

McMannis enlightened her.

"I think Ginny reminded him of our victim. To be specific, her eyes."

"It's nothing," Toledo said, waving the concern away. "Someone walked over my grave, that's all."

Ginny came back to the table.

"Well?" she asked. "Should I stay or should I go?"

She quotes Eighties songs in an alarming way, Toledo thought.

"If I go there will be trouble, and if I stay it will be double," Ginny continued.

"What?" McMannis said, as if awakened from a dream.

"It's a song, Ian. From the Eighties. The Clash." Amanda said.

"I know," McMannis replied. "I was just wondering why she was quoting it."

Toledo shook his head briefly, then said, "Stay. But maybe we should all go and talk somewhere a little more private."

'More private' was apparently just a long traipse up Bancroft Avenue to Café Strada, and one of the rarely used tables in the corner of the yard.

As darkness fell, Toledo brought Ginny up to date on the story. McMannis watched as she glanced through the evidence, including photographs. *So strange*, he thought, *she looks so damn young – so innocent – despite those terrible images casting a glow up at her from the tablet.* After about thirty minutes, Toledo had finished.

"So, what do you think?" he asked.

"I think," Ginny said, tapping the stack of evidence like some master-detective about to enlighten her slow subordinates, "I need to take a visit to Hillsborough."

Thirteen

It took two hours for Ginny to drive there the next day.

Toledo had seconded her to the case as a police cadet. Normally they were used for grunt work like searching through garbage for discarded guns or drugs, but nothing in the rules said a cadet could not be undercover.

Nothing in the written rules, anyway.

Ginny decided that Ophelia was her best route into the family, as she was the closest to her in age and experience. Ophelia worked in a daycare center in the area separating the comforts of Burlingame from the luxuries of Hillsborough. Exactly why she worked at the place was a mystery to Ginny. *Obviously, she doesn't need to*, Ginny thought as she leant against a car, watching as the line of BMWs, Mercedes and – slumming it for the day – Lexuses – *or is that Lexi?* - rolled silently to a stop.

The mothers looked ominously like Twenty-First Century Stepford Wives. Two main groups. First, the young women, often alarmingly perfect - from their daintily manicured toenails to their not-a-strand-out-of-place hair. They wafted softly across the parking lot in the late afternoon California breezes. Occasionally one glanced over at Ginny, wondering what exactly this obvious transplant from the other side of the Bay was doing on such hallowed ground. But it was the women in their late thirties that amused Ginny most. The ones who were visibly afraid of being traded in for a younger model. The ones haunted by whispering reminders of the passing years.

They managed to keep time at bay admirably, but its indelible marks snuck up on them in devious ways. The hint of crows-feet around their eyes, the beginnings of too much fat around the hips, breasts just a little south of where they had been at their perky best just years before. Ginny watched, secure in the knowledge that she would never be like one of them. *Or at least*, she thought, *I think I will never be one of them.*

She sighed, closed her eyes, and raised her chin toward the sky, feeling the slight chill in the air.

"Excuse me."

The voice was quiet, uncertain, and almost apologetic.

Ginny paused, then opened her eyes, lowering her face slowly.

"Yes?" she asked.

"I think you are leaning against my car."

Ginny looked down toward the car, as if unaware she was leaning against anything, let alone another person's vehicle.

"Am I? I'm sorry."

She now looked directly into the woman's eyes.

Ophelia Shaffer was about 5'7" and well-proportioned. She was beginning to show some of the excess weight exhibited by her parents, but just a hint of it. She had long brownish-blonde hair that was either completely unstyled or resided in that awkward region between styles. Her eyes were piercing – green in some lights, blue in others, always, Ginny conjectured, remarkably beautiful. Her mouth was small and delicate, as if compensating for the power of her gaze. Her breasts were large and full, neither accentuated nor hidden by her clothes. Small, delicate hands had a few slight scratches from dealing with toddlers all day but were otherwise smooth and untouched.

Ginny saw all of this in a second. She was drawn to the woman. Not the electricity of instant attraction, but rather the pull of intrigue.

"I'm Ginny Alridge."

"I know. I'm Ophelia Shaffer."

"I know."

"And that's my car," Ophelia continued, sweeping her hair back from her eyes.

Not exactly the way I wanted this to go, Ginny thought. *And so much from being under cover. She recognized me from the media stories years ago.* Being so young, three years seemed like an age to Ginny.

"I'm sorry," Ginny said. "I thought maybe I could help sort things out."

Ophelia studied her with intelligent eyes.

"Well, we need things sorted out. I agree with that."

A pause.

"You became famous because you went to Tahoe, found a murderer, and your girlfriend was killed. Three of you went up there. Only one came back."

"Yes," Ginny replied, feeling the tears well in her eyes despite herself.

"I'm sorry."

Somehow, Ginny thought, *she is finding out about me. Not the other way around.* But then she remembered something Toledo had told her. How you could tell as much about someone from the questions they asked as the answers they gave. She had never been entirely sure about this. *Well, now is the time to try.*

"Her name was Selena," Ginny said.

"Selena," Ophelia said slowly, accentuating each sound as if hearing it for the first time.

"That is a beautiful name. Was she beautiful?"

"Yes."

"As lovely as you?"

She did not use the word beautiful that time.

"Far more so."

Ophelia took a half step back, as if restless with this situation.

"You said you could help sort things out. How could you ... sort them out?"

It would have been better to have a ready answer to that.

"I don't know. I'm not a detective or anything. I just thought – I could help."

"And find out if my brother is a killer?"

Ophelia said this quite loudly, with a volume that some of the other mothers obviously heard.

"Don't answer that," Ophelia said, walking quickly around her car and getting in on the driver's side. "Let's get a coffee. You must be used to that, coming from Berkeley."

So, with bizarre speed Ginny Alridge inculcated herself into Ophelia Shaffer's trust and was going to some unknown café with her. Or at least, she thought she was going to a café. But Ophelia drove them away from Burlingame, up into the slopes and trees and winding luxuries of Hillsborough. Ginny glanced sideways at the woman, wondering for a moment whether she was trusting her a little too much, and a little too fast. As if in reply Ophelia turned toward her and smiled, then shifted into a higher gear as the BMW accelerated around a curve.

Fourteen

Toledo glanced toward his phone and sighed as he saw a Berkeley campus number flashing at him.

"Hello."

"Is that Detective Toledo?"

"It is."

"This is Joel Alridge here."

"Professor. Good to hear from you again."

"Same here. Detective?"

"Yes."

"Seen my daughter lately?"

"You mean Ginny?"

"Yes, Ginny. I have only one daughter."

Stupid question, but at least it bought some time.

"Ginny? Well, yes, I have."

"Ah!"

The last word was pointed. Not exactly accusatory, but not friendly either. Toledo knew that Berkeley professors were unused to being treated lightly. Even modest and essentially down-to-earth specimens of the species like this one had a nagging suspicion of their own divinity.

"I saw her two days ago, in fact."

"Yes, she said she was coming to see you. She left yesterday morning, saying she needed to go somewhere as part of a case. She never returned home last night."

After the Tahoe case, Ginny moved back home from her shared student accommodation. She had her own end of the family house, but the professor and his wife kept casual tabs on her.

"She didn't?"

"No. And I was a bit surprised to hear her talking about 'the case' as if she was part of it."

Toledo did not want to get into an unwinnable debate with the man. He decided to take the passive-aggressive approach.

"She is about to graduate from the academy. She is acting as a cadet on the case."

Silence.

"I see. Thank you, Detective Toledo."

Toledo frowned. It was strange that Ginny had not checked in with him after returning from Hillsborough, assuming she had returned. Toledo called McMannis.

"Ian? You haven't heard from Ginny, have you?"

"Nope. Not since yesterday evening."

"She did call you from Hillsborough?"

"Yes. The reception was bad though. She said something about being in the hills with Ophelia, and that everything was okay. Not to worry. Then I lost the signal. She never called back."

Toledo frowned.

"Why would she say that everything was okay? What reason would we have to think that it wasn't?"

McMannis was silent.

"Perhaps she knew she wasn't coming back last night – and knew that people might wonder where she was, might become worried."

"Perhaps. Let me call Amanda."

Toledo did so, but she had heard nothing from Ginny either. In one sense, it seemed ridiculous to worry about Ginny's non-return to the East Bay after meeting up with Ophelia. After all, she probably came back through San Francisco, with its numerous distractions. Perhaps she was staying with a friend.

A text came through from the uniformed officer who was watching Mark Shaffer at the hospital.

CONDITION WORSE. SHAFFER DESCENDING INTO DEEPER COMA

Great, Toledo thought, *that's all we need – a major suspect who perhaps we can't interview for the next few months. He might even die – then what?* He twiddled with his pen for a moment, realizing that this was not exactly the kindest of thoughts. *But if he did do what it seems very likely he did – coma and then death is getting off lightly.* Prison, Toledo knew, would not be kind to a young man like Mark Shaffer. Everything that gave him status in the outside world – his money, his education, his looks, his luxurious lifestyle – would be weaknesses, perhaps deadly ones, in the perverted, inverted existence of a state penitentiary.

Toledo looked across his small but tidy lounge. It showed signs of a place travelled through rather than a destination. The chair he was sitting in was well used, but the couches were worn by time rather than people. The cushions were still plump, as if new, and it was only the sun faded areas that showed their true age. *A bachelor's lonely pad,* Toledo thought, without a hint of regret or self-pity. Melancholy, yes, but not real sadness. He was, cliché of clichés, married to this job – and all in all, it was a successful marriage. The glow of the first years had worn off, like the physical passion of new love that is so electrifying, and yet so fleeting. Now, secure in his position as a detective, a deeper love had developed. Toledo was not only good at what he did, not even just very good, he was one of the best.

He walked over to his stereo and flipped on a Stan Getz record, enjoying as he always did the sensuousness of mechanically reproduced music, rather than the soulless precision of the digital age. Toledo liked the occasional scratches on his prized records as it lent them individuality.

The fact that you could fit all his music collection onto a single memory card was fascinating, if a little distasteful. *There is pleasure in a bulky record that no amount of convenience could ever give.* Toledo knew he was the butt of many jokes around the department regarding his Luddite attitudes and took them mostly with good spirit. He enjoyed the rumors of eccentricity, maybe even a little craziness.

The jazz caressed him gently and he sat back into his chair, allowing Getz's lilting tenor sax to remove him from the world of bodies, suspects, and blood stains. At least for a while. The music washed over the detective, cleansing him of the filth that the dregs of human behavior muddied him with. He drifted into gentle sleep.

He woke up two hours later. *Still nothing from Ginny.* Toledo felt worry creep up on him, despite it being absurdly premature. Just as he was about to call McMannis, the professor saved him the effort.

"Cassius?"

"Yes?"

"Heard anything from her?"

"No."

"It has been twenty-four hours."

"I know."

"Do you think we should start looking for her?"

"And where should we start?" Toledo asked, a little impatient.

"The Shaffer home?"

"Fine. I will call them first though."

Rather than using police dispatch, Toledo tried 411. It was ridiculous, he knew, but maybe the Shaffers were old enough to be simply a listed number. He was right. They were.

He dialed the number.

"Hullo."

"Is that the Shaffer household?"

79

"Yes."

The voice was young, almost imperceptibly soft.

Toledo was just about to ask whether Ginny was there when a loud thump came down the line, as if the quiet-voiced person on the other end had dropped the receiver. Toledo strained to hear what was happening, as scrapes, bumps and static competed with one another. Then another voice, much louder, and with a German accent.

"Telephone. Too late. Too much information. Don't give it out. Take it in. Give it here."

The phone clicked and there was silence.

Toledo called McMannis back.

"Well, I got through to the Shaffer house."

"And?"

"You were an English Lit Major weren't you?"

"Yes. You know I was. As were you."

"Well, the Shaffers seem to have Mr. Jingle living with them – only this time he is German, and a woman."

Fifteen

In stark daylight the Shaffer house was even more incongruous among its pristine neighbors than at night. Toledo and McMannis slowed down and stopped at the top of the driveway, then peered down into the virtually impenetrable gloom below.

"Do you think we should park up here?" Toledo asked.

"I don't know. It does look like you could drive down and never be seen again. Perhaps it would be safer to leave it here."

"It is just an overgrown yard, not Dracula's castle," Toledo said and paused. "Better safe than sorry I guess."

He parked on the road.

They walked down the driveway, around a small curve and were greeted by a smiling Ophelia Shaffer.

"Detective Toledo and Professor McMannis – we have been expecting you."

"You have?" Toledo said after a pause.

"Of course," the woman said, then turned and walked through the kitchen door and into the house.

"Do you think we should follow her?" Toledo asked.

"Your guess is as good as mine," McMannis answered, and they made their way toward the door, stopping to peer through the dirty glass. Suddenly a looming, dark shape appeared inside, and the door opened enough for them to see a face. It was the German woman. Both men flinched backward slightly, as if expecting an attack.

"Gentlemen. Gentlemen. Good greetings. Last time-- big mistake--my fault—apologies. Many, apologies, many."

And with that the door flew open.

The two men walked slowly into the house. Just inside was a small room with a couple of couches and a television. A two-way fireplace gave a glimpse of brightness within the kitchen, which in turn led into a much larger, formal dining room. It was here that the first signs of wealth appeared. The furniture was a deep red mahogany and it stood on a lush Persian rug. The ornaments were exquisite and the glasses hanging from a wine-rack glinted with the sparkle of pure crystal.

The Shaffers were arranged around the table and there, at the very end, sat Ginny, for all the world like the head of the family.

"Ginny," Toledo said, trying to hide the annoyance in his voice, "you have a lot of people worried about you."

"Worried?" the young woman replied. "Why have they been worried?"

"You came over here ... and didn't come back." Toledo said.

"I was just – visiting."

Toledo looked around the table and saw that, despite his first impressions, the family was not complete. Jerry Shaffer was absent. He had mistaken a young man sitting by Ophelia as the patriarch. It was the brooding brother, and he had a shock of prematurely grey-to-white hair. *He resembles an overweight, homeless Andy Warhol.*

"Guests—most welcome—guests must sit."

"Thank you, Miss Beringer," McMannis said.

Toledo gave a quick look of gratitude. He had forgotten the name.

"Oh. Ruth, Ruth. Please. Formality—ugly—not needed."

And with that pronouncement she mimed spitting on the floor. She drew the two chairs out from the table as if they were weightless and deposited McMannis and Toledo in them like overgrown babies.

"There—that much better. Now—food—food for all."

She went back into the kitchen. There was silence around the table until the younger people burst out laughing. Mrs. Shaffer gave them an annoyed look, and they soon quieted.

"Well, she is funny, mamma, you must admit that," Ophelia said, looking toward Ginny and giggling again.

"She is not funny," Mrs. Shaffer said. "She is just German."

This was cause for another round of laughter. Toledo glanced toward McMannis; eyebrows raised.

"She does, I admit, have a most interesting way of speaking."

The laughter subsided.

"So, Detective Toledo – are you on the hunt tonight, or is this a social call?"

"Actually … neither – we came looking for Ginny here. A rescue mission." Toledo answered smoothly after a pause.

Finally, silence. Toledo and McMannis were the uninvited guests, and they knew it.

"Well, you found her," Mrs. Shaffer said, a touch of irony in her voice. "You rescued her."

"Yes." Toledo replied. "We rescued her."

The young man by Ophelia sighed, poured himself a glass of wine. McMannis noticed a slight tension appeared as he did this. The family watched him with a mixture of interest and speculation as to what might happen next. Once he had finished pouring, with a flourish that brought the wine up to the brim, all eyes turned to the matriarch.

"I think this calls for a drink," said the young man.

He brought the glass up to his lips.

"Doesn't everything call for a drink with you, Teddy?" Ophelia said, timing it perfectly to the moment the wine passed into his mouth. He gulped down the whole glass.

"Yes … it does!" Teddy replied, as if newly enlightened to some glorious truth.

The food arrived and for a few minutes the table was silent except for the sound of plates and cutlery.

"So, Detective," Mrs. Shaffer said eventually, "why didn't you arrest Mark?"

Toledo carried on chewing, swallowed a perfectly cooked piece of steak, sipped some wine, and then looked up to her.

"Because, like God, I move in mysterious ways."

This prompted a little snicker from the Ophelia and Teddy region of the table. Evidently it was rare for anyone to get the better of this formidable woman, and they were relishing every moment of it.

"You have a God complex, Detective?"

"No, he doesn't," McMannis intervened. "I just think he doesn't like to fly in the face of public opinion."

More disguised giggles and Mrs. Shaffer frowned slightly, realizing she was outnumbered by not just one, but two minds as sharp as hers.

"Mamma thinks you shouldn't laugh at such important subjects," Ophelia said. "She thinks it disrespects them."

"I'm sorry," Toledo said, apparently genuinely.

"Mamma also thinks that it reveals something about someone's libido."

"Their libido?" McMannis echoed.

"Yes, their libido."

McMannis glanced toward Mrs. Shaffer, mystified.

"I think Ophelia is referring to the fact that I am a Psychologist," she said. "Ophelia obsesses on the idea that all psychologists think about is sex, or at least the sexual impulse. I have told her countless times that 'libido', when used in psychology, does not refer to what it does in the ordinary world – but she refuses to listen."

"I don't refuse to listen, mamma. I just disagree."

84

"It takes knowledge to disagree with something. Something you do not possess."

Ophelia mumbled something unintelligible then whispered in Teddy's ear. He smiled, burped politely, and kissed her on the cheek. Toledo noticed as the kiss lingered. The detective frowned. The young man moved away from his sister.

"Detective, you have a certain … reputation."

"I suppose."

"You are famous." Mrs. Shaffer paused ostentatiously. "Or is that infamous?"

"Well, I think because I tend to work with … unsavory characters, my mother used to say. Because I work with them, however famous I might be – there is a certain infamy that rubs off."

"He is saying he deals with the shit of life, Mamma." Ophelia lent conspiratorially toward her mother as she said this.

"Which I guess makes us shit!" This from Teddy, and much louder.

Mrs. Shaffer glanced venomously at her son, was about to speak again but then shrugged and pushed her chair back. This was a silent signal, as all the family got up and left the table. Toledo and McMannis were left with Mrs. Shaffer.

"We always take a break before dessert," she said.

They made their way out onto the small, rickety deck that hung over the backyard like some worn shop sign that was ready to fall at any moment. The two men were joined by Ginny.

"What in the hell are you doing?" Toledo asked quietly but pointedly.

"You asked me to get to know the family, so here I am."

"I didn't mean move in with them."

85

"I just stayed the night," Ginny said. "Down there in fact."

She was pointing down into the now gathering dusk.

"You spent the night in the yard?" McMannis asked incredulously.

"No, there is a little room down there. Ophelia calls it the date-room because that's where they brought their dates when they were teenagers."

"Really?" McMannis said, leaning perilously over the railing to look down.

"It was very comfortable in fact," Ginny said. "Although some of the things in it are a bit creepy."

"What things?" asked McMannis, but before Ginny could answer they were joined by Ophelia.

"It is beautiful even though it is so overgrown," Ophelia said.

"Yes." Toledo said but didn't sound too convinced.

"Mark didn't kill her, you know. He couldn't harm anyone."

Toledo did not bother correcting the woman's naïve certainty. He had discovered many years ago that love creates an impenetrable wall of make-believe innocence. No-one, in Toledo's experience of families, could ever hurt anyone. *Until they do.*

"How long have your family lived here?"

"Since I was about two years old. This is the only home I have ever known. Dad bought it just after he finished his residency."

Twenty-eight years! It was a long time to live in one house and looking at the dense vegetation sprawled in front of him it looked as if it hadn't been maintained in all that time.

"And none of you has ever moved out?"

Ophelia smiled slightly.

"No," she said quietly. "None of us ever moved out. We didn't see the point. It is too beautiful."

Silence and the breeze started to pick up among the now darkening trees.

"We did go away for college – but we all came back … and stayed."

"What did you study?" Toledo asked casually.

"Oh – everything and nothing, I never graduated in the end."

No need to, Toledo thought. *Education is a luxury to the rich.*

As if in answer to his thought, Ophelia said,

"Not that I didn't want to – I really did. I just got involved in some of the wrong things."

They laughed quietly.

"Didn't we all." Toledo said. "Didn't we all."

"And anyway, Mark did enough studying for the rest of us put together. He's always been the over-achiever in the family. Or at least he was."

Toledo considered pursuing this line of questioning. Did she mean that he 'was' until he crashed his car, or until some other moment, further back, that they had yet to discover? Instinct told him to be silent for the moment. An interrogation disguised as a conversation needed to be subtler, with information gained piecemeal rather than head-on.

"Will you excuse me?" Ophelia said.

Toledo, thinking it was merely a courtesy comment, continued perusing the vegetation. Then he looked sideways and saw that she was still standing there.

"Of course. Please." He said, and Ophelia turned away, her long hair hitting him slightly in the face. She went inside just as Ginny's phone buzzed.

"Apparently, there is some cell reception standing out here," she said. "But not inside…or down there."

McMannis was leaning perilously over the railing that, like just about everything else in or outside the house, looked as if it might collapse at any moment in protest at its poor maintenance.

"What I can't understand is that with all this money they don't …" McMannis said, but he was interrupted.

"Visitors – inside – getting cold outside. No? Dessert. Very good. Dessert."

And with that the German maid pushed them back into the house. Ginny giggled a little at the nod to stereotype – Black Forest Gateau.

"All Ruth needs now is one of those German skirt and shirt combinations," McMannis whispered to Toledo, who frowned. Ginny overheard his comment and giggled some more. "Or those funny pant things…what are they called?"

"I think you mean lederhosen." McMannis helpfully informed her.

Ginny laughed more loudly but managed to control herself on an even sterner look from Toledo.

Dessert was delicious but eaten in a hurry and largely in silence. Apparently, everyone had other places to be in the house and they soon scattered, leaving the three visitors to their own devices.

"They are just leaving us here?" McMannis commented.

"Apparently," Toledo replied,

"Perhaps they think we are just moving in," Ginny said. "Many people seem to just come and go without an invite in this place. This house is actually big enough to get lost in."

"Bigger on the inside than out." McMannis said contemplatively. "Like the TARDIS."

"The what?" Toledo asked.

"The TARDIS – you know – the telephone box that Dr Who time travels in."

"Oh. OK…" But the detective was obviously mystified.

"That's what I love about you, Ian," Ginny said, putting her arm through the professor's. "Despite appearances you are so up to date with things!"

Dr Who had become something of a hit among college students with its appearance on internet streaming services. McMannis found it amusing that few of them seemed to realize that it had a long history, dating back to B/W television days before their parents were born.

"I'm OK, just so long as we don't crash into any daleks on the way out!"

Ginny essentially squealed with delight at this reference, and Toledo wondered whether she was in fact a little too young for this kind of assignment. They left the house and wandered up the meandering driveway, cursing the lack of light every time they nearly tripped. Ginny was giving Toledo a rundown on *Dr* Who, with pictures that had apparently been saved onto her phone. All three sighed a little as they got into the car.

"That was like escaping from some medieval castle," McMannis said.

"Or Dracula's," Ginny offered.

The men exchanged a glance. Somehow her comment was less ridiculous than when Toledo had said it when they first arrived.

"Well Ruth sure does have the accent," McMannis said.

Rather than turn on the engine, Toledo just sat and peered out.

"From here you'd never know that there even was a house down there," Toledo said.

The other too looked and nodded. The foliage was so dense that not even a glimmer from the house below pierced the darkness.

"Where is your car?" asked Toledo.

"Down in the school parking lot," Ginny answered after a pause, as if trying to remember.

"We'll drop you."

As Ginny got out of the car a few minutes later, Toledo asked her a question.

"These daleks...you say they want to kill everyone?"

"Everyone who is not a dalek."

After a slight pause, "why?"

Ginny shrugged and frowned slightly, as if she had never asked the question herself.

"I don't know … perhaps they just don't like anyone. Or perhaps they just like the word 'exterminate' too much."

Without further explanation, she jumped out of the car and was gone.

"Exterminate?" The detective said.

"Toledo, I'll tell you on the way home."

Sixteen

"Well, we can confirm that the Shaffers are one of the creepiest families in the Bay Area," Toledo said as they sat in the café the next morning. "But what else did we discover?"

All eyes turned to Ginny.

"Or do you mean, what else did *I* discover?"

"If you want," Toledo replied. "But first – one thing's been bothering me. You said that Ophelia Shaffer recognized you, or at least your name, when you first met?"

"Yuhp."

"But does she know that you are no longer a civilian – that you are a police cadet?"

Ophelia frowned for a moment.

"They know that I am not a police officer. They asked me whether I was, and I said no. That is the truth. Because I am not."

"OK." Toledo said, a little doubtfully.

"Well, you wanna know what I found out?"

They all nodded.

"Ophelia took me up into the hills above her house. She told me about her high-school boyfriend. How much she loved him."

"High school?" Toledo said.

"Yes, high school. She said that if you want to understand her family, he would be the best place to start."

"You met him?" McMannis asked.

"Not exactly. Ophelia took me to the place that he shot himself twelve years ago. A turn-out in the road just before it starts to descend to the ocean."

"He shot himself?" McMannis echoed.

"Why?" Toledo asked.

"She doesn't know why. She just – wanted to take me there. She said whenever anything good happens in her family it turns bad. She said that she still loved him – had never really loved anyone else."

Amanda cleared her throat, as if reminding them she was there.

"You ever loved anyone that much?" Toledo said to her.

Amanda shook her head slowly. He turned to McMannis.

"You?"

The professor smiled slightly, neither confirming nor denying.

"I know I haven't." Toledo answered when McMannis was silent.

"Ever since there's been one tragedy after another," Ginny continued. "There was one good thing that came out of this relationship though."

"And that was?" asked Toledo.

"Her son. Alan."

"Her *son*?" Toledo said incredulously.

"Yes, he is six years old. For the last couple of weeks, he's been at San Francisco General. He suffers from a serious form of asthma. So serious that he spends half his time in the hospital."

"So, they were going to see *two* family-members the other night?" Toledo said, then whistled slightly through his teeth.

"There was one person missing at the dinner," McMannis said.

"Who was that?" Toledo said.

"The girl who answered the door when Ruth charged at us. The one with the strange face."

All eyes turned to Ginny. After a moment's thought she replied.

"Oh – that's Hermia. The youngest daughter. All I know about her is that she was born – a bit slow – I think that's how Ophelia put it."

"A bit slow?" McMannis echoed.

"It looked congenital to me," Toledo said.

"Anyway, she is very shy. Never shows her face when there are visitors. It's a bit of a miracle she answered the door for you. There was another sister too – Ariel – she died at the age of fourteen about twenty years ago."

"Just like that? She just died?" Toledo asked.

"That's what I was told," Ginny said with a shrug.

"What do you think, Amanda?" Toledo asked.

"I think we are getting a bit far away from the subject," she said. "Beyond the strange forensic evidence does anything suggest this was anything but a murder based on cheating and jealousy?"

"Other than multiple samples of semen – and those are a pretty big 'other' – we've got nothing. Nothing physical anyway." Toledo said. "But there is something else. Something strange beyond the physical. Something about this family that needs to be unearthed."

"Something buried in that back yard perhaps?" McMannis interjected.

"Not literally," Toledo replied with a little rolling of the eyes. Then, after a moment, "but who knows?"

They sat in silence.

"What is with the names?" Amanda asked finally.

"You mean the Shakespearean stuff? Hermia, Ophelia?" Ginny said.

"Yes."

"Seems Dr. Shaffer was an English major in college. He wanted to be an actor or something. Realized he wasn't good enough, and …"

"And so, became a heart doctor!" Toledo completed her sentence.

"Any other Shakespeare references?" he continued. "No Desdemona or Viola? What about a Juliet?"

"Not as far as I know."

"Well," Toledo said, rubbing his eyes, "I guess we have to wait for Mark Shaffer to wake up."

Seventeen

But for the next two weeks he did not.

Toledo solved a simple domestic murder during that time. 'Argument. Kitchen. Knife in the wrong place,' was how he described it in his crime journal. In a gesture toward magnanimity, he recommended only manslaughter charges to the DA.

Yet the whole time the murder of Carol Ramirez lurked in his mind. It would be neatest, and simplest, to blame Mark Shaffer for it all. He could be tried if, or when, he ever recovered from his coma. *And he'll probably be convicted*, the detective thought as he walked across campus toward his normal haunt in Café Milano. Just as he was passing under the Sather Gate, he received a text from Amanda.

INTERESTING NEWS RE MARK SHAFFER. SUGGEST   MEETING

Toledo texted back.

WHAT? IS HE DEAD?

NO. SOME RESULTS CAME BACK. MEET ME AT SF GENERAL

Toledo sighed. While SF General Hospital was perhaps twenty miles from where he stood, it might take more than an hour to get there. As if in answer to his thoughts, he received another text from the coroner.

IF YOU WANT A RIDE MEET ME AT THE BERKELEY PD

And within twenty minutes Toledo and Amanda were speeding at about three hundred feet across the Bay in a helicopter. Their pilot liked to follow the course of the Bay Bridge and Toledo glanced down at the traffic snarled up as it crawled its way into San Francisco. Toledo avoided

95

copters as he never felt fully safe in them, but this had been too good an opportunity. *And also*, he thought as they approached the helipad on top of the hospital, *I need a new perspective on things. But probably*, he continued thinking as the helicopter was buffeted by some winds as it descended, *not quite as literally new as this.*

Soon they were sitting in the ICU, waiting to be shepherded into the room by a nurse.

"Why did we come all the way here?" Toledo asked. "Couldn't you have just told me over some nice coffee, back in Berkeley?"

"Well, I could," Amanda said, standing as the nurse greeted them. "But that wouldn't have been as much fun."

Her definition of fun gets stranger every year, Toledo thought wryly.

Mark Shaffer was lying in the same position as before. The young man's skin had a slightly yellow pallor. Unhealthy, almost dead. The gentle rise and fall of his ventilator-induced breathing was the only sign of life, but even this gave him an unnatural, almost mechanical appearance. Toledo was reminded of a CPR dummy.

"Well?" he asked Amanda.

"The thing is … we have all been assuming Mark was rendered comatose by the blow he received to the head during his crash." Amanda said quietly, as if she might accidentally wake the comatose suspect.

"And are you saying that he wasn't?"

"Precisely."

They looked down at the still figure. He breathed in. He breathed out. A monitor to the side showed a slow but regular heartbeat.

"In fact, he is in an insulin-induced coma."

"Insulin? He wasn't a diabetic."

"No – and that is why he is in a coma," Amanda said, an ironically triumphant smile on her face.

"You mean he took insulin, and this has caused the coma?"

"Exactly."

"And what about the car crash?" Toledo asked, his voice rising slightly.

"He was injured. He received a big blow to the head, but nothing that would cause a young, healthy man to be out this long. He had virtually no internal injuries."

Toledo sighed and scratched his cheek, realizing he needed a shave.

"So, Mark Shaffer injected himself with insulin? Then drove off that road in case that didn't work?"

Amanda paused for a moment, then said,

"Perhaps. All we know is that somehow insulin got into his system. Either he – or someone else – must have injected him."

Toledo peered at the young man, as if simply staring could induce him to reveal all his secrets. Suddenly a thought came to him.

"Dr. Shaffer. He is very overweight, has poor eyesight, and reddish skin. Diabetic perhaps?"

"I have already checked. He is. Come on."

Amanda skimmed out of the room, pulling Toledo by the hand.

"Where now?" the detective asked as they got to the elevator.

"Time to visit the Shaffers again I think," Amanda said, and pressed the button that would take them to the roof again.

"What are we doing? Going to parachute into them or something?" Toledo asked.

"Not exactly," Amanda said, and shepherded him back into the helicopter. "I have some friends in Hillsborough who live near the Shaffers."

The helicopter rose straight from the top of the building, hovered for a moment, and then sped away. Toledo closed his eyes, feeling the vertigo in his stomach, the bile rising.

"They live near them – and also have a helipad."

"I shouldn't have asked," Toledo said, staring down at the stream of lights heading down I-101.

Toledo tapped the pilot on the shoulder.

"Do you always follow the roads?" he asked.

"Always," the man replied. "It's a trip!"

Eighteen

The friends were not "near" the Shaffers. They were the neighbors. The two houses and their spacious grounds were a study in contrast. The shabby, overgrown Shaffer estate was bordered by the pristine perfection of a home that featured perfectly manicured lawns, a glistening blue swimming pool with hot tub, a tennis-court and two houses. The main residence was sprawling, perhaps upwards of ten thousand feet. What he assumed to be a guest house intrigued Toledo most. *Looks like an English cottage*, he thought. It looked vaguely familiar but from where he had no idea.

The helicopter descended slowly onto the helipad. It was located between the pool and tennis court, surrounded by palm trees. *How the hell do you grow palm trees a few miles from the marine fog layer?* But he had discovered many times that money, even if it can't buy you love, can pretty much buy you anything else. *Even fog-resistant palm trees.*

Once the rotors stopped turning and they opened the door, there was a strange silence. Toledo glanced over to the right, past the swimming pool and the guest house toward the dark green, tumbling vegetation of the Shaffers. It looked a world away.

"Shall we?" Amanda said.

"Be my guest," Toledo answered, and the medical examiner jumped out, stretching as if after a long flight rather than a short helicopter ride. As she turned toward Toledo a door in the main residence opened, a man came out and walked quickly toward them. He was as perfectly dressed as his lawn was manicured. Toledo knew little about designer clothes – *well, actually nothing* – he thought, but he guessed this man's clothes probably cost thousands. He was about forty-five, small but well-proportioned. Short blond-grey hair with sea-blue eyes.

"Amanda, darling!" said the man, with an exaggerated kiss on each cheek.

Toledo had already decided that the occupants of this magnificent estate must be gay, with no more evidence than the perfectly designed and maintained grounds. Gay men made Toledo uncomfortable. He knew that this was a troglodyte attitude, one that made his more liberal friends cringe. But it was what it was. He was not actively homophobic and treated everyone with the same respect – or lack of it, if they deserved it – regardless of sexuality. Yet he still felt strange around gays. More importantly, he could not read a gay man as accurately as he did nearly every other human being. His discomfort built a wall around them that he could not penetrate.

"And you must be Detective Toledo," the man said, extending his hand.

Toledo was relieved when he did not try to hug him, a relief that he saw the man noticed and found rather amusing.

"Yes, I am. Good to meet you."

They shook hands, and there was a pause.

"I'm sorry," Amanda said suddenly, "this is Ben Williams. Ben's been a friend of mine since ..."

"Decades, centuries!" Ben interrupted.

Toledo had heard of Ben Williams. He was a theatre director who once went to Berkeley and now ran one of the gay theatres in San Francisco.

"Detective Toledo." Ben said, savoring the words as if they were from some new language that he had always

100

wanted to speak, but had just mastered. He took a slight step back and perused the detective.

"I thought you would be taller."

After a moment's pause Toledo said, "nearly everyone does."

Ben glanced over Toledo's shoulder, toward the helicopter.

"Useful machines," he said. "I don't use mine often enough."

The last comment was delivered as a simple fact, without a hint of irony or pretension. Toledo smiled slightly. He immediately warmed to the man.

"So, do you want to go straight over there, or will you pop in for a glass of wine first?" Ben asked.

The 'over there' was delivered with a dismissive wave toward the dark tangled trees that bordered his property.

"Let's have a drink first," Amanda said, just as Toledo was about to refuse.

Instead of returning inside, Ben led them to the guest house. As they neared the door, and just before he saw the sign over it, Toledo realized where he had seen this house before. *The Ann Hathaway Cottage*, he thought.

"You must like Shakespeare a lot," Toledo said as they went inside.

Ben laughed.

"You could say that. Yes, we do."

We. I wonder where the other half of that we is?

"We built it about ten years ago, just after we bought the place. It was a sort of homage to Tony's birthplace, as well as to my profession."

Toledo and Amanda sat on one of the huge leather couches that graced the living room while Ben went into the kitchen, calling out various wine names for them to choose one.

"Tony?" Toledo whispered.

"His lover," Amanda replied. "They are more settled than most straight married couples I know. Tony is the one with the money. Family owns half of London from what I've heard."

"Must be nice."

Ben returned with their wine. A burgundy that mellowed Toledo within seconds. He raised the pure crystal toward the light, enjoying the depths of color.

"So, what do you think of my lovely neighbors?" Ben asked, a twinkle in his eye.

"Interesting people," Toledo replied. "How well do you know them?"

"Enough to know that I don't want to know them, any further," Ben said. "One of the weirdest assortments of people I've ever met. My main problem – as you can imagine – is the pitiful state that they keep their property in. Tony thinks there is something romantic about it. A last echo of Dickensian decay, I think he said. Whatever that means. A few years ago, Dr. Shaffer accused one of our staff of deliberately throwing lawn mower cuttings onto their property. Can you believe that? I mean, how could they identify a few scraps of grass in that jungle, for a start?"

Amanda giggled slightly. Toledo smiled.

"He even had the nerve to take me to small claims court, saying I was infringing on his property."

Amanda laughed.

"Unsurprisingly, it was thrown out."

There was silence as they sipped their wine.

"Shakespeare." Toledo said finally.

"Shakespeare?" Ben echoed.

"That's a link between you and the Shaffers."

"There is?" Ben said, apparently genuinely mystified.

"The names of their children …" Toledo went on.

And now it was Ben's turn to laugh.

"Yes, you are quite right. The names of their children. Ophelia, Hermia, Ariel, ..."

Toledo was positive that the man was about to say another name when he deliberately stopped himself.

"A little pretentious, don't you think?" Ben went on.

"At least they are trying to be original," Amanda said.

"True. True." Ben said, then glanced down toward his watch. *Rolex, diamonds, but tastefully done*, thought Toledo.

"I just wish they'd clear it up, just a little bit," Ben said. "I even offered to send our staff over there a few years ago. But they took that as an insult. An insult! I was being serious!"

Ben stressed the last word loudly and Amanda laughed at the self-parody. *I wonder whether he is making fun of the histrionic gay man – or of the stereotype that straights like me buy into*, Toledo thought.

"Sometimes I think there is some old woman shut up in that house," Ben went on. "Sitting in her decaying wedding dress, with rats scurrying in and out of a wedding feast that will never be eaten." He turned to Toledo as if expecting the detective to have been left far behind by the literary allusions.

"It does have the ring of *Great Expectations* about it, I agree. But the German maid is more a female version of Mr. Jingle. *The Pickwick Papers*." Toledo said.

"Yes!" Ben replied, trying – but failing – to disguise his surprise at Toledo's evident education. Amanda stood back slightly and eyed the two men with a vaguely amused air.

"Well, we should be going," Amanda said. "Sorry we interrupted your day at such short notice."

"Anytime for you, darling. Anytime."

And with that, Ben Williams kissed Amanda on both cheeks again, raised a friendly hand in goodbye to Toledo, and left the cottage.

Amanda looked at Toledo and burst out laughing when she saw the expression on his face.

"You always look so ... bemused around gay men. I'd have thought you'd have got used to them by now, living where you do."

"I know, I know."

They walked out of the cottage and onto the path that led away from the houses toward the road. Ben had disappeared back into the main residence and the grounds looked totally deserted.

People seem extraneous to this perfection. Toledo thought.

"Did you notice that he was about to say another name, then didn't?" he asked as they got to the road.

"What? No, I don't think he was," Amanda replied.

"Really?"

But she strode ahead onto the road. Within minutes they had descended to the Shaffers again. At first, they thought no-one was in, but on the third ring of the bell Ruth came to the door.

"Detective – most welcome – most wel-come," the German woman said, oddly dividing the word on its repetition.

"And such a pretty lady. So pretty. Wife perhaps? Marriage in future? Patter of little feet?" And with this she mimed one and then several imaginary children running about on the floor.

They both shook their heads with a little laugh.

"No? Well – shame – shame – perhaps good idea – no?"

"Perhaps," Amanda said, flashing a little smile at Toledo. He rolled his eyes in mock sarcasm.

Dr. Shaffer was waiting for them in his large office. Or at least, it looked as if he was waiting for them. Sitting behind a mahogany desk in an imposing chair, he was leafing through a Bible. They stood in the doorway, waiting for him to acknowledge them.

"Detective," the doctor said, looking up. "Do you read this?" He lifted the Bible slightly.

"Not regularly. No."

"You should."

Then he turned back to the book.

"Dr …?" Toledo said, his patience was wearing thin.

"Not for the religion in it. That's all just a fairy story. Not a very original one either. No. You should read it for the poetry. You can pick any page … any page at random … and find the most beautiful poetry. Listen. *They shall be burnt with hunger, and devoured with burning heat, and with bitter destruction. I will also send the teeth of beasts upon them, with the poison of serpents of the dust.* Great stuff."

"Yes," Toledo replied, nonplussed.

"You prefer the Old to the New Testament?" Amanda asked.

"For the poetry, yes. There is no comparison."

"What does that part mean?" Amanda went on.

"It's about desire, lust. Hunger burning us. A hunger that – ironically – devours."

Toledo looked from one to the other, then back again. He had no idea why Amanda was indulging in this conversation, but it revealed a side of Dr. Shaffer he had not guessed at. *So, I suppose it's useful just for that.*

"You prefer the Old Testament for its poetry – but the New for its … ideas?" Amanda continued.

"Yes. Who wouldn't? The God of the Old Testament is a vindictive mass-murderer who plays with the very people

105

he is meant to protect. There is none of the forgiveness, none of the ... humanity – that you find later on."

"And forgiveness is an attractive idea to you?" Toledo asked.

After a slight pause, Shaffer said, "if the sorrow is genuine then forgiveness is not only attractive – it is a necessity, if the world is to make any sense at all."

"I agree," Toledo replied.

"Anyway, I am sure you didn't come here to discuss literature. Come in please, take a seat."

They did so.

"This is the Berkeley Medical Examiner, Dr. Amanda Byrnes," Toledo said.

Dr. Shaffer rose slightly in his seat, as if to formally stand, then gave up under the weight of his body, and sank back.

"Doctor." he said, nodding.

"Dr. Shaffer, I we have some bad news for you." Amanda said.

"More bad news? I think I'm up for it."

"Your son is not in a coma because of the car wreck."

"He isn't?"

"No."

"He's in the coma because of an insulin overdose."

"An insulin overdose?"

The doctor's face was implacable, conveying little emotion. *That in itself is extremely strange*, thought Toledo.

"Yes," Amanda said, equally neutral.

"He has become hypoglycemic?" Dr. Shaffer asked.

"Yes."

"Hypo ...?" Toledo interjected.

"Hypoglycemic, detective. It means literally too little sugar. Insulin helps move blood sugar into the organs. If a person who is not a diabetic, in other words, someone who

106

has normal insulin levels, injects himself with more insulin, then his blood sugar levels can become dangerously low. It can lead to coma."

"As it has in this case," Amanda said.

"You may remember the movie with that British actor. What is his name? Irons. Jeremy Irons, that's it. *Reversal of Fortune.* The main character was accused of injecting his wife with insulin to get hold of her money. He was found guilty…"

"Then later the verdict was reversed," Toledo said. "It's a true story. The Harvard lawyer Alan Dershowitz got him off the second time round…"

"Yes, interesting case, so interesting," Dr. Shaffer said, his voice slightly higher with enthusiasm. His eyes glazed over for a moment before returning to Toledo.

"And you say that poor Michael accidentally injected himself with insulin?"

A slight pause.

"Well – he had insulin in his system," Amanda said. "We don't know how it got there."

Dr. Shaffer let this pass over him.

"There is one thing I don't understand," he said finally. "Michael has been in a coma for nearly three weeks. Why have you only just discovered this?"

"We weren't looking for it."

"You mean no-one had taken his blood sugar levels?"

"Well, they had, it's just no-one looked carefully enough at the results."

Toledo smiled inwardly. Amanda was playing the part perfectly – the slightly defensive young doctor being lectured by her elder and better. *Drawing him out. Revealing what is under that cool surface.*

"Well, I know you are not responsible, but I do think that is strange."

107

He is angry, thought Toledo, *angry because – because he thought he had got away with it after the first few days. He injected his own son.*

The detective was sure of it. *But proving it will be a different matter.*

"You know, I suppose, that my son has had a drug problem for some years. He may have got some of my insulin by mistake, thinking that it was …"

But here the doctor's imagination ran out.

"Some other drug?" Amanda said, supposedly helping him.

"Yes, some other drug. You understand that we will need an accounting of your insulin." Toledo said. Then, after a pause, "merely for the record."

"You will receive it within the hour." Shaffer said.

Not that there is the remotest chance of any being missing, Toledo thought.

"Will that be all?" Shaffer asked.

"Yes. For now." Toledo turned and was walking out the room when he turned. "Well, there was one more thing…"

"Just like Lieutenant Columbo!" Shaffer said, smiling.

"What was that from?" Toledo asked.

"What was what from?"

"That piece that you read to us."

"Oh. Deuteronomy, 32:24. You should read it." Shaffer replied, raising the Bible again.

He knew the reference by heart. No need to look at what chapter and verse.

A thought ran through Toledo's mind continually over the next hour, as they left the Shaffer house and made their way back to Berkeley. Just as the helicopter started to descend onto the roof of the Berkeley PD, Toledo shared his thoughts with Amanda about the strangeness of Dr.

Shaffer knowing the Bible so well, and the probability that he murdered Mark. She turned toward him.

"But why would Dr. Shaffer want to kill his own son?"

"There could be several reasons. With him dead the whole shame of the murder case will disappear. The family is saved from any more embarrassment. Or perhaps his son knows something – something that Shaffer knows will come out in the court case when Mark has nothing to lose."

"Or perhaps Mark really did inject it accidentally," Amanda said.

"You don't think that any more than I do."

"No," said Amanda regretfully. "I suppose I don't."

Nineteen

The next evening Toledo called everyone together for what he liked to call a 'case management meeting'. Amanda always said these sounded like they were treating a patient rather than solving a murder case, but Toledo kept the name anyway. As the detective was a man of strict habits, they were surprised to receive a text inviting them to THE SPAGHETTI FACTORY, SEVEN SHARP. THE ONE IN JACK LONDON SQUARE.

McMannis was first, and seeing that no one else had arrived, he wandered over to the tiny cabin standing in the center of the square. Transported from Alaska, it was supposedly the actual cabin where Jack London had spent a lonely Arctic winter in the early 1900s. McMannis stooped slightly and peered inside. Some very 21st Century trash had made its way past the wire mesh designed to protect the interior, while allowing enough space for the spartan space to be visible. But despite the slightly depressing dinginess characteristic of Oakland, the cabin still evoked the harshness of life in the far North. *He must have written those stories just to stop from going crazy*, McMannis thought, then stood up straight and stretched. Seagulls cried fanatically above him, as if they could will scraps of food into existence. He looked up at them. *Perhaps when I get out*, he thought.

Ginny was the next to arrive, and she stooped down to look inside the cabin.

"Bit of a tight squeeze," she said, shaking her head.

"Well, people were smaller back then."

"But not *that* much smaller," Ginny replied, standing up straight and stretching.

"Let's go in," McMannis said.

The young woman slipped her arm through his, and they slowly sauntered toward the restaurant. They went inside and found Toledo had already booked a table slightly remote from the rest of the establishment, so they could talk more freely.

Within half an hour everyone was there.

"I see it this way." Amanda said, sweeping her hair back from his face. "The boy in the coma killed the girl in a jealous rage. He then took some of his father's insulin to kill himself. And decided to make sure by driving off the road at the same time. Like most murderers, he wasn't too lucky, and didn't kill himself in either way."

After a moment's pause, Ginny said,

"Why didn't he just put a gun in his mouth and pull the trigger?"

"Jesus!" McMannis said.

"She has a point." Toledo said a moment later. "Some people have a sense of poetry about death," Amanda went on. "Taking his father's own insulin is an ironic way of dying."

"It would only be ironic if his father had something to do with why he was killing himself," Toledo said. "Something to do with the murder."

"Maybe," Amanda said, but she sounded doubtful.

"You mean something beyond the Oedipus Complex?" McMannis offered.

"There are definitely things about that family that we do not know," Ginny said.

"Such as?" Toledo replied.

"If I knew what they were, we wouldn't not know them," Ginny said.

That comment took a moment to process.

"You mean like Donald Rumsfeld?" McMannis suggested.

111

"What?" Amanda said.

"There are things we know. There are things we don't know. They can be divided into two types. Things we know we don't know. And things we don't know that we don't know."

"Well, that makes things clearer." Ginny said.

"So ... let's start this again ...what do we *know*?" Toledo asked.

All looked to Amanda again. At times her scientific training was essential for seeing through the fog or, as in this situation, summarizing the complex.

"First," she said. "Caroline Ramirez was murdered by person or persons unknown. On the night of her death, she had sex with at least three different men. She was stabbed in the perianal area with a carving knife. Whoever did it wrote *This is what happens to cheaters? Pigs!?* on the wall. The main ..."

"We don't know that for sure," McMannis interrupted.

"Don't know what?" Toledo said, annoyance in his voice.

"That the people who murdered her also wrote that on the wall. It could have been someone else afterward. Someone who found her, who knew about her . . . romantic entanglements ..."

"Someone who knew that she slept around," McMannis agreed. "And left that as an ironic statement for the police. That's why pigs were mentioned."

Everyone was silent for a second.

"And that would explain the question mark," Toledo eventually said.

"But who would want to do that?" Ginny asked. "I mean, they'd have to be very sick – or have something pretty big against her."

"Another lover?" Toledo answered.

"Someone wrote it. We know that much. Someone unknown." Amanda said, determined to get beyond this speculation. "After her death," she continued, "we discovered that Caroline had an interesting personal life. Also, once the main suspect was arrested – and then released …"

"Do you have to remind me of that?" Toledo said gloomily.

"He had a mysterious car wreck. Sometime the evening of the wreck a lot of insulin appeared in his system."

"But not his father's insulin," McMannis interrupted.

"The man is a doctor," Toledo said. "I think he could get hold of some insulin without us knowing."

"Or just used his own," Amanda went on. "A diabetic uses varying amounts insulin – it is not like it is checked very carefully."

There was silence for a moment.

"We are assuming that the *cheaters* written on the wall is referring to romantic cheating." McMannis said. "But there are other types of cheating. Business cheating, cheating the …"

"IRS perhaps?" Toledo said sarcastically.

"Just an idea."

"No, you are right," the detective replied. "We have to keep an open mind on everything."

"The sexual component does suggest ordinary cheating though," Amanda said.

More silence.

"I think we need to visit our strange family more regularly," Toledo said eventually. "A kind of procession of friendly callers. Eventually, something will come out …"

"We'd be accused of stalking them," McMannis said.

"No," Toledo went on. "There are enough fights within that family that we can play one off against the other. We can be invited into the household by the participants in those fights. They will believe that we can be used to their advantage."

"Kind of a weird approach," Ginny murmured.

"It's a weird case," Toledo said. "Amanda, do you think those friends of yours would mind a few visitors to their cottage over the next few weeks?"

"Not at all," the medical examiner replied, smiling. "In fact. I think they would rather enjoy it. Being the idle rich can get terribly boring, so I'm told."

"I would risk it though," McMannis interjected.

"Risk what?" Amanda asked.

"Being idle and rich," the professor replied, and they all started laughing.

Twenty

The next day Toledo settled into the perfect reconstruction of the Ann Hathaway cottage standing on the perfect lawn. As he sat outside enjoying the sun, he thought he saw someone on the Shaffer side of the fence, looking at him through the trees. But when he looked more closely, all he could see was the mass of vegetation. He planned to stay a couple of days - very visible, but never encroaching upon Shaffer space. The reaction from individual Shaffer household members, or lack thereof, would be informative.

On the first evening of Toledo's stay Ben Williams invited him over for dinner. Realizing that he could not refuse, yet feeling nervous anyway, Toledo went at about seven. The inside of the house was even more spectacular than the outside. Solid mahogany was the most common material – from an ornate formal stairway to library-size bookshelves, and on to the dining room, the wood acted like some relaxing fabric that supported, and cosseted all those lucky enough to enter the home.

Toledo was surprised when he was placed at one end of the table with Ben at the other. Like some cliché of a European aristocratic couple who could no longer stand one another, they were situated about thirty feet apart. A maid brought them several courses of food and replenished their wine glasses. Much of the dinner was spent in pleasant but insignificant small talk, until Ben stood up, and walked slowly down the room.

He sat by Toledo.

"You must be wondering where my partner is."

"No, I wasn't," Toledo replied, after a pause.

"That's a shame because I have no idea myself. Another glass of wine?"

"Please," Toledo said.

Ben turned and took a bottle from the side table, then looked back toward Toledo.

"You haven't asked when I last saw him," Ben said.

"Should I?" Toledo replied, wondering where all of this was going.

"Maybe," Ben said. "But then, I don't think it has anything to do with your case, so why should you?"

As Ben poured the wine, Toledo asked,

"So, when did you last see your ...."

"Companion– I just call him my companion."

"Your companion. When did you last see him?"

"On the day that Caroline Ramirez was killed."

Toledo took a sip of the wine, put his glass down.

"That is – an interesting coincidence," said the detective.

"Isn't it just." Ben replied.

Toledo found the man's tendency to use 'English' English vaguely annoying. Like his sexual orientation, the habit created a barrier around him that was difficult to penetrate. Toledo knew that the words that a person used - and didn't use - revealed a lot. He had studied the subject. But if it was slightly different language, even just a form of English different from his own, a linguistic fog surrounded Toledo. He was nonplussed.

"There was no planned trip? Back to England perhaps?"

"Not that I know of. And anyway – his passport is still here."

Toledo drank some more wine. He felt the beginnings of a buzz, decided to drink no more.

"Sometimes he goes on little ... excursions." Ben said.

"Normally he leaves some idea of where he is going, and with who . . . but not this time. And he has never been away for so long."

116

Toledo suspected the man was playing some bizarre game with him. Something told the detective that he *did* know where his partner was. What probable reason he could have for lying about the matter was mysterious.

"So how much do you really know about your neighbors?" Toledo said, deciding to change the subject,

Ben paused momentarily, peering at Toledo over the top of his glass.

"That suggests that you think I am hiding something," Ben said quietly.

"Not at all. I was just wondering if anything else – if anything else had occurred to you, since all this started."

"Not really. I do know they are living at the limit of their means. Perhaps beyond it. Most people in Hillsborough, as you have probably gathered, have so much money that they barely think about it. The cost of things, I mean. Our friends next door – I have it on good authority – have only just finished paying off their mortgage on that monstrosity. Most people in Hillsborough buy their houses with cash. Once…." Here he paused, as if uncertain whether to continue. "Once – I have it on good authority – they actually received a foreclosure notice, because they made no payments for three months."

"But he is a doctor …" Toledo remonstrated.

Ben laughed sardonically.

"Yes – and doctors have to *work* for a living. Most denizens of Hillsborough haven't worked a day in their life. Investments. Trust funds. Old money. New money from the Internet bubble – cashed in before it burst."

"The Shaffers don't have as much money as other people here," Toledo said reflectively.

"And for that reason, it is important to keep up appearances."

Toledo glanced out of the window, toward the Shaffer house.

"They don't do a very good job of it," he said, gesturing slightly with his wine glass toward the darkness.

"There is one thing you might be interested in," Ben said.

"And what would that be?"

"I'm going to have a little nap. Meet me back here at midnight – and I will show you."

With that he sauntered out of the room, leaving Toledo alone. The detective paused for a moment then stood up and made his way back to the guest cottage, wondering what the rest of the night might hold. *And why midnight? Does he think this is a horror movie, or something?*

At 11.50pm Toledo returned to the main house, where Ben was standing beside the door dressed in dark clothes. Toledo had been wearing black anyway.

"We going on a reconnaissance mission, or something?" Toledo asked.

Ben looked at him carefully for a moment.

"That is exactly what we're doing," he said, then walked away from the house, toward the fence between his property, and the Shaffers.

Toledo half-expected him to stop and say it was all a practical joke, but Ben carried on walking right up to the fence. It was pitch black on the other side – the trees hiding whatever light the moonless sky might give. Despite himself, Toledo felt a little shiver of anxiety. He had seen and occasionally done things that most people could not imagine – would not want to imagine – but the simple unknown of tangled vegetation in the dark of night gave him pause.

In the gloom, he saw Ben looking at him. As if sensing the detective's reticence, the man patted Toledo on the shoulder.

"Don't worry. I've done this dozens of times."

And with that, he hopped over the fence with surprising dexterity, then offered a hand to Toledo. The detective refused it and jumped over himself, although not with quite the ease of his host. Another silent promise to spend more time in the police department gym sulked its way across Toledo's mind, but he was soon concentrating on following Ben's footsteps as the man moved quickly and silently through the lower portions of the Shaffer property.

Why has he done this even once before? Toledo thought. *Let alone dozens?*

Ben slowed down as the house came into sight and pointed to something up ahead.

"What's that?" Toledo whispered.

"Don't you see it?" Ben said, equally quiet.

"No..."

Suddenly a deer flashed across the rough pathway in front of them, causing Toledo to cry out a little with surprise. Ben stifled his laughter.

"I'm sorry," he said. "There are a surprising number of wild animals still left up here. Some people say," he continued, as he started walking again, "there are mountain lions. But I doubt that."

Well, that doubt makes me feel better.

Finally, they were in one of the small patches of ground that had been cleared of vegetation. They stopped here for a second.

"Ben?" Toledo finally said. "Ben . . . where exactly are you taking me?"

Ben was about to walk away but Toledo grabbed his hand, making it clear he would go no further without an answer.

"You must realize that anything you show me can never be admitted into evidence – I have no warrant."

119

"No-one will know we have been here," the man said as he pulled his arm away. "And this isn't going anywhere."

Ben set off again, and after a moment's pause, Toledo followed. *After all, I can hardly turn around now. What if something happens to him?*

The house stood as an impenetrable blackness against the slightly lighter sky.

"Come on," Ben whispered. "It's just here."

They walked along the side of the house, took a sharp left up some steps and came to a small doorway. It was so recessed that it would be quite easy to walk straight past if you did not know that it was there.

"What is this?" Toledo asked quietly.

"I think they call it the date room," Ben said, as he carefully turned the handle on the door.

They stepped inside, and Ben switched a small lamp on. It provided just enough light to see the contents of the room, but not much more.

Toledo paused as he looked up at the face of Joe Montana. A cardboard cutout of the great quarterback was incongruously stuck to the ceiling. It had bent slightly just above the waist, making it look as if it was making a bid for freedom. Beside it, several posters of less well-known players of the same era.

"I can safely assume they are Forty-Niner fans," Toledo whispered.

"Yes," Ben replied, voice at full volume.

"And there is no need to whisper in here. These walls and ceilings are like stone, even if they are not actually made of it."

Toledo visibly relaxed.

The room was larger than it looked from the outside, stretching quite a way back under the rest of the house. A pull-out couch in the middle and a desk with bed-pillows

120

piled haphazardly. Other sports posters on the walls and ceiling, tools of uncertain origin and use. Medical textbooks, several decades old with a similar amount of dust on them. A slightly musty, unpleasant smell that Toledo recognized but could not quite identify.

"What's the smell?" He asked.

"Rats," Ben replied matter-of-factly.

"Rats?"

"One of the downsides of living in a massive house sitting in dense vegetation. Rats. It's quite easy to kill them. Unfortunately, it's not so easy to find their bodies. The Shaffers have rats in the walls . .and floors."

Toledo glanced up at the ceiling, as if expecting to hear the patter of feet suddenly.

"And this … is the date room?" Toledo asked incredulously.

Ben chuckled.

"Apparently so. But after all – all cats are gray in the dark."

Toledo looked around the room more closely.

"Ben, thanks for bringing me here – it's been a fun … well, not fun … an interesting night. But I still don't see what relevance this is to – the murder of Caroline Ramirez."

"I'm sorry," Ben replied. "I forgot how fact-based you police are. Sometimes don't you find that the atmosphere of a place can lead you to the facts? Much more than the details."

"Not really," Toledo answered.

"Come on then," Ben said after pausing and sighing. "They are back here."

The man led the way through a curtain that was draped precariously, half hanging from a long, ominous hook dangling above. The space behind it was a little emptier, but soon they came to another door.

"Go inside," Ben said.

Toledo looked at him. Instinctively the detective reached for his gun, dangling it loosely by his side as he slowly, cautiously turned the handle and opened the door. It was pitch black, then he heard a click as Ben switched the light on beside him.

"Oh. my god!" The detective said, as a wave of nausea overcame him.

Twenty-One

Unknown to Toledo, who was too distracted at that moment to care anyway, exactly twenty feet above him Ginny Aldridge was leafing through a photo album. Her new friend Ophelia was in the bathroom. Ginny realized that Ophelia knew that she was only a fair-weather friend – *or murder-case friend would probably be more accurate –* but this did not change their natural empathy. In her casebook (she was following Toledo's practice of keeping a personal diary of each investigation), she had written that "a relationship based upon artificial and limited grounds can grow organically, into something quite different."

As if to prove her point, Ginny considered how she had first met Professor Ian McMannis, now one of her best friends. Even Toledo was too, in his way. *And then there is Amanda* ... but no, that was a bridge too far. Ginny trusted Amanda but could never be cozy with her.

She heard the toilet flush and smiled as Ophelia came back into the room.

"Do you like them?" Ophelia asked.

"Yes…" Ginny answered, as if the question was somehow too obvious to warrant a reply.

"Personally, I think looking at other people's photo albums is about as interesting as …", but the woman was lost for a comparison. Eventually she asked, "What are you looking for?"

"Nothing in particular."

In fact, Ginny was looking for something. Anything that might be out of place. But the pictures, going all the way back to the fading colors of 1970's Polaroids, offered nothing. This was strange. It was as if the photographs had been carefully arranged to look completely ordinary, but with a seamlessness and lack of loose-ends that in fact made them artificial. Everyone, and everything, was in its place. Too much in place.

Ginny closed the album and smiled at Ophelia, who was now sitting on the couch beside her. The door to the room opened and the extremely pale face of Hermia, the girl who had opened the front door for Toledo and McMannis on their first eventful visit to the Shaffer house, peered into the room. She looked from Ophelia to Ginny, and then back to Ophelia, a mixture of shyness and panic on her face.

"I'm sorry. I didn't know anyone was in here."

"It's OK Hermia, you can come in ..."

But the girl raised her hand in refusal, smiled meekly, and closed the door.

It was the first time that Ginny had seen her close. On her other visits to the house, the girl had been a waifish figure, always leaving rooms when she arrived or glimpsed at the far end of a corridor or wandering apparently aimlessly in the back yard. Like a lost ghost. Now Ginny was sure that she was not merely pale, but positively ill. Surely something congenital. Hermia's eyes were unnaturally wide apart, while her nose was far too small for her face. The bone structure was *slightly off, not sure how precisely, but there is something wrong.* The hair was sparse and lank, almost the same color as her skin.

And it was the skin that was her strangest feature. Possessing an uncanny whiteness, it exhibited the near transparency of a very old person's skin. On an undeniably young face it was disturbing, even alarming. *At any moment, it looks like it could simply slip off,* Ginny thought, and shuddered a little despite herself.

Ophelia giggled slightly.

She does tend to have that effect on people," Ophelia said, "especially close up. That's the reason that she tries to avoid strangers like the plague. Anyone outside of the family really."

"What is … wrong with her?" Ginny said.

"She has something called Werner Syndrome."

"Werner Syndrome?"

"Yes. It involves premature aging. It's inherited. The genes for aging are kind of – turned on – before they should be. That's why her skin looks that way."

"But there is something else…" Ginny said.

"Actually, there are all sorts of different variations of it," Ophelia said, brushing her hair back from her face. "Dozens of related genetic conditions. One of them causes her face to look that way. The eyes. The nose."

"Jesus," Ginny said quietly.

The two women sat quietly for a moment.

"How old is she?" Ginny finally asked.

"Fifteen."

"But she looks much older, in her twenties at least …"

"Part of the condition."

"And where did she come from? She's not your sister, so …"

Ophelia smiled enigmatically.

"No, she's not my biological sister. My parents adopted her when she was two. When doctors discovered the condition – and her real parents no longer wanted her."

"Oh…"

Ophelia looked carefully at Ginny.

"I know, you'd never guess my parents were so kind, right? Not the type to adopt a child who will become so … strange … that by agreement, will never be seen in public."

"Well, I wasn't …"

"But there is more to my parents than meets the eye. They are far more loving and generous than you would think."

Ginny looked at her quizzically.

"You find that hard to believe?" Ophelia asked, returning Ginny's gaze.

"A little. Although I have learned – am learning – there is nearly always more to people than what we see."

Ginny looked outside into the darkness.

"But yes…it is hard to believe."

Ophelia went over to the window.

"That's strange," she said.

"What is?" Ginny said, getting up and walking over to her.

"You see that tree there?"

"There are a lot of trees," Ginny said.

"OK – I mean that tree there – the one with the faint light on it."

Ginny looked and pretended to see.

"That faint light on the bottom branches – on the leaves – there is only one place that can come from."

"And that is?"

"The date room. Light on that tree means the light in the date room is on. Someone must be down there. Well – good luck to them – whoever it is."

Ginny did a quick mental survey of who it might be. No likely candidates sprang to mind, but then, *I'm always expecting someone new to be introduced anyway – some brother or sister or cousin that they had not thought important enough to mention.* As she thought this, Ophelia was looking at her, smiling slightly.

"I used to spend quite a lot of time down there, when I was younger."

"You're not exactly old now."

"No," the woman said, looking back outside at the slightly illuminated tree. "I'm not."

Her words were wistful, as if some quiet truth lay behind them that could be discerned only if a person looked carefully enough.

"When is your son due to get back?" Ginny asked.

"My son? Oh … Alan."

Almost as if she didn't know who I was talking about.

"Alan – he is due out of the hospital tomorrow. Poor thing. It's his lungs. They never fully developed. Premature."

"That's sad." Ginny looked at her carefully and decided she could pry a little more.

"His father – does he have any role in his life?"

"His *father*. No, none at all. His father is dead. You already know that."

"Yes, I'm sorry," Ginny murmured, her rather obvious ploy having failed.

"Ginny," Ophelia said, sitting her back down again on the couch. "You know I like you, don't you?"

"Yes."

"No, I mean *really* like you – if we had met at some other place, some other time – I think we would have become friends."

"I agree."

"So, you will take what I have to say as a friend – separate from all of this …"

And Ophelia spread her arms wide, as if to encapsulate something intangible yet all-pervasive.

"Yes. I will."

Ophelia sighed, looking out at the swirling blackness, as an ocean fog started to stream in from the coast.

I forget the ocean is just a few miles away, over the hills, Ginny thought.

"Leave this place and never come back. If you don't have to. And you are not an official part of any of this, are you?"

127

"No. I'm not a police officer," Ginny told the truth, while still lying.

"Then do that," Ophelia said, holding her hand rather tightly. "Go and be a student, or whatever you are away from here."

Ginny tried to withdraw her hand but found it immobile for a second as Ophelia peered into her face with a mixture of pleading and fear.

"Go," Ophelia said, releasing Ginny's hand finally. "And never come back."

Twenty-Two

Over a twenty-year career – fifteen of those as a homicide investigator - Detective Cassius Toledo had seen some very strange things, but nothing could have prepared him for the sight that greeted him when Ben switched on the lights.

The little room had shelves arrayed on all three sides. On each shelf were large glass jars. In each jar, illuminated eerily by recessed ceiling lights, was a baby. But no ordinary baby. In the jar directly in front of Toledo was a baby that – and he was thankful for this – at least had two arms, two legs, and a head. The only problem was that it had no face. Vague indentations of where the eyes should be, the hint of a slit for a mouth and two large holes served as nostrils. But no real nose. No ears.

To its left, as if to provide aesthetic contrast, was a baby that was all face. Its very large head tapered to something like a neck, but then the body itself was about five inches long. The legs and arms resembled the tendrils of some monstrous jellyfish. It looked like a grotesque tadpole with huge, sightless eyes.

"Jesus!" Toledo finally said, quietly but distinctly.

One more, he thought, *then I am just going to glance at the rest.*

The third jar contained one, or maybe two, or perhaps three babies. Toledo could not be sure. There were three distinct heads, although one was stunted and lacked eyes. Below them a torso that started singly but ended up branching off into a kind of twisted morass of limbs and flesh that was darker than the rest. It reminded Toledo of a tree after a forest fire. Twisted and tortured into an impossible shape, then frozen in time.

129

"What are these?" Toledo asked absurdly.

"Babies." Ben replied.

"I know that!" Toledo said, much louder. "I mean what kind of babies, and what the hell are they doing here!?"

"Genetic mutations. Very rare apparently. Dr. Shaffer collects them. I don't know where from. But he gets them … and keeps them here."

"Does he do research on them or something?" Toledo said, finally snapping out of the initial shock and disgust as his detective side switched back on.

"Not that I know of," Ben replied. "I think he is just a heart doctor. This is his … hobby."

"Some hobby," said Toledo, glancing at a smaller jar containing what appeared to be a part-fish, part-human fetus. Dimly remembered days of Freshman Anatomy told Toledo that all humans went through a fish stage as embryos – but this poor specimen looked as if someone had taken a baby's head and sewed it onto a fish body. The thing even had fins, scales, and a tail. A tiny human nose sprouted near where the gills would be.

In the jar next door was a two-headed baby. *But take one of the heads away and it would look quite normal,* Toledo thought.

"Enough," he said, turning away from the weird collection.

When a two-headed baby is a wonderful return to near-normality, it is time to get out of there.

Ben turned the lights off.

As their eyes adjusted to the new gloom, Toledo wondered where to fit this latest revelation into the overall scheme of things. On face value it didn't seem to have much relevance. *Many people have strange hobbies. Dr. Shaffer's is just a little stranger than most.* Something suddenly occurred to him.

"Turn on those lights again."

130

He was right. Most of the babies whose features were reasonably normal were clearly Asian.

"Thank you," Toledo said, and this time flicked the switch himself.

Twenty minutes later they were back at the guest cottage. For some reason, Ben made it obvious that he wanted them to return there rather than the main residence.

"So, what do you make of that?" Ben said, relaxing back into the large couch.

"I really don't know."

"The fact that they are in the date room is a bit weird too," Ben continued.

"In what way?"

"Did you notice that chair just outside the door?"

"Yes."

"Well, I think Shaffer takes that chair into his collection room and just sits there and looks at them."

The thought of someone enjoying looking at that grotesque scene gave Toledo a little chill.

"Maybe he goes there when he wants to be ... alone," Ben said quietly.

"Alone? You mean ..."

"It is an agreement among the family, a silent one, but an agreement nevertheless, that any ... any such activities ... go on down there."

"Meaning?" Toledo asked.

"Dr. Shaffer sits in his chair and masturbates."

"What?!" Toledo said, wiping his hand across his eyes then up into his hair. He was simultaneously exhausted, disgusted, and perturbed.

"And how do you know all this?" said the detective finally.

"Being rich and idle is not all it's meant to be," Ben said. "You need to fill your time somehow."

"You fill your time by spying on your neighbors?"

131

Ben paused for a moment, opened another bottle of wine, and smiled.

"Yes."

"Are some of those ... Hiroshima babies?"

"I have no idea," Ben said. "Although I guess it's a fair assumption. Spectacularly valuable, so I am told. Worth more than anything else in the house. Perhaps more than the house itself."

"Then why does he keep them there?"

"Hiding in plain sight," Ben said.

This man would make a good detective, Toledo thought.

"I mean – if you were burglarizing the place and took one look in the date room, what would you think? Would you go any further?"

Toledo thought for a moment.

"No, I wouldn't," he replied eventually.

"By the way, I have something for you," Ben said.

"What?"

The man reached into his pocket, pulled out a rag and tossed it over to Toledo.

"And this is?" The detective asked.

"In the old days, we used to call it a come towel," Ben said. "I accidentally picked it up when we were over there just now. You might test it for DNA to see if my theory is right."

"Well accidents do happen, accidents do happen," Toledo said, raising his glass in a mock toast.

Twenty-Three

Amanda checked the genetic match again. There was no mistaking it - a perfect correlation between the semen on the small kitchen towel that Toledo had rather mysteriously given to her and one of the specimens found on Caroline Ramirez. As was his way, Toledo gave no hint as to what evidence might be on the towel – he had just given it to her cold so there would be no bias. She hadn't even known what case it came from, even though there really was only one murder that the detective was presently dealing with.

Exactly how he had gotten hold of the towel she had no idea. It was, as she glanced down at its dirty, crusty countenance, a rather disgusting specimen. Nothing overtly horrible about it – but it seemed corrupted, *corrupting maybe*.

She frowned, swept her hair back from her beautiful face and checked the match, for the third time.

She picked up her phone and texted the news to Toledo.

Great, the detective thought as his phone started beeping loudly, *just the wrong time*. Toledo was standing near the edge of the most overgrown part of the Shaffer yard, within a few yards of the date room. He knew that he was breaking just about every protocol in the book by standing there, but his instinct had told him that Ben's voyeurism was a useful tactic. Toledo had just been rewarded for his patience because he saw Marta bustling her way along the side of the house then into the room. Obviously, it was never actually cleaned, so what reason the German maid could have for being in there was a mystery.

The door had just closed when his phone beeped, and in his haste to stop the noise, he dropped it on the ground. As he picked it up, he was glad to see that Marta had apparently not heard it – or if she had, was ignoring it.

Just as Toledo was about to move closer toward the date room, he heard the kitchen door open far above in the house. Someone came out and was soon walking down the outside steps. The walk was fast and sure with none of the cautious stumbling that Toledo already knew normally occurred when anyone negotiated the path.

The detective's brow furrowed in surprise as he saw Teddy, the leather-bound elder son of the family, make his quick way along the pathway. Just as he was about to turn the corner that led to the date room Teddy stopped and looked over to where Toledo was standing. He appeared to look directly into Toledo's eyes although, as the detective had long ago learned, this did not mean he saw him. The young man might sense instinctively that he was being watched, but no more than that.

The moment passed, and Teddy went into the date room.

Curiouser and curiouser Toledo mused.

Well, in for a penny, in for a pound – as my Anglophile host would say... and with that, the detective started to move toward the small window that gave a pathetic amount of light to the dungeon like room. He stopped for a moment, still hidden. *Best to give them some time to get going with whatever they are doing*, he thought. What he thought they must be doing seemed very unlikely, *but no less unlikely than anything else that happens around here.*

A couple of minutes passed, and he went to the window. The curtain was half-drawn, and he could only see a small, but interesting portion of the room. Marta was lying on the pullout bed spread-eagle, totally naked. Teddy was kneeling in front of her, his face buried somewhere between her legs. *Well, those are German breasts* Toledo thought with a little smile as they bounced on top of the man's head. He watched for a moment longer. *Marta and Teddy are having an affair .... or at least having sex.*

Looking at it objectively, Toledo supposed that it was not so unexpected after all.

The bored young son of a rich family. The lonely middle-aged German maid. It sounded like the beginning of a romance novel, or a porn film.

Or both.

He could hear vague sounds coming from the date-room. The detective put his ear up to the glass and listened.

"Little one! Yes! Der liebling! Liebling! Da! Da!"

Well, at least she is consistent.

Toledo turned quickly and moved back into the vegetation. He mulled the case for a few moments. The news from Amanda about the DNA match showed many people here were involved in strange relationships. *Terribly strange. What other possible combinations might there be?* All of it just added to the possible complications in the Ramirez case. The circumstantial evidence for a dense web of lies, deceit and wrongdoing was becoming stronger by the hour. Also, it seemed less and less likely that Mark Shaffer, after growing up in this environment, would hold such quaint ideas as desiring a girlfriend's fidelity. If it really was Dr. Shaffer's semen on Caroline, then what? Was he having an affair with his son's girlfriend, unknown to Mark? Or were they working together on the murder? *And while we know that the semen on the towel and on Caroline match – we don't know that they are actually from Dr. Shaffer.* A simple DNA test would solve that however.

THIS IS WHAT HAPPENS TO CHEATERS? Surely more ironic than serious.

Toledo stepped back toward the window, glanced inside again. The couple had changed positions – the

135

German woman now on top with the young man's legs showing from the knees down. *He's braver than me*, Toledo thought, and turned away for the last time.

Twenty-Four

Three hours later, as he luxuriated in the fine threads of the king-size bed that was somehow squashed into the bedroom of the cottage, Toledo felt the tell-tale vibration of his cellphone. *Just ignore it*, he thought, but then sighed and turned over, reaching blindly for it on the bedside table. His eyes took a moment to focus. Toledo had been noticing this tendency more often recently. *I am getting old,* he thought gloomily.

When, finally, he could read the text, it made him instantly alert. He even shook a little.

MARK SHAFFER DEAD. SUSPICIOUS CIRCUMSTANCES. DR. SHAFFER IMPLICATED.

The Ramirez Case had been closed, by persons unknown, although the finger of blame pointed at the suspect's father.

But how?

As if replying to his thought, Toledo heard an approaching helicopter. In a few seconds it had landed, and a few later he was sitting next to Amanda.

"God knows what this will do for our budget." Toledo said as the helicopter rose above the trees and gave a panoramic view of mansions and the freeway to the right, with the utter darkness of the Pacific just to the left.

"The top floor thinks this may become a media case, so its OK." Amanda replied.

Toledo sighed.

"That's all we need."

Some crimes, mostly murders, for mysterious reasons became media cases while others, with perhaps virtually the same underlying facts, were totally ignored. The Laci Peterson case was one of the most recent examples. Man kills pregnant wife in order to be with mistress. Happens dozens of times a year in a country as large as the USA. But something – the photogenic nature of the couple, the time of year (Christmas), the disappearance of the body – led to national and then international coverage. These media cases became the complete focus of police departments involved with them, and budgets were often thrown out of the window to get the cases solved. Police, lawyers, even judges had one eye on the case and another on after the case, and potentially lucrative second careers. It nauseated Toledo, but he accepted the reality. Ramirez was a likely media case, and that is why he was now sitting in a helicopter speeding toward San Francisco General Hospital, rather than stuck in a police car in the incessant traffic on the 101.

On the way to the hospital Amanda filled Toledo in on the details. Dr. Shaffer was found in Mark's hospital room doing something to the life support machinery. Exactly what he was doing was not yet clear. While the nurses were politely, but directly questioning the doctor, Mark Shaffer had expired. His heart had stopped because the setting on his breathing apparatus had been adjusted downward. Starved of oxygen, and damaged anyway, the heart simply stopped.

"So, they think that Dr. Shaffer simply turned the breathing apparatus down?" Toledo asked.

There was a pause for a moment.

"Well yes," Amanda said. "Unfortunately, there are none of his fingerprints on it – and no gloves were found, either in the room or on him."

This time Toledo delayed.

"How did he do it, then? With his elbows?"

138

"We don't know … but it is obvious that he *did* do it. We just have to find out how."

Not exactly a scientific approach to investigation, Toledo thought. *But hey, whatever works.*

An hour later Toledo was in an interrogation room at San Francisco Police Department with Dr. Shaffer sitting opposite. Other than having been relieved of his tie and shoelaces, the doctor looked as unflappable as ever. Toledo decided that the friendly approach would pay most dividends. Any hostility would cause the man to clam up even more than his naturally cautious personality already made likely.

"I'm sorry about the tie – and the shoelaces," Toledo said, with a little smile.

"It's all right," said the doctor said, returning the expression. "I understand the reason for it. Although I think I am rather large for shoelaces to take my weight if I tried to hang myself." Dr. Shaffer chuckled for a second, then was silent. Toledo smiled slightly.

First time I have ever heard him make anything like a joke. Shows a certain nervousness.

"You understand that your son has … passed on, Dr. Shaffer?"

"Passed on?" Shaffer repeated, as if the words were new to him. "Oh, you mean that my son has died. Yes, I am aware that my son has died."

After another pause, the doctor continued.

"You must think that I am cold, or at least indifferent to his death, Detective. That is not the case. It is just that I've prepared for this moment for a long time. The moment he lapsed into the coma, the likelihood of him ever recovering was remote. My profession enables me to deal with such unpleasant but unavoidable realities with equanimity. Like yours, I suppose."

139

"Dr. Shaffer, you are not here because of some inappropriate response to your son's death – you are here because you were found tampering with his life support system before he died. From what I have been told – it must have been like slowly drowning."

"Not entirely accurate, but near."

"What is not accurate? You weren't tampering with the equipment?"

"I meant – calling what happened to Mark like slowly drowning. Not entirely accurate. More like suffocating in a room with the air slowly being taken out of it."

Looks like he is seeing that in his mind.

"Back to the equipment, Dr. Shaffer. Were you tampering with it?"

"If by tampering… you mean adjusting, then I suppose I was."

"You were adjusting it?"

"Yes. I saw that something was wrong with his breathing. Well, at first I saw that the lividity of his skin was off – lack of oxygen – and then I saw that he was breathing too slowly."

"There is a timing mechanism on the equipment, Dr. Shaffer. It shows that the breathing apparatus was turned down about thirty seconds after you entered the room. There are cameras in all the corridors – as you probably know."

"Yes, I have had admitting privileges at San Francisco General for several decades. I am a cardiac surgeon, Detective Toledo, I know that the equipment was malfunctioning when I entered the room. I did not do anything to cause it. That was … my son."

Malfunction! Yet in that last sentence, Dr. Shaffer showed genuine emotion. *Either he is a great actor, or he is genuinely upset at his son's death.* But then, as Toledo knew, sincere grief at a person's death did not preclude a
140

person from being a killer. You can hate someone, then regret killing them – or feel hatred and guilt simultaneously.

"Dr. Shaffer. Would you be prepared to take a polygraph test?"

A long, stupid Hail Mary....

Shaffer looked at Toledo with a briefly incredulous, and then amused look.

"Polygraph tests are highly inaccurate – as you probably know. Also, as I just discovered that my son has died – it is unlikely that there'd be accurate readings for that reason alone. My heart rate and blood pressure are likely to be increased by that news."

But not by much, Toledo thought wryly.

All this was simply for form's sake. Toledo had enough, more than enough, to charge Dr. Shaffer with the homicide of his son.

"Is that all you have to say?" Toledo asked.

Dr. Shaffer looked slightly surprised.

"Apparently," he said.

"Then we will be charging you with a violation of California Criminal Code 187 – specifically the homicide of Mark Shaffer, a human being." Toledo paused for a moment and then said, more quietly.

"You killed your son."

Shaffer looked at him steadily, the blue eyes unblinking. He raised his hand and scratched at his beard for a second, almost contemplatively.

"You have the right to remain silent; anything you say can and will be used against you in a court of law. You have the right to speak to an attorney. If you cannot afford an attorney, one will be appointed for you. Do you understand these rights as they have been read to you?"

Shaffer's eyes stayed on Toledo.

"You didn't read them to me. And they were already read to me back at the hospital. But yes, I understand them."

Toledo paused, looked down at the papers in front of him, and shuffled them for no apparent reason.

"Are you prepared to carry on asking questions?"

"No, I don't think I am. I want to speak to my lawyer."

Toledo smiled slightly. Shaffer returned the gesture. If the doctor was worried, he certainly did not look it. The detective stayed sitting at the table, glancing at his phone, saw a message from McMannis.

THIS COMPLICATES THINGS. SUGGESTIONS?

Toledo replied.

STICK WITH GINNY. I FEEL OPHELIA KNOWS MUCH MORE THAN SHE IS LETTING ON. I WILL CONCENTRATE ON THE OTHERS.

With the doctor safely in jail, some others should crack – or at least be liable to speak more openly than they have been.

Toledo looked over at Dr. Shaffer. He was examining his fingernails in minute fashion, as if they contained the solution to some deep mystery.

I am not sure if he really did do it. Or if he did, whether he meant to.

And as the detective watched, he realized that Shaffer was not looking at his fingernails, but rather at his fingers. They shook slightly, and the doctor was concentrating on keeping them still. He looked up at Toledo, smiled again.

"Aging or Parkinson's, I wonder?" the doctor said.

"Who knows? Maybe my hand slipped."

Toledo put his hand up to silence him.

"I'm sorry, but you really can't say anything to me – not unless you have decided to waive your Miranda Rights."

"Sorry … sorry," Shaffer said, and returned to his quiet but intense contemplation of his hands. Detective Toledo opened another binder and stared at some of the written statements. Even though Shaffer had invoked Miranda, there was no reason for him not to sit here, as long as he did not ask any questions. So many suspects are glued to shows like *Law and Order* that they think the police must leave the room in this situation. *But it is not true, I can sit here as long as I like.*

The silent standoff continued, neither man willing to give an inch.

Twenty-Five

"He's dead? Mark is dead?"

The woman's tears were flowing freely now, and Professor McMannis shifted uncomfortably in his chair, not wanting to look at her. Ginny seemed unmoved by the display of shocked grief and emotion. She was sipping her latte with care, as it was hot. Beyond that, she looked at Ophelia.

"I'm sorry," Ginny said, and reached out to pat the woman's hand.

"But how did he ...?"

"It was ..."

But McMannis cut Ginny off.

"We are not quite sure yet."

Ginny glanced over at him quizzically and he slightly shook his head. She just raised her eyebrows and looked back to Ophelia.

The pretense did not last, however. Ophelia received a text.

"This is from Mom, she says ... Dad has been arrested for Mark's murder?! Is that right?"

In typical Bay Area fashion, the other Starbucks customers had been astutely ignoring the conversation over the last few minutes, but Ophelia said the final sentence so loudly that everyone must have heard. Two young men at a nearby table looked at one another, at Ophelia, then back to each other and then, as if by osmotic communication, stood up and moved to an outside table.

"Yes, that's correct," McMannis said quietly.

"That stupid bastard!" Ophelia said venomously, then quietly herself, "I told him that if it ever came out ..."

She was looking past Ginny and McMannis now, her eyes full of tears with an intense anger glowing from them.

"If what came out?" McMannis asked.

"I suppose it doesn't matter now," Ophelia said. "Come on, I'll show you."

Soon they were driving fast up into the hills toward the house. McMannis had been a little unsure about getting in a car with this woman behind the wheel, but she drove with remarkable care. The Shaffers were characterized by uncontrolled and often chaotic behavior, mixed with an odd detachment. Here Ophelia was showing the latter, and McMannis marveled at it as she negotiated the hairpin curves nonchalantly.

They arrived at the house. From the cars present, McMannis calculated that the rest of the family was also there, but all seemed dark when they went inside.

But then it always seems dark in here, the professor thought.

Ophelia led them in silence to the very top of the house. She opened the door carefully and they looked inside. Sitting a few feet away from a TV set was her son, Alan. He looked impossibly small beside the large screen, and his hands moved quickly on the controller. He was lost in the video game. As far as McMannis could see it was a zombie game. The monsters stumbled toward the boy, and he shot them adeptly. Often, they simply exploded, while others paused before collapsing into a heap. Their bodies vanished, before new ones took their place.

Not quite that simple in real life, McMannis thought. *Though my life would be a lot simpler if it was.*

Just as Ophelia walked closer to her son, and he looked up, McMannis received a text. Normally getting a text in this house was akin to striking the jackpot in a lottery, so he was rather surprised.

145

PAPERS GRADED. ARE WE TRANSLATING THEM TO A CURVE OR KEEPING THEM AS IS? McMannis stared at the test, mystified.

"Everything OK?" Ginny asked, as she looked at her friend standing awkwardly halfway through the doorway.

"Oh, yes," he eventually said.

After all, he thought, *you are at least nominally still a professor.*

The message had been from his GSI, referring to some end-of-semester papers from an upper division class. There were only eight students in the class, so how the GSI thought they could possibly grade on a curve was unknown.

Still – math and folklore don't go together.

"Sorry, it's nothing, just a message from my other world. My other life."

"Sound like you are an alien or something," Ginny said.

As ever, she puts her finger right on it.

The whole exchange drifted right past Ophelia, who had removed her son from the game. He was standing by her side reluctantly, occasionally glancing over his shoulder to see the zombies marching inexorably toward him, apparently joyful at their unexpected liberation from machine gun fire.

"Don't you see it?" Ophelia said.

McMannis looked. He did not.

"It might be helpful if I knew what I am meant to be seeing," he said.

Impatient, Ophelia allowed Alan back to his game, who returned to it eagerly after a slightly bemused look at his mother. One zombie was nearly on his character, and he blasted it to bits before carrying on shooting at it quite needlessly, as it vanished from view. The little boy was still shooting at the empty space on the ground of his video

146

game when Ophelia closed the door and took them to her bedroom.

All three sat down on her king-size bed. McMannis felt awkward, but Ginny was right at home.

Ophelia reached under her bed and brought out a photo album. *Strangely old-fashioned*, McMannis thought. Ginny saw that it was the same one that Ophelia had already shown her. *I think I've looked at more photos in albums over the last few weeks than in the rest of my life put together*, Ginny thought. Ophelia was leafing through it quickly. Finally, she found the page that she was looking for.

"Hadn't you wondered?" she said with an odd smile. "Wondered about Alan's father? About that story of him killing himself?"

"Do you have a picture of him there?" McMannis asked.

"Yes. I do!" Ophelia replied, her eyes flashing triumphantly.

Jesus, these people are nuts, McMannis thought.

"Here," Ophelia said, and handed the album over to Ginny.

The detective and the student looked at the photograph. Both frowned in mystification. Looking up at them from the page was a photograph of the recent murderer, even more recent victim – Mark Shaffer.

"I don't think you've given us the right page," McMannis said. "That's your brother. Not your boyfriend"

"Yes, I know!" Ophelia said loudly, then much softer. "But my brother *is* Alan's father. He is both Alan's uncle and father. We like to keep things neat and simple in the Shaffer family."

Ginny giggled nervously for a second, then stopped when she saw that the woman was deadly serious.

"You are saying that you and your brother – had a child?" McMannis said slowly and quietly.

Years of moonlighting for the Berkeley PD meant that very little surprised Professor Ian McMannis, but this was something he did not expect.

"Alan is – your brother's child?" Ginny said quietly, as if saying the words would test their validity.

"Yes." Ophelia said flatly.

"Oh."

Ginny whispered the last word.

"Did he …?" she continued.

"Rape me? Is that what you are trying to say?"

Ginny nodded silently.

"I suppose that would be much easier to handle wouldn't it? Make it much easier all round. Especially now he is gone. But no, he did not rape me."

"Were you – drunk or something?" McMannis now asked, trying to latch onto something that would make this news a little less sickening.

"Drunk? No. Well – sometimes. But not most of the time."

"This was not a … single occasion?" McMannis said.

"No, not at all. For a time, Mark and I were in love with one another."

"You were in love with one another … you were in love with your brother?" Ginny echoed.

"Yes, I was in love with my brother!" Ophelia shouted, standing up. "Will you stop repeating everything I say like some stupid child?!"

Questions were rushing their minds. New dimensions to this whole case. Past moments now took on new meaning. Certainties turned to doubts. Doubts to certainties.

"How long did this go on?" McMannis asked.

"About two years." She was quiet again now. "Then I got pregnant, and he lost interest."

"And after you had Alan?"

"My lovely brother pretended that the whole thing had never happened. Even when Alan's strange diseases started to show up – even then he did not admit anything. I saw him reading a book once on the Egyptians, explaining how the tradition of brothers and sisters marrying had caused them – eventually – to fall from power. But they did last several thousand years, so how we were we to know that …."

She was interrupted by Alan, who came staggering through the door, apparently unable to breathe. Ophelia took an inhaler from her bedside table and gave it to the boy. A few deep breaths, and it was as if the attack never happened.

"Thanks, mom," the boy said, then scurried out.

"I keep them in every room in the house. He always forgets to carry them."

God, McMannis thought, *what must she have been going through all these years?*

"Does anyone else know?" Ginny asked.

The question was obvious, but McMannis was surprised by the matter-of-fact way in which she asked it. The contrast between Ginny's angelic features and this almost brutal emotional toughness was always starkest at moments like this.

"Does anyone else know?" And this time it was Ophelia's turn to echo someone's words incredulously. The woman laughed and walked quickly out of the room. McMannis and Ginny looked at one another, as if unsure what had just occurred.

"I'll be fucked!" Ginny said quietly but vehemently. She got up as if to follow Ophelia, but McMannis held up his hand and shook his head.

149

"No, let her go. The thing is," he said, as Ginny sat down again, "do you believe her?"

"Do I believe her? Who the hell would make up a story like that? Who would *want* to make up a story like that?"

McMannis shrugged.

"I mean – what good would it do her?"

He was silent again. *What good would it do her?* But for all these uncertainties, something did not sound right. *Something is missing.*

McMannis glanced over at a photograph of Alan. What had seemed like a perfectly normal looking boy now took on a more sinister aspect – as if his origins were written on his face. *Or supposed origins.*

"Where do you think she went?"

McMannis raised his eyebrows. He had been in this house often enough to know that people could appear and disappear with an eerie suddenness, as if there were hidden doors every few feet.

"Do you think she is all right?" And with this, Ginny stood up, anxious to go and look for Ophelia.

"As all right as anyone is in this crazy place."

Ginny was about to walk out of the door when Ophelia came back in, quiet and shy.

"I'm sorry," she said. "I didn't mean to run off like that."

She seems more embarrassed about the running off than she is about having a child with her own brother, McMannis thought incredulously.

"Bad manners," Ophelia murmured, as if answering his question.

Ophelia sat down on the couch, glanced over at them in an inquiring way. Eventually she spoke.

"I suppose that's how people look at someone after they have been convicted of some terrible crime. I remember reading that somewhere – this woman was convicted of killing her own child, and she said that it was the looks, the disgust mixed with hatred, mixed with fear, that were the worst part of it. She felt cast out."

"You are not a murderer," McMannis said quietly.

"No," Ophelia replied. "But I might as well be. Incest – the final taboo. It is easier to explain killing someone than having sex with your brother."

"But it wasn't just having sex," Ginny said.

Ophelia smiled slightly but said nothing.

"You had an actual relationship with him."

Ophelia's smile weakened.

"You were in love with him?"

"In love? I suppose you could call it that. After all, we are meant to love our siblings – it is just a small step toward loving them in a … different way."

McMannis frowned at Ophelia, and then said, "Most people would think that is a giant leap."

"True." Her voice was distant.

"Did your boyfriend actually …?" Ginny asked.

"Oh, yes. He shot himself. He found it rather … difficult to deal with."

"Found what rather difficult?" Ginny went on.

Ophelia paused, smiled a little.

"We had a misunderstanding. About a time. He thought that I had said seven when I said ten. So, he went – he went down there – at the wrong time."

Ophelia glanced down, gesturing with her hand toward the floor.

"The date room?" Ginny asked, already knowing the answer.

"Yes, the date room," Ophelia replied.

There was silence for a few seconds.

"He walked in on us – Josh, my boyfriend – he walked in on my brother and I."

151

She was still smiling in that vaguely manic way, her eyes shining.

"I tried to explain to him. Tried to show that ... but it didn't work. That night he went up into the hills and shot himself. Shot himself in the eye."

"In the eye?" McMannis echoed.

"Yes, in the eye. As if he had wanted to get rid of what he saw. Destroy it completely. Destroy what had seen it completely."

Ophelia was now looking past them, somewhere out in the dark. *What terrible things is she remembering?* McMannis thought.

"Did you find him?" Ginny asked.

"Find him? Oh, you mean Josh? Yes – I found him. I knew where he was going. Well, I guessed. I arrived just a few minutes after he had done it. The windshield was shattered – at first, I thought that he had just been in an accident. But no. He had shot himself in the eye, and because of the angle, the bullet had gone all the way round his head, then back out of the other eye, and through the glass. The hole it had gone in was quite neat, but the one where it had come out."

She looked at them intently.

"The one where it came out was huge – it destroyed most of that side of his face. I can see it now as if it had just happened."

She reached out for McMannis, touching the left side of his face gently, contemplatively.

"Afterward, Mark said it had been for the best."
Silence.

"The strange thing was – I think it was that night that I conceived. It must have been the shock of looking up and over Mark's shoulder and seeing him standing there, silhouetted in the doorway with his mouth half-open in astonishment. I wanted to tell him that he looked stupid,

152

wanted to tell him to shut his mouth. And at that moment Mark came inside me and I had an orgasm – one that I have never experienced – before or since. An electric jolt bursting through my muscles. Endless pleasure. And I conceived."

"A massive rush of adrenaline," Ginny suggested.

McMannis looked from one woman to the other.

"Endless pleasure." Ophelia said quietly. "Followed by endless pain."

The door suddenly flew open, and Ruth ran in.

"Mr. Mark – he is dead! Mr. Mark – he is dead!" She shouted; her eyes red with tears.

"Yes," Ophelia said quietly. "We already knew."

Twenty-Six

"So, Mr. Carlisle – if that really is your name – what is the real reason you came to see me?"

"I'm sorry," Police Officer Carlisle said, squirming under her gaze.

"What is the real reason that you came here? You are no more depressed than I am."

One hell of a bedside manner, Carlisle thought, *or should that be couchside manner?*

"Dr. Shaffer, I really don't know what you are …"

"As I said, you are no more depressed than I am."

Carlisle looked over at the psychologist. She had a self-confident face, softened slightly by a certain vulnerability around the eyes. Makeup skillfully applied could not hide the effects of advancing age, but they leant a vulnerability she would not otherwise possess.

"You seem remarkably sure of my symptoms – or lack of them."

"They are simply too perfect – like you have read a textbook and skillfully mimicked each and every symptom of major depressive disorder."

"Fair enough," Carlisle replied.

Expecting another comment, the psychologist glanced down at the empty chart on the desk in front of her. But he did not say anything else. He merely looked at her, a hint of an ironic smile on his face.

"Do you know how many people have come wandering through that door just to look at me?" The woman asked.

Carlisle slowly shook his head.

"My son is accused of murder. Then my son has an accident. Then he is dead. And my husband is arrested for the murder. And then people – people like you – they come to gawp and laugh. Come out of amusement or curiosity of some sick mixture of all of them. Can you imagine what that feels like, Mr. Carlisle?"

"I cannot," he said, frowning a little in mock concern.

She looked at him steadily, then her brow furrowed as a little doubt crept in.

"I am correct in assuming that you *are* one of those damned people."

"Yes," Carlisle said. "You are."

She just cannot read me, he thought.

"Mr. Carlisle I'm …"

"Johnny, please call me Johnny."

"Johnny, I must apologize – my situation – this …" Her voice faded as tears started to well in her eyes. "Could you perhaps make another appointment? This one – and that one – there will be no charge."

Carlisle laughed nervously, as if embarrassed that the woman could make such a faux pas – assuming that money was an issue.

"I will call for another appointment, Dr. Shaffer. I thank you for your time."

And with that the police officer stood up, nodded slightly at the woman, and left the office. He walked down the plush, carpeted corridor, through the foyer and out into a now gloomy late afternoon as the fog started to drift in from the ocean. He called Toledo, worried that he had not found out enough.

"Toledo!"

"Yes?"

"Toledo … it is Officer Carlisle!"

"Ah."

Toledo waited.

155

"And what did you discover?" the detective finally said.

"I think that this lady has had one sleepless night too many."

"Meaning?" Toledo replied.

"Meaning – she worked out that I was not depressed straight away – then second-guessed herself and ended up like some grad student apologizing for getting too wrapped up in a session. Too emotional."

"Do you think she knows anything?" Toledo asked.

Carlisle paused as he got into his car, relaxing into the seat.

"Negative," he finally said. "Or rather – negative with a slight uncertain. The problem with that family is that they are all so crazy weird that their normal seems to be hiding something – simply because it is so far away from anyone else's normal. Anything your end?"

"Not really," Toledo said, glancing at the two-way mirror, behind which the good doctor was quietly conversing with his lawyer. Occasionally they laughed slightly, as if sharing some secret forever beyond Toledo's understanding. The lawyer's shoes had probably cost about a week of Toledo's earnings. Something about that annoyed the detective, even though he had long accepted that it was his lot to be paid only a fraction of what his intelligence and skill were worth. *The price of a clear conscience*, he thought, almost wincing at the naiveté of this cliché.

"Well, I guess I'll see you later," Carlisle said.

"Roger," Toledo murmured.

"And Toledo?"

"Yes?"

"Did I do all right? This being my first undercover assignment?"

"Perfect. Just perfect." Toledo said and slid the phone back into his pocket.

In his car, Carlisle flushed with pride then frowned a little. He was not sure Toledo would ever call him again.

Toledo walked back into the interrogation room.

"Not disturbing you I hope," he said with a silvery lack of sincerity.

"Not at all, Detective Toledo, not at all," the lawyer replied.

Why does he keep on calling me 'Detective Toledo' rather than just 'Detective' or 'Toledo'? There is something mocking about it.

The lawyer smiled slightly, as if reading his thoughts.

Toledo sat heavily in his chair, feigning the fatigue of imminent defeat.

Of course, really, I am just getting started.

"Dr. Shaffer, can we move onto another subject?"

Shaffer glanced at his lawyer, as if he was the font of all wisdom.

The lawyer nodded.

"Certainly," the doctor said. "How else can I help you?"

"Dr. Shaffer – do you know the room that your children refer to as the date room?"

For a second – less than a second – Shaffer's eyes widened slightly.

"Yes, I think I was the one who christened it that – back when my oldest first became a teenager."

"OK," Toledo said. "But it is not just a place for dates is it?"

"I think it would be more accurate to say that it is a room for *after* the dates, Detective."

Toledo could not help but smile. Shaffer had a disarming charm when he chose.

157

"Well, whatever we call it, other things happen in that room, don't they Dr. Shaffer?"

"Other things?"

"Other activities."

A moment's pause.

"I assume so – it's been years since I have been down there. Probably. We store things down there. Mostly old toys. Things like that."

"Really? You seldom go down there?"

At this question, Shaffer's lawyer leaned ever-so-slightly toward his client and stiffened at the same time.

"Years." The doctor paused, as if considering. Then he nodded. "Maybe it's only months."

"Is there a point to this, Detective Toledo?" The lawyer asked, needlessly.

"My point is," Toledo said, leaning forward, "in the back of that room, behind some curtains, there is a bizarre collection."

"A bizarre collection?"

"Yes, very bizarre. Unique I'd say."

"Unique?"

"Yes."

The lawyer was looking from one to the other, like a television camera slightly behind the action in a fevered game of tennis.

"These, doctor," Toledo said. He took four eight-by-ten photographs from the bottom of the casefile in front of him and spread them on the table.

The lawyer shrank back a little and gasped.

Dr. Shaffer looked down at the pictures of the babies in the bottles curiously, as if they were a pleasant reminder of some gentler, simpler time in the past.

"Oh, you mean *that* collection." He said sarcastically.

You mean there is something even worse than these? Toledo thought.

"Embryology and more advanced fetal development interest me, Detective. Naturally, I do not practice in that part of medicine, but it remains a curiosity to me. A hobby, if you will."

"But it is more than a hobby, isn't it Dr. Shaffer? Much more than a hobby. Don't you have an erotic interest in them?"

The lawyer's eyes widened this time.

"What?" Shaffer said quietly, almost whispering.

"An erotic interest, doctor. There is evidence that you sit in a chair in the date room and look at this – collection – and masturbate."

The lawyer's gaze was now fixed on his client.

"I would be careful, Detective. There is still such a thing as slander I believe," Shaffer said.

"But something is only slanderous, and I believe your counselor will vouch for this, if the statement is not true."

Shaffer glanced at the lawyer, who obediently nodded his head.

The doctor regained his composure, rubbed his hand over his eyes and sighed.

"Every man is free to his thoughts, Detective. Surely you understand that. What I do – or do not do – with my collection is my business, and only mine. And it has nothing to do with my son, and even less to do with his death."

He's right, Toledo thought. *At least at the moment, he's right. But there is a link, I know it.*

"And even less, if that is possible, to do with my girlfriend's death."

Toledo was so gloomily mulling over the slowness of this case that he almost missed the slip.

"Your girlfriend's death, Dr. Shaffer?"

"His girlfriend. Sorry. A slip."

"Freudian slip?"

159

"Maybe," Shaffer said, now stifling a yawn.

"I think my client has had enough for this afternoon, Detective Toledo."

"That's OK," Toledo replied. He stood up, turned as if to go and then looked back toward the doctor and his lawyer. Instinct told him that now was the time to drop the information he had been holding back.

"But I can guarantee you, detective. Absolutely guarantee, that I do nothing but look at my collection. Just look."

Toledo nodded slightly. *I believe him.*

"Oh, there was just one more thing," Toledo said. "You might be interested to know that we found your semen both in and on the body of Caroline Ramirez."

Dr. Shaffer looked shocked, mystified, and then amused. *As if,* Toledo thought as he walked out of the room, *it would be impossible for his semen to be found there. Worrying.*

And with that the interrogation was over, at least for the day.

Twenty-Seven

The body was lying halfway down one of the ravines
that cut through Hillsborough at strange, tortured angles.
Naked, with the clothes arranged in a neat pile at the top of
the hill.

"She died from a broken neck," Amanda said, after a
cursory glance.

"Not going to make sure?" Toledo asked.

"Back in the office – yes – but here, no need. Number
one, it is pretty obvious that she is dead. Number two, you
can see from the angle of her neck, it's broken. For once,
you boys will have your way, a completely untouched body
to photograph and gloat over."

Amanda crouched down, looking carefully at the
breast that was flattened by the weight of the body above it,
the nipple protruding at a strange angle.

"They should get excited – they will get to pop her
cherry."

Toledo frowned a little. Professional rivalries between
various branches of the same organization were common,
he knew that, but the macabre joviality that often-
accompanied turf wars within forensics was more than a
little creepy. Some forensic officers were only slightly
removed from the criminals they pursued, at least as far as
their eccentricities.

The detective glanced up the slope, traced the body's
probable path through bushes and long grass. It had hit a
rotten log and somersaulted several yards in the air before
coming to rest in a little hollow. Had it continued any
further it might have descended into an even steeper area
with dense vegetation. If she had been wearing her clothes

rather than leaving them at the top of the slope, they might never have found her.

"Do you think she jumped?" Toledo asked.

"That's for you to find out," Amanda replied. "Although I think she was dumped rather than jumped."

"Dumped?"

"I think she was thrown off already dead," Amanda said, now looking carefully at the back of the body's neck,

"And they took her clothes off, piled them neatly – all to make it look like a suicide?"

"Could have," she replied. "But I am just a lowly medical examiner – and I shouldn't be here at all."

"Special dispensation, dear."

"Special dispensation – BS – they can't deal with a case like this."

"It started in Berkeley and so …"

"Cassius, I am tired, do you want me for anything else tonight?"

The detective looked over at her and shook his head slightly. Amanda was about to leave when she paused, bent down to the body's feet. She carefully lifted the big toe and scraped underneath the nail.

"Huhm. I thought so."

"What?" Toledo said.

"Sand. Just like Caroline Ramirez."

Toledo sighed.

"We do live near many beaches."

"True – but neither of our ladies were exactly the outdoor type, don't you think?"

He was about to agree when headlights appeared up on the road. The car slowed and stopped. He knew her from the silhouette before he saw the face.

Ophelia, what a coincidence that she should pass by.

"What's happening?" her voice was quiet, yet clear.

The uniform was looking her up and down.

162

Great professionalism.

"Just an incident, ma'am, nothing to concern you. Best if you drive on …"

"No," Toledo said, clambering up the slope to the road. "It's all right."

The uniform looked at him with surprise, then shrugged slightly as he reached them.

"Detective Toledo, what brings you here again?"

"It's very unfortunate," he replied.

"Unfortunate?"

Toledo gestured down the hill. Ophelia looked, then stepped closer to the edge, her eyes adapting to the darkness below.

"Is that a body down there?"

Toledo nodded.

"Anyone I know?"

Toledo pointed toward the neat pile of clothes, studying Ophelia's face carefully. At first, she did not recognize them and then something, he had no idea what, caught her eye, and she quickly looked back down toward the body.

"Ruth! Oh my God…"

She's one hell of an actress if she knows anything about this.

"What happened?"

She looked from the clothes to the body and back again several times, as if the sheer repetition would reveal something unclear on the first viewing.

"Can I go down?" she asked, but Toledo raised his hand.

"No, it's an incident scene – or a crime scene."

"Crime? You mean she didn't jump?"

"She may have. Or she may not have. It's up to us to decide – or to find out."

"You'd think if she was going to jump – she'd have chosen a more certain place."

"That's a point," Amanda said. Somehow, she had walked up the slope without either of them noticing. *Like a deer*, Toledo thought, smiling.

"I mean – off the Golden Gate or somewhere."

Amanda looked quickly at Toledo, about to interrupt the woman. The detective raised his hand to signal "I'm OK."

"But then she might not be found." Ophelia continued. "And this looks like she wanted to be found. Like she was making a statement."

"Or someone was making a statement," Toledo replied.

"Yes," Ophelia said thoughtfully.

"I think you chose the wrong career," Amanda said lightly.

Ophelia looked at her in surprise, then smiled.

"I don't have a career. Haven't you heard? My daddy's rich."

She took a step toward her car then paused.

"Can I go?" Ophelia asked.

"Yes," Toledo replied.

Ophelia smiled, got into her car, reversed to a turnout then set off back down the hill.

"That's strange," Toledo said.

"What?"

"Well, she was driving up the hill when she stopped here – then turned around and went back the way she came from."

"Change of plans?" Amanda said.

"Or she had seen what she came to see."

An ambulance was arriving, with another police car near behind.

"Let's go," Toledo said, and Amanda nodded as they walked to their cars.

164

Twenty-Eight

"The cause of death is not readily apparent," Amanda said as Toledo carefully avoided looking at the body. The coroner saw his discomfort and pulled a blue sheet over her. He glanced up just as it settled on the body, reminding him of his grandmother who always set the table for dinners like some English housewife. Anglophile, although she had never been East of Chicago, but he had fond memories of her house and faux-English ways. *Ben would have liked her.*

"Cassius? Have you been listening to me?"

Evidently not.

"I said that this on the back of her neck – these marks – they came from a post-mortem blow."

"From the fall down the slope?"

Amanda shook her head.

"Probably not – it looks to be an active blow – she was hit with something heavy. Not too strong a person – but enough to make it seem as though it might have killed her."

"So, someone is trying to make it look like a violent death, when in fact …"

Toledo was interrupted as a medical tech came into the room with a report. He handed it to Amanda. She glanced at it quickly, raised her eyebrows, and sighed.

"What is it?" Toledo asked, although he had already guessed the answer.

"Insulin-induced coma and cardiac arrest."

Toledo rubbed his eyes and sighed in turn.

"How quickly would it happen?" he asked.

"How quickly would what happen?" Amanda replied, still looking at the report.

"Death – when you are given insulin when you don't need it."

"No more than a few hours," she said. "It depends on the amount of insulin and the speed of your metabolism."

"Would it be reversible?"

"If used in the right way. Insulin-induced comas used to be used in severe cases of mental illness. Back in the Fifties and Sixties. I don't think there was any science to back it up ... it just looked impressive."

"Looked impressive?"

"Patients often had seizures and then fell into comas. They administered electro-shock treatment at the same time, while the person was in a coma. If the coma is mild, then you can give an injection of glucose to reverse the effects of the insulin. But, in this case ..." and here she gestured toward the body with her elegantly long fingers, "death was pretty quick. And nothing could be done about it. Whoever injected Ruth with insulin knew what they were doing, knew what end they had in mind."

"And now Dr. Shaffer is out of the picture," Toledo said.

"At least for this murder," Amanda said.

"What do you think the likelihood is of two people – in the same basic case – using the same method of killing, independent of each other?"

"They needn't be independent of each other," Amanda replied. "Dr. Shaffer might have killed his son and had an accomplice."

"Or," Toledo said, smiling slightly, "we have a copy-cat – someone else got the idea from Mark Shaffer's death."

They walked out of the room into the long corridor that sloped gently upward toward the main part of the hospital. They sauntered, as if on an afternoon stroll in some idyllic park.

"We have to remember that the original insulin overdose on Mark Shaffer was not successful. He was put into a coma, but not killed." Amanda said.

"How long could he have stayed like that?"

"Months, years – possibly even decades. The woman in the Von Bulow case survived more than twenty years."

"Do you think it is possible that Dr. Shaffer intended to kill his son straight away, but failed? Gave him the wrong dose?"

"No," Amanda replied, shaking her head. "He may not be a specialist, but he is a diabetic himself. And any second-year medical student could calculate a dose that is sure to be fatal."

"So perhaps he wanted him to linger? Death would mean an autopsy. Waking up would mean a trial. But coma? The perfect medium." Toledo liked to bounce ideas off Amanda, using her scientific mind to weed out his more imaginative, less likely thoughts.

"Perhaps. But either way, they are both dead."

Twenty-Nine

Professor McMannis looked over his class. Freshman seminars were a lovely idea in theory, but often degenerated into discussions more suited to a bar after a few drinks. *Or Starbucks after a few too many lattes.* This current session had moved from how urban legends spread so quickly through a campus to the likelihood of the San Francisco Forty-Niners ever winning another Super Bowl. McMannis was not exactly sure how they had got from one to other and wasn't really bothered either way. He was in a smiling and nodding mode – something these young people found reassuring. For many it was just about the only time that they had genuine contact with an actual professor, beyond looking at him from a distance in a massive lecture hall.

As one of the more vocal students lamented the lack of a Jerry Rice or a Joe Montana in the present team, McMannis mulled Toledo's decision to release Dr. Jerry Shaffer. It was a standing joke how Toledo often pursued cases by allowing the main suspects to roam free after an initial arrest. The results were too impressive to cause any more than vague comments from Toledo's superiors, but McMannis feared that at some point, in some case, it would all blow up in his face.

It had to.

And will this be the one? he thought as he nodded volubly at a male student's comment.

"So, you agree with that?" the student asked.

"In theory – yes, but in practice, it might be more difficult to actually put into theory."

Vaguely bemused faces greeted him. McMannis wondered whether he had just committed some painful faux pas. He never discovered what he had just commented upon, as his phone buzzed him, or rather, emitted the strains of a little saxophone music.

Toledo. Must be something serious to disturb me in class.

"Excuse me for a minute …" he said, smiling at the class.

They all knew about his other occupation, and most found it intriguing and even a little exciting. The students waited patiently as he read the text.

YESTERDAY EVENING RUTH FOUND DEAD AT BOTTOM OF HILLSBOROUGH HILL. HEAD CAVED IN BUT CAUSE OF DEATH INSULIN OVERDOSE. KEEPING SHAFFER IN CUSTODY AND CHARGING HIM WITH THE RAMIREZ MURDER. THAT MAY CAUSE OTHERS TO OPEN UP MORE. NO WAY HE WILL GET BAIL AS TOO MUCH OF A FLIGHT RISK. TOLEDO

McMannis smiled. Toledo was young enough to be able to use the latest technology seamlessly, but old-fashioned enough to sign off on his texts. With the discovery of the bizarre collection of babies underneath the house, McMannis thought that he might now be more genuinely useful to the case. *Anything strange, inexplicable, or just outright weird and they always look to me*, he thought. *I should be flattered, but somehow, I am not.*

The class was still looking at him. He glanced down at his watch. Ten minutes before they were meant to end. *Close enough.*

Half an hour later McMannis, Toledo, Amanda and Ginny had congregated at Café Milano. Upstairs.

"I remember when you could smoke up here," Toledo said wistfully.

"You never smoked…" Amanda said.

"There is a lot that you don't know about me. My short but intense period of smoking is one of them."

"So, what do we have?" Toledo said, glancing around to check that those at other tables were out of earshot.

"You mean – what do we have that is new?" Ginny said, her eyes still on her phone.

"Yes, what do we have that is new," Toledo replied.

"Well," and finally she looked up from the screen, "it seems that the Shaffers are an even more incestuous lot than we had thought."

"Literally so." McMannis said gloomily.

"You believed her?" Amanda asked.

"Believed Ophelia?" Ginny answered and looked toward McMannis for agreement. "Oh yes."

"As I said to Ginny at the time, who in their right minds would invent a story like that?" McMannis said.

"I don't think a 'right mind' standard is really that useful when discussing the Shaffers," Toledo said.

Amanda nodded.

"I assume that is a crime too," McMannis said.

"What? Having a baby fathered by your brother?" Amanda replied, a little consternation in her voice.

"Yes, that is a crime." Toledo said. "But not one, in these circumstances – that I guess would actually be prosecuted. Probably every adult member of the family that knew about it is guilty of a crime … because they knew and said nothing."

"Might provide some leverage…" Ginny said, brushing the hair away from her eyes and staring out of the window for a moment. "Why don't they ever clean those windows?" she asked dreamily. "It's as if they are afraid of

170

us seeing too much of what is outside. Or afraid of people seeing in."

McMannis marveled at how she could move smoothly between pragmatic, police methods and classic Berkeley bullshitting.

"If Mark Shaffer really was the father of Ophelia's child ..." Toledo looked toward Amanda inquisitively. She nodded.

"The DNA matching will be in later today," she said.

"... then that gives a serious motive for him being killed. It doesn't bring us any nearer to *why* his father killed Caroline Ramirez."

"Maybe Caroline found out about the child. A discovery that couldn't be accepted by the family. Then she was killed by one – or all of them," Amanda said.

"And the sex, the message on the wall?" McMannis asked.

"Simply a cover – to hide the real motivation."

"A bit of overkill," McMannis continued.

"As many barriers to the truth as possible," Toledo said. "To put us off uncovering reality."

"There is one problem with all that," McMannis went on.

"What's that?" Amanda said.

"Ophelia openly told us about the child, and who its father is…"

"Only after Mark Shaffer was dead."

"We are back to Dr. Shaffer killing Caroline. Then he kills his son. Then Ruth got in the way or discovered the same secret."

"And she was killed," Ginny completed the sentence. She had been so quiet that they were barely aware she was present.

"By someone else, because Dr. Shaffer was in jail at the time," Toledo said.

171

"Thus, the logical course is to wait until only one is left – and we will know who the killer is."

McMannis was correct, but his comment provoked a groan from the others.

"That works in Agatha Christie novels," Toledo said. "But unfortunately, we don't have that luxury in real life. Although at the rate we are going, that's going to happen anyway."

"You could use that leverage," Amanda said.

"In what way?" Toledo replied.

"Arrest all of them."

A moment of silence around the table.

"I could I suppose," Toledo said. "But then we would never get an answer. Mark Shaffer and Ruth Beringer's killer is among them – but then …"

The others waited expectantly.

"I suppose Dr. Shaffer could have requested the murder of Ruth from his jail cell – it really could be him."

"Requested? You make it sound so polite," Amanda said.

"I can't really see that man raising his voice over anything," McMannis said. "He lacks the energy."

Toledo chuckled ironically.

"You didn't see those bottles – and what was inside those bottles," the detective said, and an involuntary shudder passed over him.

"But surely that is passive energy. Looking at the babies. And what he does when looking at the babies. Could he really plan all of this? And why was Caroline killed in the first place?"

Each of them looked at the others expectantly.

None said anything.

Thirty

If Caroline's funeral was more well-attended than
seemed likely, this is positively empty, Toledo thought, as
he looked over the desultory little group gathered in the
"Rest Garden" that hugged the bottom of the Burlingame
hills. Mark Shaffer and Ruth Beringer were being buried
on the same day. Indeed, their plots were adjacent.
Apparently, Ruth was regarded as literally part of the
family.

Ophelia was wearing the same outfit as at Caroline's
internment, only this time with a thin jacket as some
protection against a little fall chill that had drifted in from
the ocean. Her older brother was wearing a motorbike
jacket once again. Mrs. Shaffer wore a voluminous black
dress that made her look twice her already considerable
size. She shed what Toledo saw as genuine tears during
both ceremonies.

The only surprise attendee was Ben, who arrived with
a spectacular bouquet for Mark and a slightly less ornate,
but still impressive arrangement for Ruth. Without his
offerings, both gravesites would have been embarrassingly
bare. Perhaps it was not surprising that few had come for
Ruth – as far as they could tell she had no living family
beyond two cousins that she had never met. But for Mark to
be essentially ignored was odd. Toledo glanced back over
his shoulder at Dr. Shaffer, standing awkwardly with a
large overcoat half-disguising his handcuffs. The detective
frowned. Surely it was obvious that the heavyset, barely
ambulatory doctor was a minimal escape risk. The officer
with him could probably walk faster than he could run. Yet
normally homicide suspects were not allowed to attend the
funerals of their victims, even if the victim happened to be

their son – so Toledo supposed that the handcuffs were a compromise.

None of the Shaffers shared as much as a glance during the ten-minute-long ceremonies. Each was obviously here for the sake of basic propriety and wanted to leave as quickly as possible. The fact that the murderer (s) was/were almost certainly standing just a few feet from him amused Toledo in one sense yet infuriated him in another. Glancing around, he wished he could peer into their minds briefly, mine out the secrets lurking there. But the faces were blank, almost bland. *If bad hearts hadn't made them wealthy, poker would have been an alternative.*

McMannis was late, and he lingered a few cemetery plots over in order not to disturb the ceremony. Once it was over, he walked quietly to Toledo.

"So … any interesting attendees?" the professor asked.

"Not one."

"I guess we will just have to wait for the next one to be killed after all."

"You may be right, but I can't officially say that. Let's lean on all of them a bit more – see what we can come up with."

They wandered toward the car as Dr. Shaffer was led back to the unmarked police vehicle. There was something pathetic about the aging, lumbering figure attempting to keep up with an officer who was making no effort to measure his pace to his prisoner's. For a moment, Toledo remembered documentary clips of prisoners being run from one place to another in prison camps.

"I think I'll pay a visit to the neighbors again. Find out what else our inquisitive friend discovered on his trips into the Shaffer forest."

"I will work some on Ophelia," McMannis replied.

"Some of that old womanizing magic?" Toledo said quietly, teasing.

174

"Something like that, yes."

Toledo snorted in mock disgust, and the two friends got in their cars and drove away.

By midday Toledo was sitting outside the cottage on Ben's estate. Ben had welcomed him like some long-lost friend and the detective realized that the suave, apparently self-sufficient man was in fact lonely. While Toledo's whole house could comfortably fit inside Ben's kitchen, and their lifestyles were about as different as possible, he could recognize loneliness easy enough. *I know it too much firsthand*, he thought, feeling a wave of melancholy pass over him. He forced his mind away from images of a small, empty lounge with the well-worn bachelor's chair and the virtually unused couches. *Ben's lover has been away for months and left, at least according to Ben, on the exact day of Caroline Ramirez's murder.* Surely this was an odd coincidence. *So odd to be not coincidental at all?*

"So," Ben said, sipping what Toledo suspected would be first of many glasses of wine that day, "to what do I owe the immense pleasure of your company again, Detective Toledo?"

"I was wondering what other things you have seen on your …. visits to the Shaffers."

"Not much really. The normal comings and goings of a large family of means."

"Did you see much of Mark and his girlfriend?"

"You mean the one that died?"

"Yes," Toledo said, disguising his surprise. "The one that died."

"They were fairly frequent visitors to the date room. About once a week I'd say. I don't think young Shaffer was exactly faithful and exclusive in his ways. Occasionally other girls went there with him – but Miss Caroline was the most regular."

"Did you see anything unusual?"

175

"Well, it was unusual that Mark bothered to use the date room at all. As far as I know, all the adult children of the family could have their lovers freely stay with them in the main part of the house."

"They could?"

"Oh yes..." Ben smiled. "In fact, Ophelia's boyfriend virtually lived there for a time."

"The one that killed himself?"

"Yes, the one that killed himself."

"Did you ever suspect some of the relationships within the family?"

"What do you mean by suspect?" Ben replied, pouring himself another glass of wine.

"Was there anything strange – out of the ordinary – do any of them act as if they are not part of the same family?"

Ben smiled again, laid his head back as a shaft of sunlight suddenly made its way through the top of the trees.

"I assume this is your rather coy way of talking about the distinctly unique relationship that Ophelia had with her brother," he finally said.

"Yes."

"Well, not to speak ill of the dead ... nor the soon-to-be-dead, if recent history is anything to go by, but they were a little closer than one might expect for siblings. They visited the date room quite regularly late at night, and even during the day... when they were the only ones in the house."

"Perhaps they were just going through old childhood things."

"No, they were not going through old childhood things," Ben said with certainty. "The two of them were involved in something decidedly uninnocent – if that is a word."

"Really?"

"Detective, you obviously know that they were involved in an incestuous relationship – why not just ask me if I knew about it?"

Toledo was silent.

"I didn't see them in the act or anything, but it became pretty clear from their body language that they were closer than the average brother and sister."

"How long do you think it went on?"

"Until Caroline's murder and his arrest, as far as I know."

But she said it ended years ago!

"In fact, about one week before Mark was in there with Caroline – she left and within a few minutes Ophelia went there. He never even left the room. Oh, for such *energy!*"

Ben accentuated the last word loudly and accidentally moved a little closer to Toledo. The detective instinctively edged away, causing the gay man to laugh.

"Don't worry, detective, I never force my attentions on people."

There was silence for a few second before Toledo said,

"And you never thought about telling anyone?"

"Who would I tell? And what would I tell them? As I said, I never found them in flagrante – I just knew they regularly visited a room that is used for one thing, and one thing only."

"Well, Dr. Shaffer has other uses …."

"Only marginally different from how other people utilize it."

"I suppose so."

"And yes, I knew that what they were doing was illegal." Ben said. "But the whole thing kind of fascinated me. When she became pregnant, I wondered what could possibly happen next."

"And you just stood there and watched all this?"

177

"Sometimes," Ben replied. "But I do have a camera set up in one of the trees that keeps me in touch when other things take me away."

"You have set up a camera in their trees?!"

"Well, it isn't in one of yours, Detective. There wouldn't be much use in that."

"You know that is illegal too?"

"I imagine so – I never really thought about it."

They were silenced by the sudden sound of a helicopter. Within seconds it appeared above the trees and slowed to hover about a hundred feet above the helipad.

"I think it has been more used in the last week than in the last ten years!" Ben shouted, attempting to be heard over the sound.

The helicopter landed and McMannis jumped out, ducking his head as he came toward them as if the rotors could somehow hurt him.

"It's such a shame Tony isn't here. He would love all of this!"

Three murders and counting ... and he would love it? Toledo thought, then dismissed his feelings as too maudlin. *Anyway, there is an undoubted excitement about being whisked in and out by helicopter. Beats being caught in the commute on the Bay Bridge anyway.*

"My dear Professor!" Ben said, greeting McMannis with apparently genuine affection.

The helicopter powered up again and within a minute its sound had disappeared. *No evidence it was ever here in the first place ... and Ian's sudden appearance is difficult to explain.* The thought gave him pause for a moment, and then he was lost in a stream of thoughts regarding the case. After Ben had excused himself the two men sat down.

"I have some interesting news."

"What?" McMannis replied.

"Ben says that Ophelia and Mark were having a relationship right up until the time Caroline died."

"He does! But how does he know that?"

Toledo shook his head.

"It's not necessary for you to know how he knows. He just does."

"Which puts a new light on everything."

"Somewhat."

"Why do you think she would lie about it?"

"No idea."

"Perhaps it was easier to admit incest if it was all in the past. Make it seem like someone else had done it."

"Maybe. But what it does mean is that their relationship lasted at least *seven* years."

"Longer than many marriages," replied McMannis.

"Exactly. Longer than mine, anyway."

McMannis flicked the mostly empty wine glass that Ben had left on the table. It rang with a clear harshness, even in the open air. It was unusual for Toledo to mention his marriage. He always said that it meant little to him – a fling in his twenties gone too far – but his very reticence made the professor feel it had left a greater mark than he admitted.

"Are you going to confront her with it?" McMannis asked.

"I must, don't you think?"

McMannis shrugged, pinged the wine glass again, but this time with too much force. It fell over and smashed. The professor looked around like a child who had just been caught doing something forbidden.

"Don't worry," Toledo said. "I have a feeling he has plenty more."

As if in answer Ben suddenly rushed out of the cottage. He looked at the broken glass and a brief, but undeniable expression of fury crossed his face. In a second it was gone, and he picked up the pieces of the glass with remarkable dexterity.

"No harm. No harm. No harm". He said, as if it was some healing mantra. He then bustled back into the cottage, with a reassuring pat on the professor's shoulder as he passed by.

"Did you see that?" McMannis asked.

"I did."

"I hope I don't do anything like that again!"

"Ditto."

"Why do you think Ben is so interested in what goes on in the Shaffer house?"

"Curiosity, mixed with boredom, combined with loneliness – with a touch of the wannabe detective thrown in. After all, in many ways he discovered more about this case than we have. A bit like you in our first cases."

"Boredom? Perhaps. But not lonely …" McMannis said. Toledo just shrugged.

Ben looked out of the cottage and beamed at them, his good spirits apparently completely restored.

"Soup's up!"

The expression sounded incongruous coming from his lips, and the two men were more surprised when they went into the cottage to find a perfectly laid table…with one exception. The ornate wine glasses had been replaced by red Solo cups. Ben acted as if nothing was unusual, even pouring wine into them with a delicate elegance. McMannis spent the whole lunch avoiding the laughter welling inside him, while Toledo made small talk, apparently determined to avoid two subjects: the murders that had brought them here, and the red cups that spoke of an apparently unforgivable accident.

They excused themselves quickly after the meal and made the long walk up the driveway toward the road they now knew so well.

"Apparently, they don't have too many of their glasses left," McMannis said.

"They could probably buy the company that makes them with negligible effect on their bank balance," Toledo replied.

"So, who is going to break the news to her?" the detective continued.

"I will," McMannis said. "I think she will open up more to me."

"As is often the case. Meanwhile, I think we should start looking at some other family members too. The mysterious, suspicious Hermia for one."

"Not sure how mysterious she is …"

"She is mysterious," Toledo said, "because we don't know much about her. And that also makes her suspicious. You must develop the more cynical side of your mind, Ian."

"Everyone is guilty until proven innocent? Isn't that what you said once?"

"Exactly. And even if we *think* they are innocent, they all deserve a close second glance, if the case doesn't resolve itself in other ways."

Toledo got into his car.

"I think I will go straight down there," McMannis said, motioning along the road to the Shaffer driveway.

"How will you get back?"

"Oh, I am sure someone will give me a ride."

"Happy hunting."

McMannis sauntered slowly up the road, round the gentle bend and glanced down at the house lurking among its chaos of vegetation. It had become familiar now, somehow less daunting. *Or am I being drawn too much into their world? Is it in fact too familiar?* He shrugged off the thought and set off down the driveway.

Thirty-One

"So, when were you going to tell us?" McMannis asked.

He had found Ophelia sitting at the kitchen table, sorting through newspaper accounts of her family.

"It makes sad reading, doesn't it?" she replied, looking at him with a resigned sadness.

"Yes," McMannis replied.

"When was I going to tell you?"

"Yes."

"I wasn't ..."

"You weren't?

"No. There didn't seem much point. With Mark gone."

"It might have helped us with ... might have avoided what happened with Ruth."

Ophelia looked at McMannis and smiled enigmatically.

"Can I ask you a question?"

"Certainly," the professor replied.

"Why do you do this? Why do you get involved in these cases? You have a good job at Berkeley. You could sit around drinking coffee all day, flirting with students, and writing books that no-one will ever read."

"That's it. That life is simply too boring. And when you do one of these cases, it is hard to refuse another one."

"Have you thought about giving up being a professor entirely? Becoming a police officer?"

"God ... no. This isn't my whole life."

"From the amount of time that you spend here it would seem to be. At least this case. You are married?"

"Yes."

"Doesn't your wife worry about you? Get mad at all the time you spend away from home?"

Ophelia had turned the tables and was interrogating him. Yet perhaps a genuine interest lurked beneath the evasion. A folklore professor who moonlighted as a detective *was* strange.

"My wife? Yes – she does worry sometimes. But she knows I could never be happy without this. Not now anyway."

"Do you have any children?"

McMannis ran his fingers through his hair, sighed slightly and looked beyond Ophelia to the trees gently rustling outside. He shook his head slowly.

"No … no children."

"Why not?" she asked, then, seeing the changed expression on his face, "if you don't mind me asking."

"We can't."

McMannis knew most people assumed it was a bad marriage that kept them childless. Or this side job. But in fact it was biology that had determined that they could not have children. He knew that forty miles away his wife was sitting in a kitchen – somewhat like this - wondering what had happened to her life. A woman in her mid-thirties who wanted children but could never have them. A uniquely melancholy figure. Tragic even.

Of course, I could have children with someone else.

"I'm sorry," Ophelia said quietly.

McMannis looked back to her and smiled.

"It's all right," he said.

Ophelia laughed slightly, then held up her hand at his consternation,

"I'm sorry," she said. "I was just thinking – I have a child that most people would find vile, just because of the way he was conceived – I am apparently endlessly fertile. While you and your wife cannot …"

Endlessly fertile? Surely, she has only one child?

As if reading his thoughts, Ophelia quickly said,

"Well, the one time I might have become pregnant, I did, so I suppose that makes me fertile. At least then."

Feeling the need to explain too much.

"You must be wondering about my life."

"I haven't done much else since I first met you all. You are – to put it mildly – kind of unusual."

"You've mastered the art of understatement, Professor."

McMannis recognized the characteristic hint of mockery in her use of his formal title. *Reminding me that I do not belong, either within these formal police investigations or – more obscurely – within her social world.*

"What is it that most disturbs you about me?" she asked.

Her eyes were shining mischievously, as if this was a game.

"All of it."

"What I mean is – the fact that I had a relationship with my brother, that I was in love with him, or that I had a child with him?"

"I suppose the first is – most explainable – I think it happens more often than we think. Being in love…I am not sure. Having a child – that seems most …"

"Unforgiveable?"

"Not sure that is the right word. Unimaginable, perhaps? But you pass the risk on to your child."

"A single incestuous relationship is no more likely than any other to produce a damaged child. It is generations of intermingling that causes it. His medical problems are not related. They are not genetic. And anyway – surely abortion would have been an even worse thing to do? He can't help who his parents were. So, while it would have been easier to … get rid of him … I didn't."

184

Her eyes were more serious now, searching him for an answer to a question that had perhaps long haunted her.

She needs some validation. Some sense that what she did is not totally loathsome. McMannis knew that reassuring her was the best way to encourage openness, but something stopped him.

"We didn't intend to have a child. But once I became pregnant – we decided to give it as good a life as possible."

She speaks as if there was some nobility in keeping the baby. Not just seeking validation…but absolution.

"Did anyone else know?"

The young woman smiled, glanced at the floor and then looked up at him.

"You asked that before. When you and Ginny questioned me."

"Not sure questioned is the right word …"

"As far as I know, no-one else knew. Or even suspected. Josh committed suicide and I became pregnant around the same time. They assumed I told him I was pregnant and that made him kill himself. The dates were a little off – but close enough to make the story seem reasonably likely. And anyway, who in their right mind would think a brother and sister were having an affair?"

"You were relying on it being … unimaginable?"

"If you like."

She got up, went over to the counter, and rummaged among some of the fruit lying there. Eventually she chose an apple. She came back to the table and slowly, almost delicately, peeled the fruit as they continued talking.

"Anyway – we had history on our side."

"History?"

"One of my father's hobbies is history."

"I know."

"One story he is fond of telling is how – when the Nazis came up with the Final Solution to the Jewish

185

Problem – someone asked Himmler how they thought they could do what they were planning. How they believed they would be allowed to. Himmler just replied that no-one would believe that they were doing it. The idea of killing a whole race seemed too monstrous – so unbelievable – people wouldn't believe it was happening because they didn't *want* to believe it *could* happen."

"And that allowed the Nazis to do it."

"Exactly. Himmler was correct."

"And you and Mark?"

"No-one wants to believe that a brother and sister are in love with one another, let alone have a baby. So, no-one did.""

"You seem almost proud of the fact."

She paused for a second, before saying, "not at all. It just explains it – that's all."

McMannis realized that Ophelia Shaffer possessed the same raw intelligence as her father, mixed with a similarly cold pleasure at fooling people. The fact that their own world was collapsing around them and littered with murdered bodies did not appear to phase them. In many ways it just raised the stakes, making the game more interesting.

Time for another tack.

"Do you miss your brother?"

"I miss my lover – he was never really a brother to me. When he denied our love, when he rejected it – we could never return across the bridge to being just … siblings again."

"So, you could never go home again?"

Ophelia smiled.

"Something like that."

She looked down at the apple, which was finally completely peeled. The skin sat as a virtually perfect spiral, resembling some organic spring about to release its energy at any moment.

Is she capable of murder?

Toledo often argued that any person was, given the right provocation and set of circumstances. McMannis was not as sure, and every time the detective accused him of being a naïve optimist, he pointed out that homicides had always been – and remained – remarkably rare, despite the personal chaos that many people experienced.

The professor watched as Ophelia cut through the apple and winced as he saw the knife bite into the side of her finger when it slipped. He watched as the blood seeped out, and she put her finger into her mouth.

"Sorry about that," she said after a few seconds, as if he was the one injured.

"I guess you don't like the sight of blood very much," she went on.

"No," McMannis replied quietly.

Some blood had split onto the apple, giving it a bizarre, mottled appearance. Ophelia took it, held it up and then bit into it. After a few chews she smiled appreciatively.

"Interesting flavor – blood and apple."

McMannis sighed as he watched the woman continue eating.

Oh yes, she is capable of murder.

Thirty-Two

Officer Carlisle eyes were blurring over as he went through yet another page of records. For some reason court systems in general, and family records in particular, displayed a perverse pleasure in remaining behind the times. Toledo had said that "as the Shaffers don't want to give any more of their family history, we will have to go and dredge it up ourselves." By "ourselves" he had meant Carlisle, and while the want-to-be detective sought more challenging assignments, he knew that this type of drudgery remained a central task in police work.

Being "loaned" out to Toledo in this manner was a novelty and raised more than a few eyebrows among colleagues, but after he was brought up to speed on the case the young officer wondered whether the legendary detective was really doing him that much of a favor. He did not see how anyone, even Toledo, could possibly unravel this chaotic case.

Specifically, Carlisle was looking for the adoption records for Hermia Shaffer – the twenty-year-old who looked more than forty – who Toledo now believed held something key to the case.

Or maybe he is just throwing as much shit at the wall as possible and seeing what sticks.

There was no official record of the adoption. Carlisle knew that meant little, as many adoptions were done informally, often when rich families basically bought babies from the poor. He had no moral perspective on the matter, other than the general sense that if a child is given a better life, then the exact manner of improvement doesn't need much scrutiny.

But why are they so secretive about this adoption? What had the Shaffers to hide? It suddenly occurred to Carlisle that perhaps they were hiding the details of the adoption, because no such adoption had ever happened. *In that case – where had Hermia come from?* A possible solution appeared in his mind, one that caused his brow to furrow and a little adrenaline to flow. He called Toledo.

"Detective," Carlisle said quietly, as if in a library even though the room was completely empty.

"Yes?"

"There is no sign of any adoption occurring around the time Hermia came to them. I was thinking maybe we should check birth records too. Ordinary birth records."

"Meaning?"

"Ophelia Shaffer had one child with her brother. But are we sure that it was the first?"

"You are saying that Hermia might be Ophelia's daughter?"

"There's a possibility."

"She'd have had her as a teenager…"

"If you think it's too unlikely …" Carlisle said.

"No, no… look into it."

"10-4."

For some reason, ordinary birth records had been scanned into computers, and so within a few minutes Carlisle discovered that on January 28th, 1984 a baby girl was born to one Ophelia Shaffer, aged sixteen. In the space set aside for FATHER lay the simple word, "unknown". In the years since it had never been updated, despite the development of easy DNA paternity tests.

Perhaps they already knew who the father was and didn't want to write it down.

An hour later Carlisle was sitting with Toledo and McMannis in a Starbucks in downtown Burlingame. Toledo had ordered an ominously dark drink with no less than four shots of expresso in it. Carlisle wondered how much caffeine leads to an overdose.

"But we do not know for sure that Mark Shaffer is the father…" McMannis said.

"We can find out though." Toledo replied, nodding toward the door where a sheepish-looking Ophelia Shaffer came into the café, followed by her bizarrely aged daughter. Hermia looked older than her mother at first glance, but in a strange, surreal manner that told anyone looking more carefully that she was younger, despite appearances.

She looks like that premature aging episode of Star Trek, McMannis thought, then felt a little guilty at being trite.

Ophelia sat down at the table. She slipped her credit card to Hermia.

"Can you get my normal drink, love?"

The woman nodded, made her way to the counter.

"So," Ophelia said, once she was out of earshot, "you have discovered that Hermia is my daughter, and was never adopted."

"Yes," Toledo said.

"I must congratulate you … detective? Is that right?" Ophelia said, looking toward Carlisle.

"It's good enough," Carlisle said, smiling nervously. Toledo and McCandless exchanged amused glances but said nothing.

"You must understand that I was very young, and we fully intended to put her up for adoption. But when it became clear that …."

"That what?" Toledo asked gently.

"That she was not completely … normal … and they realized that within the first day – well, then no-one wanted to adopt her."

"So, you kept her. An admirable decision." Toledo said.

"The only one possible really … and you must be wondering about the father."

"It had crossed my mind."

"A one-night stand at a party. Too much drink, and the date room was available."

Hermia came back to the table but did not sit down. She hovered just behind Ophelia's chair, waiting with an exaggerated impatience for the drinks to be ready.

"Who do you think killed Ruth Beringer?" Toledo asked matter-of-factly.

Ophelia paused for a moment, then said, "I really have no idea."

Another pause.

"Who do *you* think killed her?" she asked.

Toledo shrugged, then raised his arms expansively. "Take your pick," he said, gesturing to the whole, crowded café.

The barista announced that their drinks were ready.

"Detective Cassius Toledo, mocha with three extra shots is ready. Professor Ian McMannis, ordinary coffee is ready. Ophelia Shaffer, chai latte is ready. Hermia Shaffer, Frappuccino is ready."

The conversation lowered a little, as Hermia made her way back to the counter.

"She gave our full names?" Toledo said in a near whisper.

"She always does that," Ophelia replied.

"Why?"

"Maybe she just likes being precise," interjected McMannis.

"A little too precise perhaps." Toledo said gloomily. Public reactions to his name made him a little uncomfortable – anonymity was the instinctive stance of

191

any detective worth his salt. Yet underneath this lay a little pride, a certain pleasure at the interest he piqued. Possessing a mystique was irresistible, however much he tried to deny it.

"Professor Ian McMannis. Detective Cassius Toledo. Ophelia Shaffer."

With each name, Hermia placed the drink with an odd formality. There was one drink left – her own. She looked at the table and frowned. She had forgotten Carlisle. He put his hand up to assuage her but overlooking one member of their party was apparently an unforgivable sin on her part.

"I'm so sorry … sorry," she said, then followed up with, "Hermia Shaffer," and in one fluid motion set her drink down and sat in the chair.

"I wasn't thirsty anyway," Carlisle said, but Hermia looked at him with sad eyes.

"Well, it looks as though I ended up with two drinks." Toledo said.

And, McMannis thought, *wonders will never cease. Toledo offering to give up something with caffeine in it.*

The detective moved his drink over to Carlisle, and Hermia smiled broadly. Everyone else was silent. *All is apparently well with the world.* Toledo thought. *Wish I could see things so simply. What a strange group we must look, sitting here in silent formality. And then after we were announced. All eyes are already on us. And then….* But his thoughts drifted.

McMannis and Ophelia were talking, strangely enough, about the weather. Toledo glanced over to see that Carlisle, with an indefinable ability to put anyone at ease, was chatting amicably with Hermia. The young man was impressing Toledo more by the minute. *Such a contrast to that awkward first meeting.* But Toledo liked to think he had good instincts for spotting potential talent among new officers, and here, once again, he had been right.

192

The detective was left out of both conversations and amused himself for a minute or two looking around at the other customers. Mostly middle-aged women taking a break from shopping. A few students. A few of those non-descript individuals who appear to inhabit Bay Area cafes permanently without any apparent purpose, or occupation. They stared at their computers with an intense vacancy, as if the mere action brought meaning to their lives. A couple in the corner were going through a quiet breakup – their facial expressions eloquent, even while they were attempting to keep the volume of their voices at a polite minimum. *But at least they know what they are doing,* Toledo thought. *Us? We are scratching around at the surface of this mystery without gaining any ground.* But somewhere below the surface he knew the truth lay, if only they uncovered the right entrance.

The café door opened, and Toledo recognized the lithe, perfectly dressed figure as it moved into the room. Ben. He looked briefly nonplussed to see them, then smiled, and raised his hand in greeting. Burlingame was a small town, so such accidental meetings were to be expected, but it was the expression of uncertainty that gave Toledo pause. Not only had Ben not expected to see them there, he did not want to see them there.

An assignation of his own perhaps? After all, the mysteriously absent lover was still just that – absent – and *that massive house must get lonely on a dark, foggy night.*

Ben bought an expresso, then sat at a table not too far from theirs, yet not near enough to require communication. Close enough, Toledo guessed, to allow him to eavesdrop. The detective's eyes caught McMannis's attention and briefly gestured toward Ben. Toledo interrupted the professor's conversation with Ophelia with a pleasantry. McMannis sighed slightly, shrugged, and then accepted the inevitable. He got up and went to Ben's table.

"Ben. Do you mind if I join you?"

Fifty thousand dollars-worth of perfect dentition smiled up at him.

"Of course, young man – all your friends seem so involved in their own conversations."

Ben patted the table as if it was a couch and he was offering McMannis a seat. The "young man" seemed a little strange as there were only a few years age difference between them, but McMannis guessed that it was just another color in the palette of reminders that he did not belong here. *Or at least they do not think I belong here.* As a policeman, Toledo was obviously granted a begrudging membership, one that recognized the inevitability of his presence. Toledo's Columbo-like demeanor added to his almost caricaturist identity.

"So, are you a prisoner of Starbucks?" McMannis asked, frowning inwardly at his awkward attempt at casual conversation.

"Oh – aren't we all?"

"Well as you probably know there aren't many of them in Berkeley."

"As I have heard."

"If I am a prisoner of anything - it is of caffeine – and here is where I can get the best expresso outside of going into the city. In that sense, I am a prisoner. Like most people, I am a creature of habit."

"Life is habit," McMannis said.

"Love is habit. Who was it who said that?"

McMannis suspected that the man knew precisely who had said it, or rather, written it, but played along with the game anyway.

"I believe it was Proust. In *Albertine Disparu*," he said.

"Exactly. What we miss most about a person is not the passion, or the romance, or even the physical intimacy. It is familiarity, the mysterious power of habit. They become as

194

necessary and yet as unnoticed as breathing. But take them away and we soon notice the difference – just as a drowning person comprehends the delicious sanctity of another breath – only when the possibility of taking that breath has been irretrievably lost."

McMannis nodded solemnly, realizing that Ben was revealing things normally kept hidden.

"Is that how you miss him?"

Ben smiled, and the mask raised again as he said, "oh not really. I believe all of that in theory, but the practicality of a living with someone is much messier, don't you think?"

"I suppose."

"As a married man, you must know that."

"Yes."

"Do you mind me asking whether you have children?"

Why not? The subject is suddenly irresistibly interesting.

"No, we don't."

"That's sad."

Ben was undoubtedly charismatic, but also possessed a presumption that annoyed McMannis.

How could he possibly know that it is sad we don't have children? Perhaps we don't want them, for all he knows. And anyway, who says such a thing?

Ben was now looking at him as if reading these thoughts. He looked downward and nodded slightly, perhaps acknowledging their validity. Then he looked up into the professor's eyes, as if immediately following up with the undeniable claim that he was correct in his assumptions about their marriage.

"Anyway, to more pressing matters," Ben said. "I gather you have discovered just how convoluted and sordid family relations are among the Shaffers."

"Yes."

195

"Although you may know even more than we do."

Ben paused momentarily, then said, "perhaps I do."

McMannis saw a brief but unmistakable flash of bitter irony in Ben's eyes, as if whole volumes of knowledge that he possessed made their recent explorations laughably superficial.

"But then I've been at it for longer than you," he said, all trace of fierceness gone from his eyes.

Ben tapped at his jacket pocket and frowned.

"Would you care to join me for a smoke? I believe I must be at least fifty feet away from the premises to indulge my little . . . what is it that the French call an orgasm – le petite mort? The little death? Well, my smoking is a little suicide. Or a slow suicide, as he says."

"I don't ..."

"I know that *you* don't smoke, but I do."

McMannis paused then nodded.

"Sure – lead the way."

On their way out of the café Toledo gave him a congratulatory look, and McMannis was amused once again at how dated his friend was in his discomfort around gay men. McMannis himself didn't feel one way or another about them. The professor claimed no interest in what others did in their bedrooms, showing what Toledo argued was "a spectacular lack of imagination." McMannis said that he had better things to think about and left it at that.

Ben took out a cigarette. He offered the pack to McMannis.

"Are you sure you won't join me?"

"I'm sure."

Ben smiled pleasantly, put a cigarette in his mouth and the box into his pocket. He took out a lighter but put it back quickly.

"Wrong one."

How can it be the wrong one? McMannis thought.

196

The 'right one' having lit the cigarette, Ben smiled.

"They say that men like me – gay men that is – that we are more creative than others because we can never have children."

Ben said this after he had taken his first drag of his cigarette. What provoked such a comment was a mystery to McMannis, but he just gave an encouraging smile. Ben continued.

"Jung argued that men are more artistically creative than women because they cannot perform the ultimate act of creation – having a child. Yet a straight man can at least contribute to a baby. But a gay man – if he is to be true to himself – cannot even do that. That is why so many of us leave so much behind, when they put us into our shallow bachelor's graves."

He sounds like a reincarnated Oscar Wilde – only not quite as brilliant.

"But you are thinking a gay man can have a child – there is artificial insemination. But is that really the same?"

"I doubt it makes much difference to the child."

Ben laughed at this.

"I suppose you are right."

He inhaled deeply on the cigarette, then coughed.

"I know, I know," Ben said. "He tells me all the time that the cough is an unsubtle hint."

Why does he never use his lover's name? Or does 'he' apply to someone else?

"But I figure that you have to die one way or another – why not this one? We are all on the same road – why not indulge some pleasures along the way?"

"You have a point."

The man was obviously used to impressing people. McMannis was inoculated against being impressed by words alone – being a professor at Berkeley almost necessitated it – but Ben had a way of capturing a moment, of echoing the hint of a thought barely formed in another's brain. *A kind of instant empathy*, McMannis thought. *But one perhaps revealing an emptiness within. Or a secret that he wants to keep hidden. He inhabits others, because he is essentially an empty shell.*

"Well," Ben said pleasantly, "I am due to run auditions for my latest show two hours from now in the city – so I suppose I must start that terrible journey."

He received a text. He glanced down at it, then smiled at McMannis.

"Kind of suitable really."

"What is?"

"The play I am directing."

"Which is?"

"*The Homecoming*, by Harold Pinter. My prodigal lover has just deigned to send me a text."

Thirty-Three

"He said that his prodigal lover had just sent him a text."

"He did?"

"Yes."

"Did you see the text?"

"No – I mean he said that his lover had sent him the text. Obviously, I didn't ask to see it. Then he said that it was apt that he was about to direct a play by Harold Pinter."

"That gloomy Englishman?" Toledo said, tossing a stone at one of the waves.

"Yuhp," McMannis replied, eyeing a wave just a bit further from Toledo's target, and flinging his own stone with apparent casualness.

"And what is the play about?"

"I looked it up. A young man returns home from America with his wife," the professor said. "He has a working-class family who are all either criminals, or mentally ill. Most of them seem to be both. By the end of the play the man's wife agrees to become a prostitute working for the family."

"A prostitute? Why?"

"It's never really explained."

"How come the Brit is living in America?"

"He's a professor."

Toledo laughed at this and threw another stone, this time perhaps twice the distance of his friend's farthest effort so far.

"So, working as a prostitute for a working-class English family is a better prospect than being an American professor's wife?"

"Apparently," McMannis replied, who picked up a stone and then dropped it. Their silent and unacknowledged competition had apparently ended, with Toledo the victor.

"It's a shame you didn't see the text though. Still, at least we have another one that we can interrogate. For the last week. I have been waking up with the feeling that it has to be *that* morning that someone else is killed. But no luck."

"Luck?"

"I mean – at least another murder would provide a few more clues. As it is, we can just put Dr. Shaffer on trial for the murder of his son – and he will almost certainly cop a deal for manslaughter – and the other murders will remain unsolved. The main one – or at least the first one – completely a mystery."

"And that is what gets to you most," McMannis said as they walked up the beach toward the road. The professor realized that this was the first time he had been to Ocean Beach since the fateful journey with Ginny and Selena two years before, when they had been shot at. He still missed those times, despite the danger. *Or I miss the girl*, he thought poignantly.

"I don't mind admitting it," said the detective. "I want to know who the cheaters are and why this happens to them. And why the pigs are involved,"

"Beats me."

"Like to talk to the Ramirez girl's mother?"

"Thought she had already been talked to."

"Yes … but not by you."

"Flattery will get you nowhere, Toledo. But sure, I'll do it."

Two hours later McMannis was parking his car on a road just off 40th street in Oakland. Not the worst part of the city, yet not exactly the safest either. He glanced up and down the street before getting out of his car. The house was

200

one of the large, old Victorians once called home by an upper-class family, but it was now subsumed in the general poverty of the city. Of all the houses surrounding it, this one appeared to be the best maintained. A hint, if not a full expression, of pride.

He walked up to the door and paused before ringing the bell. On the phone, Caroline's mother had sounded forlorn, melancholy and withdrawn. Even a rather bad cell phone line had not been able to hide her sadness. But little could have prepared him for the face that greeted him within seconds of ringing the doorbell.

Mrs. Sonia Ramirez was in her early forties at the most, but her hair was nearly completely white. McMannis frowned, remembering this had not been the case at the funeral. The agony of losing a child had aged her decades, and her eyes – while filled with a tentative hope that someone from the police was finally showing an interest again – exuded an acute desolation that made him want to turn away. Looking into such eyes might sadden you permanently. But look he did.

"Mrs. Ramirez, my condolences again on your loss."

Condolences? It has been months since her daughter was killed.

But the woman appeared to appreciate the comment and smiled quite warmly as she welcomed McMannis into her house.

"You understand I'm not a police officer – I just help Detective Toledo with some cases."

Technically he was at least a sworn officer, but he wanted her to know that he wasn't "full police", as Toledo liked to put it. His more ambiguous role could relax her, although exactly what she might be able to offer was uncertain. They knew the basic facts of Caroline's life, but not the nuances, and perhaps her mother could provide these.

201

Mrs. Ramirez led McMannis into the lounge. The décor was dated, but nothing was dirty. She even had a mantelpiece above the fireplace with photographs of the family. Just one of Caroline on her own.

"You wanted to know more about her? Yes?"

"Yes."

"What kind of things?"

"Anything that might … explain how she ended up in that room that night."

"Caroline was a good girl. She enjoyed life. To the full."

"I know."

The woman paused for moment, then said, "but there were some things about her that I did not understand."

"I am sure … everyone feels that way about their children as they grow up."

"How many children do you have?"

"None. Not yet anyway. We've decided to wait." The lie came easily, now repeated so often that had had almost come to believe it.

"A good idea," the woman said. "I had my children when I was little more than a baby myself. Not that I regret them … it's just …"

And she became lost in her thoughts for a moment. She looked up at Caroline's photograph and sighed.

"Is there anything of hers still here?" McMannis asked.

"Excuse me?"

"Is there anything of hers that she left behind? Anything still here."

Mrs. Ramirez looked bemused for a moment.

"There's a whole room upstairs."

Toledo had told him that "all her things" were in the house where she was living. He was sure nothing was left in her family home. For a second, McMannis thought of sending a snarky text about this vital misinformation, but then paused – he had seen enough police investigations to know they were fraught with mistakes. It was the mist of investigation that descended on any murder case. *But for a whole room full of possessions to go unnoticed?*

"If it would be OK, I'd love to see it." McMannis said, attempting to hide his excitement at the possibility that had just presented itself.

The room was neat, surely too neat for a late teenager. Her mother had preserved it as a shrine to her dead daughter. The possessions remained, as if she was expected back at any moment.

"What are you looking for?" Mrs. Ramirez asked.

"I am not sure really. Would you mind if I just looked around on my own for a little bit?"

The woman paused. *She may see this as an incursion onto sacred ground. An invasion.* Mrs. Ramirez swept her hand to show that he was welcome.

"Feel free – if anything here might help you with finding out who really killed her…"

"Who really killed her?"

"Yes."

"You don't believe that Mark Shaffer killed her?"

"That boy was no killer. In his way, he loved her. They had their problems. Who does not? But he was no killer."

"OK."

"Well – look all you want."

She paused for a moment and her eyes filled with tears. She lowered her head as if ashamed, then quickly left the room.

McMannis looked around. A poster of Metallica on the wall, something of recent vintage by the look of it. *She was so young.* In fact, most of the room held remnants of childhood beneath the sophistication of a fledging adult. Some teen books mixed among alarming-sized college textbooks. From the spines, they looked barely read.

McMannis took one down – "An Introduction to Sociology". The first few pages were heavily lined and outlined with marker, and there were even a few comments written in a neat but childish hand. But by the second chapter these signs of diminishing, before disappearing entirely about fifty pages into the book.

He took down a couple more textbooks, and discovered the same pattern of initial enthusiasm, soon drowned by boredom.

Or did something happen that made schoolwork seem irrelevant? Pointless even?

McMannis scanned the books on another shelf. Several on genetics. Some on the sociology of blended and mixed families. Both sections of books were better used, and some even displayed the tell-tale coffee stains showing they had been carried around quite a bit. He noticed a sheet of paper sticking up from one of the books and removed it. It was a term paper titled – "A Case-Study of a Blended Family – Hermia Shaffer and the Oedipal Complexities of Adoption." For a sociology paper, it started with a rather imaginative zip.

"It has often been said that the relationship between parent and child is a difficult one, and as Shakespeare said *how sharper than a serpent's tooth is it to have a thankless child?* When that child is not only thankless, but also adopted – well, then the problems are perhaps multiplied."

She would have done better in grad school than as an undergraduate, Toledo thought. He read more of the paper.

"But what happens when the child you are claiming to be adopted, is not adopted at all, but in fact the child of an adult within the family? We may add to this a further complexity. The same daughter not only gave birth to the supposedly adopted child, but also to a child fathered by her boyfriend – who supposedly committed suicide – but is probably not the father at all. Oedipus accidentally married his own mother and had children with her. What if he had deliberately done it? Or did he perhaps know...?"

Almost despite himself, the professor within McMannis wanted to write – "you are rambling, stick to the point" in the margin. *But what is the point?* The paper described how Caroline had met Mark, how they had fallen in love with one another, how they planned – without a hint of irony apparently – to run away to get married. The first sentence was the start of an academic paper, but Caroline soon digressed into a rambling stream of consciousness. Near the end of the second page, she discussed her suspicion that Mark was the father of Ophelia's other child. It was this that finally caused McMannis to call Toledo.

"I am reading one of her academic papers."

"Sound fun."

"Actually, it's more some rambling list of hopes and fears and suspicions. In the last paragraph, she says that she knows that Mark and Ophelia are actually in love and have had a child together."

"She wrote what?"

"That Mark and Ophelia are lovers. That Alan is their son."

"Jesus. Do you know when this was written?"

McMannis turned back to the front page.

"At 3AM exactly two weeks before she died."

"How did she find out?"

"It doesn't say. Will carry on looking."

"Do so. Do so. Thanks, my friend."

McMannis scanned the rest of the room. Nothing immediately caught his eye until he saw more papers sticking out from underneath a mat on which various skin care products lay. The papers looked as if they had been put there in a hurry – an abortive attempt to hide them that had been disturbed. He pulled them out slowly, careful not to disturb the bottles.

More musings on the Shaffers. The conflict between her love for Mark and disgust at what she was discovering, both about him and the broader family. Near the end, she became ambiguous –

"If what I think about him is true, then I must tell someone. If he is who I think he is and is about to do what I think he is about to do – then whatever they say, however they try to persuade me – someone outside of all this mess must be told. It is too dangerous not to."

The "him" did not appear to refer to Mark, as a couple of pages before she wrote about telling Mark about what she suspected about him, and that he had virtually confirmed her suspicions. And there was no suspicion as to who Mark was. It was just the relationship with his sister that was hidden.

"So, who is he?" asked Toledo as they sat in Milano about an hour later.

"I don't know – but whoever it is, Caroline Ramirez was worried enough about him to consider revealing what she knew to the authorities."

"She doesn't say that ..."

"But it is implied surely."

"I suppose."

"There is only one person it could be – Dr. Shaffer."

Thirty-Four

Jail was not doing him well.

Take virtually any person, remove them from their normal life and lock them in an 8 by 6 hole with nothing to do but think about their predicament, and they are likely to deteriorate. But when that person is highly educated, wealthy and used to enjoying all that his position in society offers him, the change can be remarkable.

And so it was for Dr. Shaffer.

Well at least he has lost weight, Toledo thought as he surveyed the man sitting opposite him. Shaffer's lawyer was sitting a little further away than in their previous interrogation, as though subtly removing himself from his client.

"We have, as you may know, filed a motion for a speedy trial," the lawyer said.

"Yes, I know, but this isn't why we are here."

"My client has nothing else to …"

"Detective Toledo. What is it?" Dr. Shaffer said, holding up his hand to silence the lawyer.

"I must advise …"

"Advise me nothing," Shaffer said, and with that the lawyer shrugged his shoulders and edged his chair even further away.

"What do you have to ask me?" Shaffer asked.

"How much about the parentage of Hermia Shaffer and your grandson are you aware of?"

"The parentage?"

"Yes."

Dr. Shaffer looked down and rubbed his beard thoughtfully.

"I am not sure exactly what you are implying. Hermia was adopted, as I think you know, so I have no idea of her parentage. We have always acted – and regarded ourselves – as her parents. Alan is my daughter's child. His father killed himself before he was born. Just after he was conceived in fact."

"And that is all you know?"

"Yes."

"Would you swear to that on oath?"

Toledo had found that it was strange how many criminals, even murderous ones, paused before stating that they would repeat an obvious lie on oath.

"That would depend on the question," the doctor said after a moment's pause,

"Really?"

"Yes."

"You are aware that your oldest son and Ruth Beringer were in a relationship before she died?"

"Yes, I was aware of that."

The answer came without a pause.

"You thought nothing of that, doctor?"

"I thought plenty about it. But they are ... they were ... two consenting adults. They were thrown together a lot because the rest of the family travels so much. It is a large house. A lonely house. Their relationship was a little ... unusual perhaps. But no more."

"And you are sticking by your beliefs about the parentage of Hermia and Alan Shaffer?"

"My beliefs?" the doctor answered, vaguely mystified.

"Yes."

"Surely, they are simply facts. Unless you have some other ideas. Please. Enlighten me."

"I wanted to know your opinions, doctor."

There was a lull in the conversation, one that the lawyer obviously saw as an opportunity.

"Is this … interview at an end now?" he asked.

"There are some other matters," Toledo said, "but they can be dealt with by my colleague." He got up and left the room.

"Well," he said to McMannis, who was leaning against the wall just outside the door, "no time like the present. Your turn at bat."

"My turn?"

"You have to start somewhere."

McMannis gulped, and suddenly felt simultaneously hot and cold.

"And you think this is the best place to start?" he asked, as quiet as a whisper.

"Yes, I do. I think Dr. Shaffer may respect your education."

McMannis laughed, saying "oh, the MDs respect a Ph.D. the least – they feel we shouldn't call ourselves 'Dr.' – even though we were the first ones, long before physicians ever used the term. In fact, …"

"Professor McMannis," Toledo said, with mock formality, "you are engaging in a filibuster. Your quarry awaits."

McMannis saw that it was no use arguing. He took one step toward the door, grabbed the handle, and paused for a second before going inside.

"Professor!" Dr. Shaffer said, as if greeting an unexpected, but very welcome friend.

"Doctor." McMannis replied.

The lawyer looked toward the two-way mirror and shook his head.

"Professor McMannis, I am aware that you are a sworn peace officer – and thus able to conduct an interview like this if you want, but I must state, for the record, that I am uneasy with having an amateur explore such a serious matter. Dr. Shaffer might be on trial for his life."

"I am aware of that. And if Dr. Shaffer has any objections I will gladly …"

"No objections at all," Shaffer interrupted. "None whatsoever."

"OK," the lawyer said, apparently resigned to being ignored.

McMannis paused and took a deep breath. The doctor's enthusiasm to be questioned by him was a little unnerving. *As if he thinks I pose no threat.*

"Dr. Shaffer, you may be aware that my specialty is folklore – modern folklore in particular. Urban myths – that type of thing."

"Yes, I am aware of that."

"After World War Two there were rumors, based at least partially in fact – as most of these myths are – that many babies born in the Japanese cities of Hiroshima and Nagasaki were grotesquely deformed due to their mother's exposure to radiation."

"I've heard that."

"And if your date room is anything to go by, you have more than a passing interest in these babies."

"Of what possible relevance is this to my client's case?" the lawyer asked loudly.

"Would you say that doctor?" McMannis continued, completely ignoring the lawyer.

"It is undeniable."

"Did you – acquire these babies on your trip to Japan? The one when Ruth Beringer accompanied you?"

"I did. There is no secret to that."

"But was not the transportation of these babies illegal?"

"I have no idea. Legal or not – it was irrelevant to me. I wanted them. I paid for them. I took them. They came with me back to America."

"Without being declared?"

210

"Yes – without being declared. Professor, I am already charged with murdering my own son – feel free if you want to add charges of illegal importation of scientific artefacts, if you want."

"Did Caroline Ramirez find out about your collection, doctor?"

Dr. Shaffer laughed a little. But McMannis, sitting opposite him, and Toledo, closely watching on the computer screen, realized it was the first time they had seen anything but a stoic expression on the doctor's face.

"She may have discovered them. I have no idea. Mark and she did spend a lot of time in the date room. Perhaps she went exploring. I don't know."

McMannis was silent. Toledo congratulated himself on his friend's training. Often a suspect felt the need to fill a silence with words, and sometimes – although accidental – they were of a revealing nature.

"But if you are suggesting that I would harm Caroline, let alone kill her, because she found the babies – that is totally insane. I liked the girl. Liked her a lot. She was good for Mark."

"You found she distracted him from other women?"

"Yes."

"Women you felt he should not be with?"

A slight pause.

"If you like, yes."

McMannis was silent again. The lawyer tapped his pen impatiently for a few seconds, and then was silent after Shaffer glanced at him.

"The problem is," McMannis eventually said, "that the Hiroshima babies are a myth."

What the hell is he doing? Toledo thought. *He never said any of this to me!*

"They are?" Dr. Shaffer answered, and his ironic, detached demeanor slipped for a moment.

"Yes. A myth. While some deformed babies were born after the nuclear bombs were exploded over Japanese cities, they were never collected and stored in bottles. There was never a collection of them."

Dr. Shaffer was looking intently at McMannis.

Is he taking this bluff? McMannis thought.

"If those babies are not Hiroshima babies – where did I get them from?"

"That is what I am wondering, doctor. That will be all for now."

With that, McMannis got up and left the room.

"What the hell was that?" Toledo asked after leading him down the corridor a little way.

"That was a bluff." McMannis replied.

"How are the babies …?"

"If they are *not* Hiroshima babies – and they are not, as Shaffer was unsure of what to say when I said that they are a myth. They aren't by the way. If they are not, then he is getting those babies from somewhere."

"And so?"

"Perhaps he is more responsible for those babies than we think."

"Now you are losing me," Toledo replied wearily.

"I don't know," McMannis said. "I was playing on a hunch that came to me as I was sitting there. Something tells me those babies are – that they have a more sinister origin. One Shaffer wants to keep secret at all costs."

"Including murder?"

"Hypothetical then – suppose Caroline Ramirez somehow films. or photographs, Dr. Shaffer doing – whatever it is that he does – while looking at the babies. If such evidence were made public, it would ruin him. He would lose everything. His family would lose everything."

Toledo paused then nodded, "I suppose people have been killed for less. Much less in fact."

212

"And suppose she found out that those babies – she found out the mysterious something, that I can't quite put a finger on? Suppose this college dropout, from the wrong part of town, saw an opportunity to make money from an undeserving monster?"

"And she blackmailed him? But miscalculated who he was by a fatal amount."

"Exactly."

"Then why did he kill Mark?" Toledo asked.

"He knew that Mark would never keep silent about the death of his girlfriend …"

"But killing a virtual stranger is very different from killing your own son."

McMannis frowned, shook his head.

"I know. It is." He said finally.

"But it does answer some other facts such as the multiple semen samples on – and in – Caroline's body," the professor continued.

"How does it do that?"

They had made their way out of the police department now. They were both surprised to find Amanda and Ginny sitting on a bench, a little way down the road.

"What brings you to these parts?" Toledo asked.

"We heard that the Professor was doing his first official interrogation," Amanda said, "and we just couldn't resist finding out how it went as soon as possible."

"Well?" Ginny asked, hooking her arm through his.

"Well, let's just say that I took a seat-of-the-pants approach and went off a bit on a tangent," McMannis said.

"A bit!" Toledo exclaimed.

"You were meant to be finding out how much the good doctor knew Caroline Ramirez and ended up discussing the validity or myth of Hiroshima babies."

"I still think the babies are an irrelevant detail. Sickening, but irrelevant." Amanda said.

213

"Maybe," McMannis replied, "but then maybe not."

The four of them walked down toward Union Square and stopped off at a van selling coffee, before settling on a bench. McMannis filled the two women in on his theory so far, then started explaining the rest of it.

"So, Mark Shaffer has consensual sex with Caroline on the night of her murder," McMannis said. "Afterwards, Dr. Shaffer plants semen from two other men inside her and makes it look like some crazed sex killing. Covering up the real motive."

"And the writing on the wall?" Amanda asked.

"The coup de grace. The ultimate way of putting us off the scent."

"And where did he get the semen from?" Ginny asked.

"A friend at a fertility clinic," McMannis answered, quickly and assuredly.

Ginny laughed, but McMannis looked to Amanda for confirmation.

"Wouldn't it be relatively easy for a doctor to gain access to semen that way?"

"If he knew someone working in the clinic, I suppose it would," Amanda replied. "It's not as if they are very secure places."

"Not much of a black market for stolen semen," Toledo said.

"But," McMannis said, with a sudden uncertainty in his tone, "it does not explain why he killed Mark. Or even *who* killed Ruth."

"Insulin does point toward Dr. Shaffer," said Toledo.

"Perhaps *too much*," McMannis replied. "And aren't there easier ways for a doctor to kill someone?"

All eyes once again turned to Amanda.

"We are not magicians who can kill without leaving a trace of how we did it," she said. "But yes, there are ways that are more – more difficult to identify."

214

"Perhaps," McMannis interposed, "Caroline came to him not only with what she knew about the babies, but also what she suspected about Mark and Ophelia."

"Which would put Mark back in the picture as a possible suspect in her murder ..." Ginny said.

"No," McMannis continued. "Caroline wrote about Mark admitting what had happened with Ophelia. That somehow, they had got beyond that."

"That is meaningless," Ginny replied. "Mark wouldn't have told her she had just discovered something that made him want to kill her. He would act cool about it. So, she'd suspect nothing."

"Either way we come back to Dr. Shaffer," Toledo said. "He had something to do with Mark's death – and whether Mark conspired with him to kill Caroline is irrelevant – he was part of it. Ruth's death from an insulin overdose – while Shaffer was safely in jail – suggests he's got someone working for him on the outside."

"Insulin is the common theme," McMannis said. "I assume you checked Caroline's body for insulin?"

Amanda stared at him then closed her eyes and sighed.

"Shit," Toledo said resignedly. "I have a feeling my least favorite part of being a detective is about to rear its ugly head."

Thirty-Five

Why exactly does the lead detective have to be present? Toledo thought for the twentieth time that day, as he stepped through the privacy screens that had been erected around the grave site. Exhumation is often a grisly affair, although sometimes strangely clean. A human body does not decompose according to any predictable schedule, and there was at least one element of surprise that came with the opening of the lid.

In this case, it was not to be a full exhumation. "Just a quick sample." Amanda had said, stating that the whole affair could be over in less than a minute.

But some minutes are longer than others, Toledo thought grimly as the coffin was carefully brought to the surface. Two coroner's officers opened the lid with quick efficiency and all those around the coffin took a step back as the smell hit them. All except for Amanda. Apparently immune to the sickly, sweet smell of human putrefaction, Amanda bent down, and with a deft hand thrust a needle into the corpse, just below the heart.

"It's lucky that she wasn't embalmed," she said.

The syringe looked like it was designed for something much larger than a human being, and its odd size lent a grotesque element to the already bizarre setup.

That doesn't look like blood, Toledo thought, glancing at the brown-yellow liquid that filled the syringe.

"All done." Amanda said, and a little touch of Caroline's shoulder signaled that she was done with her. The lid was replaced, and the coffin descended back to its home, the wires holding it to the hauling equipment almost sighing with relief as it disappeared.

216

"That took less than a minute?" Toledo grumbled as they walked away from the grave.

"You look completely green, Cassius," Amanda said with a mischievous little laugh.

"I am sure I look better than I feel."

"Well, I am nervous about what we will find in here," Amanda said.

She raised the syringe to Toledo, who waved it away with his hand. They walked in silence for a few moments before he said,

"I think we probably know though."

And four hours later, as he sat in his lounge chair and relaxed to some mellow jazz, he received the expected text. While Caroline Ramirez would have died of the numerous stab wounds inflicted upon her, they really had not been needed. Amanda texted that her blood contained enough insulin to kill her within "a couple of hours".

Detective Toledo knew loose ends still existed as he entered the labyrinthine structure of the San Francisco jail. *But actual cases are not like those in books*, he thought, as Dr. Shaffer looked up at him. *There are nearly always some parts of them that are never explained. Especially ones as complex as this.*

"Dr. Jerry Shaffer. You are being charged with breaking California Penal Code Section 187, by the unlawful killing of Caroline Ramirez, a human being, on or about the 13th of March, 2004. You are also being charged with the unlawful killing of Mark Shaffer, a human being, on April 16th, 2004. You are being charged with the unlawful killing of Ruth Beringer, a human being, on or about May 23rd, 2004."

Shaffer looked more tired than shocked at the charges, but his expression changed as Toledo continued.

"Further, you are being charged with being an accomplice to felony sexual assault, specifically the

217

impregnation of Ophelia Shaffer, then aged seventeen, on or about September 1ˢᵗ, 1986. You are being charged with being an accomplice to an unnatural, incestuous relationship, specifically the ongoing sexual relations between siblings, namely Ophelia Shaffer and Mark Shaffer, now deceased, from September 1986 through March 2004."

"What?" Shaffer said, almost whispering in amazement.

"Other charges are pending."

The doctor glanced down, and when he looked up into Toledo's eyes, he had regained his composure.

"Surely three murder charges are enough. Why make them top heavy with the others? Overkill, don't you think?"

The speed that the man regained composure impressed Toledo, but also showed he was more ruthless than the detective previously suspected. Even though most people knew a homicide charge was likely by the time it came, few reacted with such disdain. It reminded the detective of Shaffer's son, who took news of being suspected in his girlfriend's murder in a casual, almost patrician manner. Two types of people displayed such an attitude. First, the outright psychopath who, despite a superficial cunning that made him instinctively evade capture, is essentially as unconcerned about his own fate as he is of his victims. Second, the innocent. Or rather, the innocent who believe in an innate natural justice that will foreclose any chance of being found guilty. But such beliefs belonged with the naïve, and while Mark Shaffer was young enough to be seen this way, his father's cynical, ironic eyes reflected a shrewd awareness of the world.

Perhaps, Toledo thought, *Dr. Shaffer is presenting a third suspect type, who receives a murder charge as if it was a demand for an overdue bill. Annoying, a nuisance even – but nothing more.*

Toledo left Shaffer sitting in his cell and hurried out of the jail. He always took a deeper-than-normal breath when he stepped outside of it. Whether air-conditioned or not, a jail or prison always reeked of despair and paralysis. McMannis met him outside and they walked in silence for a minute before the professor spoke.

"Much of this is circumstantial, at best."

"I am aware of that."

"Even being found in Mark's hospital room – there is no proof he did anything to harm him. The defense might argue the contrary, in fact. Perhaps he was trying to save him."

"Again … I am aware of that," Toledo answered.

They walked silently for a little way.

"But, unlike many cases, we have a great deal of motive – the good doctor is positively overflowing with motive for these murders. And as you know, while juries are instructed that the prosecution does not need to show motive – something in human nature almost demands one. And in each of these cases, Shaffer had clear motivation."

"But without the first murder? The others disintegrate."

"Which side are you on?" Toledo asked.

A moment's pause, then McMannis said, "the truth. Always the truth."

Toledo laughed.

"How did I know you were going to say that?!"

They walked down the road, still skirmishing over the case. Any casual eavesdropper might have thought that the two men held some animosity toward one another. Professional, if not personal. But they would be wrong. Toledo always liked to bounce ideas and theories off McMannis, knowing that the naturally analytical and skeptical mind of an academic was the ideal sounding board. More than a few ADAs and defense lawyers listened

219

into their conversations with greater attention than they admitted to.

They reached McMannis's car – an old Volvo that he insisted on driving, despite his wife's protests that they should buy a newer vehicle.

"Any plans for tonight?" Toledo asked, even though he knew there would be none.

"Oh no – just a quiet night, what we usually do on weekdays.

The royal 'we', Toledo thought. *Or rather, the 'we' of companionship. Of marriage and safety and security.*

The bitterness of his thoughts surprised him, but as his own single existence had become more obviously permanent than temporary, an imagined, longing nostalgia for a life he had never known grew. For all the difficulties and exasperations of married life, at least the couple had one another. *A sense of home.*

Toledo cast his mind toward his own house. A single light in the lounge that faced onto the urban park gave him glimpses of family life. Teasing hints, as only silence greeted him every day when he unlocked the door. A few years ago, he considered leaving music on all day so he could experience the illusion of activity when he returned, but he had decided that would be too illusory, and ultimately depressing. Pets? Well-meaning friends suggested them as a surrogate for family, but he was away too often for a dog and cats just lent an involuntary shiver. McMannis often said that he envied his freedom. *Maybe. Maybe not.* But Toledo also knew that the professor pitied him a little, especially at moments like this – when the easy comfort of a *we* illustrated the chasm between single and married life.

"I believe the dinner invitation is still open – not tonight, but at some point." McMannis said. "Give us a couple of days' notice."

"To give you time to hide the corpses?"

"Exactly."

Both men were relieved a potentially awkward moment had passed painlessly.

"One question before I go … where do you think the cases will be tried?" McMannis said, his hand on the door handle. "Or will they be separated."

"Berkeley. For Caroline. If he's convicted there . . . no hurry for the other trials. They'll have to occur in San Francisco, and then San Mateo County."

"OK."

With that, McMannis got into his car and drove away. He looked in the rear-view mirror at Toledo, who remained standing where he had been – a lonely figure, hands deep in his jacket pockets, the wind buffeting his thinning hair as he stooped a little in the gusts.

Thirty-Six

Something was troubling Toledo about the whole case, but he felt a little easier when the results from the DNA test on the semen found inside Caroline finally came back. It needed a more complex and time-consuming process, due to sample degradation. It matched Dr. Shaffer's DNA. *And that leaves an even stranger situation – the mysterious semen belonging to another man from the same family.* He was happy that his suspicion of Dr. Shaffer was correct, and a circumstantial case had turned into one with very direct physical evidence. *Modern juries require CSI-type evidence – well, here they have it.*

A week after the DNA match, the mystery deepened further as all known male relatives of Dr. Shaffer had given samples for testing quite willingly, and none came back positive. Toledo used his influence to push his sample up the enormous waiting FBI lab waiting list for closer analysis. Within a few days they informed him that the John Doe sample was not only related to Shaffer – "the good doctor is actually his father," – as Toledo had texted to McMannis. The professor sent a reply to the whole group – Toledo, Amanda, and Ginny.

UNKNOWN CHILD. I THOUGHT IT WAS PROFESSORS WHO WERE MEANT TO SPREAD THEIR SEED AROUND.

A quip to which Ginny replied that according to her parents they were virgins before they had met, so university faculty should not be disparaged in that way.

"How did that come up in conversation?" Toledo asked when they all met later that day in one of the less attended Berkeley cafes – The Mediterranean.

222

"I cannot remember – but somehow it did," Ginny replied with a little smile.

Toledo received a text and sighed deeply as he read it.

"What is it?" McMannis asked.

"Dr. Shaffer's legal team…"

"Team?" Amanda echoed.

"Yes, team – he can afford it – has offered to plead guilty to manslaughter on the three homicide charges, and for the lesser counts to be dropped. The DAs from the three counties involved have accepted the offer. They issued a statement that, considering Dr. Shaffer's health condition and probably prognosis, it was not in the interests of justice to pursue actual trials."

"What health condition?" McMannis asked, looking toward Amanda.

"I know what all of you know – he is a diabetic. Perhaps it is progressing. Eventually it does kill most people who suffer from it, despite treatment."

"And jail can't exactly be helping," Toledo interjected.

"So, they figure that he will die in prison either way," McMannis suggested. "What is the point in the expense and energy of actual trials?"

The group was silent for a few seconds.

"One thing does bother me though," Toledo said.

"What's that?" McMannis asked.

"That we're never going to get the full truth on the incestuous relationships. And we still don't know who the fourth semen sample belongs to."

"Perhaps he will come clean now," McMannis replied.

"Yeah – and I'm becoming the Pope tomorrow," Ginny said.

"Most plea deals stipulate that the accused has to tell the whole story – to the satisfaction of the prosecutor," Amanda said.

"But I feel that in this case everyone wants to just sweep this case under the carpet," Toledo replied. "Dr. Shaffer numbers too many powerful and influential people among his patients for the full facts to be forced out of him."

Silence again.

"You might use your notoriety ..." McMannis said.

"By that you mean fame?" replied Toledo, playing at being offended.

"Yes. You might use your fame to push it all a little further."

"That's a good idea," Ginny said.

"I think by notoriety the professor meant your tendency – alarming to most people above you – to simply ignore orders when you want to. You might release information – selectively. Tidbits for the press. Keep them hungry." Amanda suggested.

"You have a devilish mind beneath that beautiful exterior," Toledo replied.

Amanda paused before saying, "I will take that – cautiously – as a compliment."

"You should leak," Ginny said. "After all – there's still some wandering around out there who at the very least raped, and most probably took part in, the Ramirez murder."

A sobering statement, Toledo thought.

"Have they passed it by the victims yet?" Amanda asked.

"What do you mean?" Toledo replied.

"They will need their permission before accepting any such deal."

"The victims are dead," Ginny said.

"The family of the victims."

"That means the Shaffers." Toledo said.

"And the family of Caroline Ramirez," McMannis said. It vaguely annoyed and embarrassed him how easily they seemed to get forgotten. *Or perhaps because I talked to her mother – that made it more real for me.* McMannis wondered whether there was a racial component to it as well. Clearly, none of them was overtly racist. It was more that they felt more comfortable among the educated, white and affluent territory of the Shaffers, than the poorer Oakland regions that Caroline Ramirez once called home.

"What do you think they will say?" McMannis said.

"The Shaffers? God knows. The Ramirez family? They'll be conflicted. They will be tempted to agree, just to put the immediacy of this nightmare behind them. But manslaughter? How could it be called that? What justice is that for her?"

"At times, you can be almost eloquent," McMannis said.

"Thank you."

"Almost," the professor reminded him.

"The choice made by the Shaffers may be revealing," Toledo continued. "Who says what. Who disagrees."

He received another text.

"And guess what? They are asking us to persuade both families to accept the deal. McMannis to Mrs. Ramirez again, with Amanda. I will join Ginny at the Shaffers. And we are to just find out what they want – not persuade them."

Thirty-Seven

The early evening light was fading when they arrived at the Shaffers. An hour later, when Toledo called Mrs. Shaffer to ask what time was convenient, she immediately invited them for dinner. Toledo suggested that might invade their privacy too much, but she merely laughed, saying they were almost family friends now. *Some friends,* Toledo thought, but accepted politely.

The table was set haphazardly, and the empty spaces once occupied by Mark and Dr. Shaffer loomed ominously. But it was the absence of Ruth, and her bustling, near-manic energy that was most noticeable. The kitchen was untidy and vaguely dirty, with canisters, plates and pans spread out haphazardly. Asian food had been delivered, one dish of which had been put onto a plate, but the rest was still in its boxes.

"It seems that we have a choice to make."

"Yes," Toledo replied.

"It is a rather unusual choice."

"Yes."

"I don't think anyone else at this table – beside you and … your friend here – actually believe that my husband harmed anyone. We are victims – yes, but victims of who?"

Ophelia swept her hair back from her face and mumbled something quiet and unintelligible to Teddy, who smiled slightly. Hermia was toying with her food, apparently resolved not to look anyone in the face. Alan was lost in his child's world, humming, and playing with the food in front of him.

"The question is – do you want a full trial for your husband. Do you want …?"

But Toledo ran out of words. It was too strange a situation. He had asked victims whether they wished for a trial many times before, but none with the convoluted relationships that greeted him as he looked around the table. Everyone, except for the child Alan, was both an undeniable victim and a potential perpetrator, and he did not relish interrogating Mrs. Shaffer on her knowledge of Ophelia's children. Somehow, he doubted that she would implicate herself, yet the evidence was too overwhelming to deny any knowledge.

"Detective, maybe you and Ms. Ginny would like to stay the night? The roads here are treacherous in the dark, and the fog is thicker than normal tonight."

"We don't have …"

"We have plenty of room, and any necessities can easily be provided for."

Toledo looked toward Ginny. She shrugged slightly and widened her eyes, as if to say, *who knows what we might find out?*

It would be highly unconventional but as Toledo broke so many police conventions, this was hardly a limitation.

"We would love to," Ginny said, and after a questioning look from Shaffer, Toledo said, "sure. That would be great."

"Good. That settles it. These questions can be discussed at more leisure. After our minds have had time to process them."

"You mean when we are asleep?" Ginny asked.

"Exactly," the psychologist replied.

"You believe that dreams are actually a way for the brain to filter out what is irrelevant from the useful? And to solve problems that are too difficult for us to think about consciously?" Ginny continued.

"I do."

She is playing the eager student well, Toledo thought.

"I thought that the latest theory is that dreams are just random images – thrown up by the reptilian part of the brain, as it desperately tries to understand what the human part of is experiencing." Teddy said. "Nothing more or less."

"There is that theory, yes," Mrs. Shaffer replied. "But I do not subscribe to it." She said the last words with a definitive tone, and Toledo noted her perfunctory and dismissive attitude toward her son with the gentler handling of Ginny.

There is no love lost between any of them.

"Anyway, I think Dad should get everything that's coming to him if he did kill Mark and that girl," Teddy said, then wound a noodle around his chopstick thoughtfully.

"He did not," Mrs. Shaffer replied icily, "and I thought we said we weren't going to talk about that at the dinner table."

"No, *you* said that," said Teddy. "We did not agree to anything."

Mrs. Shaffer continued to gaze at him venomously.

"I think it would be better though, don't you?" she said finally.

"Whatever," Teddy replied and downed a full glass of wine with one gulp.

They all ate in silence for about a minute. It was Ophelia who spoke first.

"I keep thinking Ruth is going to come in at any moment and start collecting the dishes, and then announce what is for dessert like we are in some old English stately home."

Some of them glanced at the kitchen door, as if the very thought would somehow conjure up the dead woman.

"But she won't, ever again," Ophelia said.

"Hermia what do you think of it all?" Teddy suddenly asked.

"Wh … what?" The girl stuttered.

"What do you think of it? Do you think that Dad should be tried for murder, or should he just be sent to prison for manslaughter?"

"I …"

"Come on, you've gotta have an opinion of some sort."

Hermia looked helplessly at her mother, then at Mrs. Shaffer, then back to Teddy.

"I'm sorry," she said as she got up and ran out the room.

"That was a shitty thing to do," Ophelia said, glaring at her brother.

Teddy poured himself another glass of wine.

"I know," he eventually said. "I'm sorry. I just miss her, that's all."

"Jesus!" Ophelia snorted the word in disgust.

Mrs. Shaffer toyed with her food, then dropped her fork. Toledo had been surprised to see that she was not using chopsticks. The sign of a less affluent childhood perhaps.

"I might suggest that the ladies should retire, so the gentlemen can smoke," Teddy said ironically in a faux-European voice. "But as that would leave myself, Detective Toledo and Alan – perhaps that wouldn't be too good an idea."

Mrs. Shaffer sighed loudly.

"Do you count yourself as a gentleman, detective? I certainly don't. Count myself, that is. Not you. I don't know about you. And Alan? Well, I could say the jury is out on Alan, wouldn't you say?"

229

Ophelia stood up, slid her chair in, and walked slowly out of the room toward the door that led to the balcony. Mrs. Shaffer left in the other direction, heading toward the far wing of the house that held the master bedroom suite. Toledo nodded toward her, and Ginny nodded back, rose and followed Ophelia.

"Dividing your attack. Good tactics." Teddy said.

Toledo smiled thinly at him, and strode out of the room, catching up with Mrs. Shaffer within a few seconds.

"Detective. Would you like to talk?" she asked.

"I would."

"Come in," she said, holding the door to the suite open.

It was the first time Toledo had seen this part of the house, despite his numerous visits. As with the rest a sullen sense of decay and foreboding pervaded, although one strange object hanging on the wall caught his attention. In a quite large picture frame was a piece of card, with a CD split into several pieces stuck onto it.

"You are wondering about that?" Mrs. Shaffer asked.

"Yes, I ..."

"That was my husband's contribution to a summertime project we had many years ago – when the children were still children. We all produced a work of art, and then we judged the winner. That was his work of art."

Toledo looked at the frame once again.

"And very interesting it is," he said finally.

"No, it isn't. It's a piece of crap. I think Jerry deliberately made it so bad to make fun of the whole idea. He never liked arty people. Thought art in general was a big con trick. He couldn't even bring himself to compliment the kids' art."

She gestured to three pictures further down the wall. One was a sunset scene. The next two superheroes – *or are they supervillains?* – having a fight. The third, and the only one that Toledo looked at for more than a second, showed a young girl looking out of a window. A man and a woman were kissing in the background. All you could see of the girl was the back of her head, but something about its angle and the way her hands were holding onto the window ledge told the viewer that she was anguished by what she saw.

"That is Ophelia's," Mrs. Shaffer said, reaching out and touching it gently. It was one of the only times Toledo ever saw a tender gesture within the Shaffer family.

"Mark's was the fight?" Toledo asked.

"Yes – and Teddy spent about ten minutes on the sunset. He has always put the least amount of effort into everything he does. Come, sit down."

Toledo sat on an old but very comfortable leather couch. Mrs. Shaffer took the chair nearby and sighed as she relaxed into it.

"I nursed Ophelia and Teddy in this chair, Detective. Does that seem strange?"

"Strange?"

"I am far away from them now. We can sit at the same table and talk, but it is as if we are not even speaking the same language. As if we are shouting at one another from a great distance, and only catching a few words out of many."

"I suppose."

"I feel you are basically a good man, Detective. You are superb at your job. It is a difficult job, one of the most difficult. And one you are not rewarded much for. But you do it because someone must. You have – I hope you don't mind me saying this – sacrificed a lot to be so effective at your job. You have never married?"

"Once for a couple of years in my early twenties, but we were just kids really…" Toledo said after a pause.

"Children?"

"No children."

"But…" Then she stopped and looked closely at Toledo. He felt as though he was being inspected.

"But you feel as if your cases are your children?" she asked eventually. "You look after them, nurture them, and see them grow to their full potential – then send them out into the world, or rather, into a courtroom, so they can mature and blossom …"

"That's a strange way of describing a murder case…"

"But aren't I right? Don't you see them in that way?"

Toledo paused for a moment.

"Yes, I suppose you are right."

"So, the interrogation you are just about to do with me is …"

"It's a conversation, not an interrogation."

"Oh. Why?"

"The only time I call it an interrogation is when I have read someone their Miranda Rights. When they are under arrest."

Mrs. Shaffer laughed a little.

"Oh please, Detective. I may have been raised in a small apartment the whole of which could be fit into this room – but I am not quite that naïve."

Interesting that she would bring up her background in that way. She sees it as a weakness.

"Well, whatever we call it – I do have some questions for you."

"Right." Mrs. Shaffer sat up straighter in her chair, as if now performing the role of one-being-interrogated.

"First …"

"But perhaps first of all I should tell you all I do know – to save you time." Mrs. Shaffer said.

"OK."

"I am aware that Teddy was having a sexual relationship with Ruth. I didn't like it, but as Jerry said –

what could we do about it? They were both consenting adults."

"You could have fired her."

"But that wouldn't have been fair. Her … her time with Teddy did not affect the standard of her work. She was an excellent cook and housekeeper."

"OK."

Silence for a few seconds. She was clearly struggling with what must come next. Toledo let her take all the time she wanted.

"Then there is the other thing," she said eventually.

"The other thing?"

"Mark and Ophelia."

"Yes. Mark and Ophelia."

"About fifteen years ago – when Ophelia was about sixteen, and Mark fourteen – I became aware, *we* became aware, that something was not right between them."

"Was not … right?"

"Yes. Was not right. A glance, a touch, a feeling, an atmosphere. At first, I thought we must be imagining it. Then I thought that it had something to do with their age. Maybe some transferred, delayed Oedipal and Electra Complexes that somewhere landed on the sibling, rather than the parent."

She paused, sighed.

"I thought they would grow out of it. But then – they didn't. It developed."

Toledo was silent. He knew a rookie detective would jump in here and ask why the Shaffers had not intervened, why they had not told someone, why they had not put a stop to it – all of which would lead to the woman clamming up. All he needed to do now was to listen, a silent witness and vessel into which she could pour a guilty conscience a decade in the making.

233

"It was only a year later that we had any direct evidence. I walked in on them kissing in the lounge. They covered it up very well, but facts – as someone once said – are stubborn things. And the fact was that I had seen my two oldest children passionately kissing one another ..."

While he did not want to disturb her flow, Toledo felt that he must.

"Two oldest? You mean Teddy is the youngest?"

"Yes. He looks older than them, doesn't he? Too much drink, and too many drugs. They take a toll. So yes, I caught my children kissing one another and had I been a minute later – who knows what I would have seen?"

Probably nothing, Toledo thought. *They had the date room for that.*

"It was then that Ophelia got pregnant with Hermia. Yes, Detective, I knew all about that from the beginning. The adoption story seemed sensible at the time – God knows why. The boy she had slept with at the party did not want anything to do with her..."

The woman's voice faded away. Toledo watched her carefully, wondering whether he should push her a little further. *Does she really believe that Ophelia got pregnant with some random guy at a party?*

"When it became clear that ... that something was wrong with Hermia ... I ..."

"You what?"

"I started to wonder."

"Wonder what?"

"Was the supposed boy at the party actually my own son, down there in that damn room?"

"What did you find out?"

"We didn't find out anything."

"You never did a DNA test?"

"No . . . no DNA test. We didn't want to know perhaps. We convinced ourselves that Hermia's father was

234

a drunken pickup. We accepted it as a fact – willed it into being as a fact. And we said it so long that we ended up believing it."

For a moment, it sounded almost probable to the detective.

"And anyway – soon after Hermia was born their . . . their relationship ended. Both started dating other people. We assumed it had just been a stage that had run its course. A terrible, perverted stage – but one with a natural beginning, middle and end."

God, she really doesn't know about Alan.

"And that is all you know?"

"Yes. That is all I know."

Toledo was about to tell her but decided to ask about the date-room babies first.

"What do you know about the . . . the collection in that little section off the date-room?"

"You mean the babies?"

"Yes, the babies."

"As is the case with many doctors, my husband is an eccentric. He has eccentric tastes. Eccentric interests. One of them is genetic mutations that cause abnormalities in fetal development. The more extreme the better."

From the way she had given this information, Toledo knew she was telling the truth.

"Mrs. Shaffer – why do you think your husband raped and killed Caroline Ramirez, killed your son Mark and then Ruth Beringer?"

"I don't think he did."

"The evidence – at least for Caroline – is irrefutable."

Mrs. Shaffer laughed slightly.

"That one piece of evidence is the part that I *know* for sure is not genuine. It can't be. Believe me, Detective, it cannot be…"

"What do you mean?"

235

"My husband has not been capable of ejaculation for many years. About fifteen, in fact."

"Fifteen?"

"Yes – almost exactly around the time we discovered our children were in love with each other."

Again, experience told Toledo that she was telling the truth.

"Mrs. Shaffer – because a man cannot ejaculate in one situation, with one person, does not mean that he cannot in any ... with anyone."

She laughed again, a tendency that was grating on Toledo.

"Detective, he could be given the best sex this side of heaven and not ejaculate."

"Really?"

"Yes. You know, I am very surprised at the lack of information you all have. You have reputation of being something of a Sherlock Holmes, you do know that?"

Toledo just raised his eyebrows and shook his head.

"I was just joking about his impotence starting when we found out about Mark and Ophelia, Detective. Well, it did start then – but not for that reason. Detective, fifteen years ago my husband was diagnosed with virulent forms of testicular and prostate cancer. He had his testicles and prostate removed."

Toledo closed his eyes for some time. *Just when it is starting to clear up, this case becomes even weirder – and we get further away from the truth.*

A hope glimmered before him.

"But when suspects are processed at the jail, they are physically checked ..."

"Prosthetics, Detective."

"Prosthetics?"

"Yes. My husband has prosthetic testicles. I persuaded him that it would be good for his psychological recovery from his surgery."

And the hope was quickly removed.

"But that doesn't mean that he did *not* kill that girl, or Mark and Ruth for that matter – it just means it cannot have been his semen found in her, or on her, or whatever…"

She almost sounds sorry for me.

"But it definitely *was* found both in and on her. There is about a billion to one chance that it is not his semen."

"Well, maybe. I just know it didn't get there through him ejaculating. Any more than you could have a menstrual period, Detective. He simply is not equipped."

"Then where did it come from?"

"I don't know – but not from inside him."

At least not at the time of the murder, Toledo thought. *At least not at the time of the murder.*

Toledo took out his phone and sent a group text.

EVERYONE BACK TO BERKELEY. NEW INFORMATION. EVERYTHING ON HOLD.

He received an OMG from Ginny, a WHAT A SURPRISE – NOT!!! from McMannis, and an ambiguous, I THOUGHT SO ☺ from Amanda.

"Just what the doctor ordered." Ginny said after she read the texts.

Toledo just smiled and sank back into the seat, taking a well-earned nap as the uniform drove them back to Berkeley.

Thirty-Eight

The rest wanted to descend immediately on Berkeley City Jail, to ask why Dr. Shaffer confessed to at least one murder that he could not have committed. But Toledo nixed the idea. They would wait for the DNA results to come back, hopefully for the last time. Three days passed, then a week, and still nothing. On the eighth day, Amanda called them all together.

"It's like this. Its best if I drew a diagram of it all."

"Be my guest." Toledo replied.

"Well – here goes."

Sample	Location	Identity	Chances
Semen 1	Stomach/anus	Mark Shaffer	1 in 2 billion
Semen 2	Stomach	John Doe 1 (Jerry Shaffer father, Mark Shaffer half-brother)	1 in 800,000
Semen 3	Vagina	John Doe 1 (Jerry Shaffer father, Mark Shaffer half-brother)	1 in 800,000
Semen 4	Vagina	Jerry Shaffer	1 in 2 billion

"So, what we have is three, not four individuals. One of them, Semen 1, is definitely from Mark Shaffer, or there is a 1 in 2.5 billion chance that it is not him. Semen 4 is from Dr. Shaffer."

"Well, that's great." Toledo said.

"Semen 2 and 3 are from the same individual, who I call John Doe 1. The interesting thing is that he is Dr. Shaffer's son, and Mark Shaffer's half-brother."

"With the information we now have, how can Dr. Shaffer's semen have been found on Caroline?" Toledo said.

"Someone must have put it there. I bet at some point Dr. Shaffer gave a sperm sample, and our John Doe 1 got hold of it. And put it on Caroline."

"And we are now sure that he is the Mark's half-brother?"

"Yes, absolutely."

The group paused for a few seconds, as they took it all in.

"So, who is John Doe 1, and why is Dr. Shaffer protecting him?" Ginny said.

"I think it all relates to that mysterious 'he' that Caroline Ramirez talked about in her last paper," McMannis interjected. "It's obviously not Dr. Shaffer at all. It is our John Doe 1."

"It is someone who knows our every move before we do," Toledo said. "Someone with access to a sample of Shaffer's semen."

"More than that - he is someone determined to kill off the Shaffer family, one by one," McMannis said.

They were about to break when Amanda held up her hand.

"How is it that the semen on Caroline matched the towel from the date room?"

"Maybe our John Doe 1 put it on the towel and planted it there. He wants to get at them from all sides." Toledo answered.

"That makes sense," McMannis said.

"OK," Toledo continued. "McMannis back to Caroline's mother – we have to go through everything she ever wrote on, read, or even thought about. Somewhere in there is our John Doe 1. He must be. I am going to visit Dr. Shaffer to see what is going on with him – why he is taking the rap in this way. The two of you," he said to Amanda and Ginny, "just hang loose for now. But have your cell phones on you at all times."

They all agreed, and half an hour later Toledo was sitting opposite Dr. Shaffer.

"Dr. Shaffer, I strongly suspect that you had nothing to do with any of these murders."

"You do?" the doctor replied quietly.

"Yes."

"Then you are dropping the charges?" the lawyer interrupted.

"Before that – do you know who our John Doe 1 is?"

By way of showing the different situation, Toledo had shown the doctor Amanda's diagram.

"I do not."

"Do you know how he got a sample of your semen then?"

"In the sixties, I took part in a study. Thirty dollars for a sample of your semen that would not be used during your lifetime. Thirty dollars was a lot in those days for a med student …"

"I see."

"I assume that somehow he got hold of that sample."

"He? I know you know who it is."

Shaffer looked at Toledo. His eyes told the detective that he did indeed know exactly who John Doe was but made it equally clear that he would never give up the name.

"You didn't have any other children, other than the ones you have here?"

"Not that I am aware of, no. But a man can never be completely sure of that, can he?"

"Doctor, the rest of your family's lives are at risk. Your life is at risk."

Shaffer merely shook his head slowly.

Toledo received a text.

"Well here!" he shouted at the doctor. "Perhaps this will stir your memory!"

He thrust his phone across the table.

OPHELIA SHAFFER DEAD. APPARENT SUICIDE. SAME LOCATION AS BOYFRIEND'S SUICIDE.

"My God! Oh, my God!" Dr. Shaffer said and burst into heaving, whole-body sobs.

"If he does remember anything, just let me know," Toledo said to the lawyer and waved him away when the man started talking about the need for immediate release.

"I think he will safer here, don't you?!" Toledo said as he left the room.

He didn't wait for an answer.

Chapter Thirty-Nine

According to old case photographs, Ophelia parked her car in the same spot as her boyfriend's had been found.

"Well, at least she made sure," said one of the uniformed officers present.

Toledo frowned at this comment, but a quick glance explained it.

A hose led from tail pipe into the back window, and yet the woman had shot herself too. Quite a large caliber

241

handgun in the temple. Her head was virtually obliterated. Much to Toledo's annoyance, Detective Spander – who he had last seen at the site of Mark's drive off the road – was peering into the car.

"Toledo," he said, not looking up, "this is a beautiful car – shame she made such a mess of it."

"You are such an asshole sometimes, Spander," replied Toledo.

"Well, as you have arrived from the Gods, I guess I will leave," Spander said. "By the way, I don't think it was a suicide."

"Why?"

"No powder burns on the hands. She shot herself without a gun in her hand."

For all his bullshit, he's a good detective, Toledo thought.

"Thanks," Toledo said as the other detective started back toward his car.

"Don't mention it."

Spander got into this car then drove near to Toledo. The window buzzed down.

"I have one question though."

"And what is that?"

Toledo felt he was going to regret his brief spurt of friendliness.

"If your John Doe gets rid of the rest of the family – do you think the car will go into a police auction? A scrub inside and some detailing and she'll be as good as new."

He paused for a moment.

"The car I mean."

"I know."

"Well, later then."

Spander needlessly spun his wheels and sped off.

Toledo saw the CIS cars making their slow way up the hill. He decided to go to the Shaffers' house and persuade them to leave. *If this is murder*, he thought as he raced down the slope, *more of them have been killed than remain alive.*

The lights of police cars were reflecting off the fog long before he arrived at the Shaffer address. Brief, ghostly glimpses of blue and red slowly became brighter and more frequent, eventually materializing into actual vehicles as he rounded the corner where the driveway led down to the house. Two cars at the top, two at the bottom. A couple of unmarked detective vehicles, and his own made seven. As he walked down the driveway, he saw a news van arrive, its satellite dish strange against the primitive wilderness of the Shaffer trees.

Mrs. Shaffer was sitting in the lounge, her hand in a female uniformed officer's. The officer was speaking quietly to her, and the psychologist occasionally nodded her head with little smiles.

Just humoring her, Toledo thought.

"Ah, Detective, I have been expecting you."

"Mrs. Shaffer. I …"

"No need, Detective, no need. Ophelia has taken her own course. Now we must take ours."

Toledo had seen many reactions from family members to a loved one's death, but never one quite as cold and detached as this. *Perhaps she is just frozen by shock, beyond emotion.*

"Mrs. Shaffer, I think it would be prudent if you and the rest of the family left this house. Until we know exactly what happened with Ophelia, I feel you are in considerable danger. You should be in a safer place."

She paused for a moment, sighed then raised her arms as if to show the emptiness of the room around her.

"I am quite willing to leave. But the others are gone."

The uniformed officer looked up as Toledo moved closer.

243

"What?"

"The other members of my family are already gone. Teddy took Hermia and Alan earlier today."

"Took them where?"

"Somewhere safe."

"Mrs. Shaffer, do you know the whereabouts of your son and grandchildren?"

"I do."

"And they are safe?"

"As safe as can be."

Toledo sighed and sat down on the couch.

"Mrs. Shaffer, you are aware that two members of your family, and two others closely associated with your family, have been murdered over the last few months?"

"Yes, I am. It is all I ever think about. But you say the person responsible for at least three of those murders is in custody."

"Your husband is no longer a suspect and will be released soon."

All Toledo could see was a sharp mind calculating the consequences of a new situation. No relief, no sadness, no fear, no anger – just simple, cold calculation.

"My husband is no longer a suspect?'

"He is not."

"And when will he be released?"

"Soon. Mrs. Shaffer, did your son take your grandchildren before or after the tragic news about Ophelia?"

She paused for a moment.

"I am not completely sure. This afternoon has been a blur."

"It was not in reaction to the news?"

"No. We just felt it would be better if he left. If they all left."

244

"You . . . you and Ophelia were going to stay here alone?"

"Yes."

The uniformed officer stood up and led Toledo gently away.

"She is obviously suffering from severe shock," said the officer. "She is just answering the questions automatically. You won't get any sense out of her."

I won't get any sense out of her, but not for the reasons that you think, Toledo thought. He went back to the couch and sat back down. Mrs. Shaffer looked at him glassily, as though not really seeing him. Toledo sighed and closed his eyes.

Thirty-Nine

Amanda talked to the mother downstairs while McMannis rifled through more of Caroline's papers. While there were some oblique references to Mark and his family, they were not as specific as the previous notes had been. He turned to the computer and switched it on. The login automatically came up with "Caroline". He thought for a moment and wrote "Ramirez" as the password.

It was correct.

Not very security conscious, this girl. Too trusting. A trust that may have led to her death.

Most of the documents were college-related – an outline of a university career that started promisingly but became mired in a life simply too complex for concerted studying. Caroline had been drawn into the world of the Shaffers with all the certainty of prey caught by a constricting snake. The family had slowly tightened its grip until escape was impossible. In retrospect, it was poignant and sad. Yet also inevitable.

She did not stand a chance.

There were hundreds of documents and time was of the essence. McMannis scanned the filenames for possible leads. He remembered that in those far-off days when people kept phone numbers in books rather than on their cellphones, those with something to hide often placed them in the unusual, seldom used letters such as Q and Z. Even trained investigators tend to ignore those letters instinctively. He felt a bit foolish doing so, but he scrolled down to the very end of the file list and found a single name under Z, "Zoo Animals".

He clicked on the file, half expecting to be embarrassed at the mundane document that he was sure would appear.

He was wrong.

"Last Friday night, Mark and I went to the date room and made love. The rest of the family was out, but he insisted on going down there, even though his own bed is much more comfortable, and there isn't that smell up there. But the date-room it was. Near the end, I could swear I saw someone looking in through a window. I saw it over Mark's shoulder, and as he was moving on top of me at the time it was just a brief glimpse. When we finished, I told him about it. At first, he said that it must be the ghost that several people claimed to have seen in the area, then said he was joking and that I must have been imagining it. I wasn't. I know I wasn't. We went upstairs and slept in his bed. Ruth brought us breakfast in bed – bacon, eggs and some gross sausage that was white and only half-cooked. Mark told me it was German sausage. I told him it looked like a sausage that had been cut off someone. We spent most of the day watching movies and lounging around. That evening – back to the date room. Why his obsession with making love there? He was rougher this time, but I still enjoyed it. He fell asleep and I just lay there thinking. Once again, I sensed someone watching us, but saw nothing in the window this time. I decided to go outside and look around a bit. I walked down the path a little way then saw something in the trees – a small red light flashing on and off. It took some time to find it, but when I did it was a camera. A small, obviously very expensive camera pointing straight at the date room. Just as I was about to take it down, I heard something further into the trees and went after it. Something, or someone, was moving very carefully away from the house – down to the bottom of the yard. I stayed far enough behind not to be seen, but close enough to keep track of it. I got to the edge of the garden and saw a man walking across the lawn toward the neighbor's mansion. I stayed hidden in the trees. I was just about to leave when the man came back out, but this time with a large bundle slung over his shoulder. He must be very strong as he walked easily with it across the lawn. He pushed it over the fence, picked it back up and then went further into the trees with it. I followed him for a little way, but then went back to the Shaffer house when I thought he had heard me. Just as I was leaving, he dropped the bundle on the ground. Mark was still asleep when I got back. I was going to tell him about what happened but couldn't. Will write more next week."

McMannis frowned and wondered for a second what the "bundle" could possibly be.

He texted Toledo.

CAROLINE RAMIREZ DISCOVERED THAT BEN SPIES ON THE DATE ROOM. SHE ALSO SAW HIM MOVING A BODY-SIZED BUNDLE FROM THEIR GROUNDS DEEP INTO THE SHAFFER FOREST. SUGGEST SEARCH OF THE SHAFFER GROUNDS IS NEEDED.

He added the "body-sized" to get Toledo going, but it didn't seem too far-fetched.

About half an hour after Toledo received the text a canine unit arrived at the Shaffer home. It took the cadaver dog less than five minutes to find the body. It was not fully buried, but the cloth it was wrapped in, and the leaves had somehow kept out the air. The body had been mummified rather than decomposed. Toledo asked for a photograph of the face so he could "stay with Mrs. Shaffer". The uniformed officer, who was not fooled, went away mumbling something about a homicide detective being squeamish of a corpse being like a doctor afraid of the sight of blood.

"Death transforms a face, but I'd know those features anywhere." said Toledo as he looked at the picture.

It was Tony, the long-lost lover of Ben Williams. The man who had supposedly just returned home.

Toledo reached for his radio.

"I need an APB on Ben Williams, suspected of homicide …"

McMannis, who had been whisked by helicopter back to the neighbor's residence, wryly considered how long Toledo had spent with the new homicide suspect without apparently noticing anything beyond an eccentric curiosity about strangers.

"Caroline Ramirez saw Ben Williams discard the body. And unknown to her, she was observed as she was looking." McMannis said.

"The camera …!" Toledo said, as he finished reading the document on Caroline's computer. "It was good you brought this along."

"I thought I should go through every document on it. Just in case."

McMannis looked around the room.

"Are we the only ones here? Where are the rest of them?"

"Mrs. Shaffer is in there with a uniform, being counseled on her grief."

"You don't sound too concerned."

"Not too sure how much *she* is concerned in fact. Not very much grieving going on."

McMannis waited for a moment, then said,

"She has lost her son and daughter in the space of a few months. Perhaps she is just overwhelmed."

"No. There is something else."

They both looked up as the sound of a helicopter swooping in suddenly enveloped the house. A searchlight briefly flashed outside. Toledo got up and looked out of the window.

"A news copter. That's all we need!" Toledo said.

"Where are the others?" McMannis asked, as the helicopter sound faded away.

"Well – Teddy, and Hermia, and Alan all left for … what did they used to call it … parts unknown? Yes – they left for parts unknown earlier in the day."

"Doesn't Mrs. Shaffer know where they went?"

"At first, she said that she did. But when I asked her again, she wasn't so sure."

"Jesus. This is all falling apart," McMannis said.

Toledo looked at the photo again.

"And I spent several days in this poor man's house – under the nose of his murderer."

"His guest cottage, to be precise."

Toledo smiled sardonically and McMannis returned the favor.

"How old do you think he is?" Toledo asked.

"Mid-forties? Perhaps a bit older. He has looked after himself."

"Come on," said Toledo. "We are going to pay a visit."

The detective got up and strode out of the door. McMannis knew better than to ask for an explanation when he was in this mood, and just followed along. The two of them fairly sprinted up the driveway, along the road and then back down the gentler slope to Ben's residence. Both were out of breath when they arrived.

"When this is all over … we must … get fit again," Toledo said, taking breaths between each phrase.

"Who said we were ever fit in the first place?" McMannis asked.

Toledo grabbed the doorhandle, but McMannis stopped him.

"Shouldn't we at least ring the doorbell?"

"I have strange premonition that he's not in," the detective replied.

"Just to be sure."

"Be my guest."

McMannis rang. There was no answer.

"The next question is whether we have probable cause to enter without a warrant," McMannis said.

"Who is the detective here?"

"We don't want it all thrown out."

"I heard Mrs. Shaffer say she was worried that Ben might hurt the children of the family – specifically Hermia and Alan. I mean, he's killed two of them already."

"One. Mark."

"Two. Mark *and* Ophelia. My least favorite detective pointed out there were no powder marks on her hands. And it fits in with his pattern of overkill."

"What?"

"He kills people more than once. Stabbing and insulin, insulin then car crash, insulin then broken neck then fall down a ravine … hose in the tail pipe then shooting – it's just a variation on a theme."

"Interesting."

"Well, are we going to carry on standing out here playing with ourselves, or are we going inside?"

As an answer McMannis opened the door and led the way. There were a few lights on, but the house was mainly dark. It was immaculate, with not an object out of place.

"This place never looks lived in," Toledo said with lowered voice.

"I suppose in many ways it wasn't. Ben Williams was already dead, if you accept the theory that murderers are

251

simply destroying something they loathe within themselves when they kill others."

"I don't, but it's a good theory."

They walked along a corridor and into an office. A notebook computer was open on the desk.

"Shall we?" McMannis said.

"I'd better look into it – in case there is any question about the probable cause," Toledo said. He switched it on. Both the login and password sections were blank.

"Try "Ben" for the login and "Williams" for the password," McMannis said.

"No-one would be stupid enough to ..."

But the detective was silenced by his own keystrokes as the computer desk-top appeared on the screen.

"Woah!" Toledo said.

"What is it?"

"Recognize those eyes?" Toledo asked.

The desktop background was a close-up of a pair of eyes. So close that just the eyes and the bridge of the nose were visible. McMannis looked carefully for a few seconds, then nodded.

"Dr. Jerry Shaffer."

"Precisely," Toledo replied.

"Let's see what this is," the detective said and clicked on a file named "Faces". It contained several GIF files, each one with a name from the Shaffer family. He clicked on ALAN. A head shot of Alan appeared, but it began to morph slowly through a series of stages until Dr. Shaffer's face appeared. When Toledo clicked on Shaffer's face, it morphed back into Alan's. He tried each of the other files, with the same result.

"Jesus!" he said quietly.

He clicked on the final file. The one marked simply "?".

Ben's face appeared, before slowly fading into a white screen. A two second delay then Dr. Shaffer's appeared on the screen with a deafening, maniacal scream. The sound filled the whole room and both men jumped backwards. As the sound echoed into silence, Shaffer's face dissolved into Ben's. But the changes were not complete. Ben's face became steadily younger, through his twenties, teens, childhood and back to a single, fuzzy image of a baby. The screen then went black.

"I think I understand," Toledo said.

"You do?"

"The Shaffers had another baby. One long ago. About forty-five years ago. When they were still poor students and could not afford a child. So, they adopted him out."

"You mean Ben is Dr. Shaffer's child?"

"Yes."

"And decades later he came back – moved in next to them – started a whole life – for what?"

"Revenge maybe. Perhaps it was a complete accident at first, a complete coincidence. Then he discovered, somehow, who the Shaffers really were. He saw the life he had been denied as a child…"

"But he is far richer than them…"

"Or maybe he *became* that rich to get close to them."

"A murderous Gatsby?" McMannis suggested. "And the green light at the end of the dock is the flickering lamp in the date room."

Toledo clicked on the "?" file again. This time they were expecting all that would happen, and they looked at the images with analytical eyes.

"That comes from a very sick mind," McMannis said as the screen became black again. "A dangerous mind."

"One moved from a potential to a very real threat. There is no member of the Shaffer family who is safe."

Toledo rested back into the chair and closed his eyes.

"And his wealth explains how he got hold of the semen and the insulin. And I have experienced first-hand how expert he is at getting in and out of places unseen. I guess that his lover found out what he was doing, and so he was disposed of. Caroline? She was simply in the wrong place at the wrong time. Then he saw a way of using her death for multiple purposes. He had been planning some . . . some way of destroying the Shaffers – but what better way than to have them destroy themselves? Or to make it seem that way. Mark and Ruth were merely tools – ways of convicting Dr. Shaffer and sending him to prison for life. I'm not sure about Ophelia though. Perhaps he has just decided to kill all of them – now several are gone already."

"You are mostly correct, Detective. But not entirely."

The gentle voice came from behind them, and both men turned quickly.

Ben Williams was standing about ten feet away, a gun levelled at Toledo's head. Instinctively, Toledo reached for his gun, but Ben moved a step closer and shook his head.

"Please, Cassius. I like you. Don't make me shoot you. Just slowly, very slowly, take your gun out and place it on the floor."

Toledo hesitated for a second, then complied.

"I believe you are not armed, Professor. But – just in case …"

He stepped forward again and patted McMannis down. The professor met the detective's eyes for a second, but Toledo shook his head ever so slightly at the silent inquiry. Ben Williams obviously knew what he was doing. It would be too risky.

"A wise decision," Ben said, as he stepped back from McMannis. "There is no need for this to get messy. Sit down, please."

McMannis did so, and Ben sat on a couch nearby. He was apparently relaxed but the gun was held steady on them.

"So. These great reckonings in little rooms . . . I am quoting here . . . these great reckonings in little rooms are coming to an end. Gradually, but inevitably."

They were silent for a few seconds.

"You are Dr. Shaffer's son?" asked Toledo.

"Yes. I am, as they used to say, his bastard son. I am the result of a drunken party and conveniently empty bedroom. I was not adopted, however. I was raised by my biological mother. Unfortunately, she was not quite as successful as my father. She married when I was about eight, and for the next seven years I was raped on average . . . two to three times a week. My stepfather raped me. Then when I was fifteen, he disappeared."

"He disappeared?" Toledo said.

"Yes. Just like that."

"You ... made him disappear?"

Ben just smiled at that. He laid the gun down on the couch, picked up a bottle of wine. He then took a corkscrew and rather casually opened it. As he did so, he spoke.

"You are wondering, Detective. You are wondering whether you would have time to overpower me before I could get hold of the gun. You are wondering that. But – and I think I know you well enough…"

He had poured a glass of wine for himself by this time, and the gun was firmly back in his hand.

" – to know that you would not be stupid enough to try it. This is not a book after all. You cannot heroically overpower the mad, bad faggot and save the children and grandchildren, and thus the day…"

His eyes widened slightly, and his voice rose. Both McMannis and Toledo saw the violence that he was only just keeping in check.

"I would never call you that," Toledo said quietly.

"What – mad and bad?"

Toledo shook his head.

"Oh – you mean *faggot*? How quaint! Oh, I know you don't like men like me, Detective. Not because of what we do in bed, but because you don't quite *get* us. Isn't that right? That marvelous intuition of yours falls to pieces when you see the wiggle in our walk. Is that it?"

Toledo just looked down at the floor.

"And you professor. The quiet but unconventional one. What do you think of me? The self-loathing homosexual perhaps?"

"Not at all. I am a folklorist, not a psychologist."

"Folklore is a kind of mass psychology is it not? A study of societal delusions?"

How sad he used his mind in the way he has, McMannis thought.

"I suppose you are right. But it is more …"

"What did you mean about saving the children and grandchildren?" Toledo asked, louder than before. "I'm sorry to interrupt. I was just wondering."

Toledo received a text.

"Do you mind if I read this?" the detective asked.

"Be my guest. Just don't reply."

Toledo took his phone out of his pocket.

"Wait – I would like to read it."

Compliant, Toledo handed him the phone.

"Your pass code, please."

"Two, two, five, one, nine, six, four."

That's not it! McMannis thought, but mysteriously, the number opened the phone.

Ben read the text. It was from Amanda.

256

DR SHAFFER WAS JUST RELEASED. HIS
LAWYER FILED A WRIT OF HABEAS CORPUS
AND THEY HAD TO LET HIM GO. HE IS ON HIS
WAY BACK HERE.

"Good news?" Ben asked, handing the phone back to
Toledo.

"Not exactly."

"Well, I am sure it all evens out in the end. Oh – and
what was your question?"

"I was asking about you saying that we might save the
children and grandchildren. What did you mean by that?"

"I was planning on bringing them back here for the
climax and finale, Detective. But as I have been
interrupted, I am not too sure."

"Too sure of what?"

"Teddy refused to co-operate – he actually came here
to ask whether he could borrow one of our houses up in the
Sierra. I couldn't have him go that far, so I had to leave
them … had to put them in a secure place. One that is
underground. Not too sure about the amount of air down
there. They might be a problem with the tide too."

"The tide?"

"It's rather annoying. This wasn't meant as a clichéd
cliffhanger – will the detectives get there before the air runs
out? About as much suspense as whether the sun will rise
tomorrow. I really did just put them there for safe keeping."

"Alan is just *six years old*." McMannis said.

"I know. It's a shame. What is that phrase that the
military use? Collateral damage? Yes, that's it. Collateral
damage. I don't intend to harm him. But if that is the only
way at getting at the legitimate target, so be it."

"Alan is just a small child." McMannis said.

257

"Yes. I know. And I wish you wouldn't keep on saying it. I was a small child too when I was abandoned and then raped. I died a little death every time, Professor. A *petit mort*. But a real one in this case. At least his death will be quick, and relatively merciful."

"But surely ..." McMannis continued, but a look from Toledo silenced him.

"Again, you should take your friend's advice."

They were silent.

"Where do we go from here?" Toledo asked.

"What would you suggest?" Ben answered. "You know something about children being sacrificed for the wrongs of adults, don't you Cassius?"

"What?"

"Your father, Cassius. He took that leap, didn't he? Kind of cliched ... to jump off the Golden Gate Bridge."

Toledo stared at the man's face. It was a cold mask.

"I was raped as a child by my stepfather – and you were abandoned by your real father, Cassius."

"Please, just call me Toledo."

"Abandoned by your father, Toledo. Left to wonder why, always wondering why he didn't stay. Didn't face the music of his addiction. Do you think he regretted it? On the way down? Those three seconds that it takes to hit the water. Knowing that whatever other bad decisions you have made, that this is the worst. And nothing can be done about it. Not even by you, Cassius. Not even the great Detective Toledo can solve that question."

Toledo was silent again, and despite his fear McMannis smiled slightly at the strength his friend was showing in not taking the bait. Finally, the detective spoke.

"I suggest that you take us to wherever you have put Teddy and Hermia and Alan. We'll release them. We then take you to get the help that you so obviously need."

Ben paused for a moment before laughing, and then said,

"What help would that be, Cassius?"

"It is obvious that you were – damaged in some way by what your stepfather did to you. Damaged so that you see things – in a different way, a distorted way. When he … touched you … he hurt you inside as well as out."

"Detective, I knew there was a reason that I liked you! You are so … polite. He didn't rape me until I was ten. I was lucky in that way. So yes, he *hurt me inside* – but I have been hurt more by others, all while enjoying the activity."

"You enjoy that?" McMannis said, unable to help himself.

"Yes. Oh, you think that I was 'made gay' perhaps – by being raped by a man as a child? That makes no more sense than saying a woman raped by a man when she was a girl made her straight. No, Professor, I was born gay. It is one of the few parts of my life that I am happy about."

"How did you find out who Dr. Shaffer was?" Toledo asked.

"When Tony and I moved into our house, and I looked for something to do. I was taken a break from theatre. I decided to find my real father. Hired a private detective. It only took him a few days. You can, I am sure, imagine my surprise when I discovered that I was living *next door* to him! Almost too much of a coincidence. But then life has a way of coming first circle, don't you find? I don't believe in a God exactly, but surely this was Fate talking to me – placing the good doctor, putting my father virtually within plain view."

Both Toledo and McMannis were searching their brains for any tactic that might draw him closer to taking them to where the family was hidden. But, as a psychologist had once said to Toledo, attempting to reason with a crazy person was like arguing metaphysics with a shark. Yet something had made Ben tell them about where he had put them, and that gave hope. If no part of him intended to rescue them he would not have bothered. *Or rather*, McMannis thought, *there is some tiny part of him that is not sure about killing them or allowing them to die. We just must uncover that part and make it grow.*

"I assume you are telling us all this because you have no intention of letting us leave here. Not leaving while alive at least." Toledo said.

"No," Ben said, and paused before saying, "I have no desire or intention to hurt you. You have not harmed me in any way. If you attempt to stop me – then it will be a different matter. But I don't think you will."

"Good. Can I ask you some more questions? To satisfy my professional curiosity?"

"Certainly."

"This is what happens to cheaters? Written on the wall?"

Ben laughed.

"Just part of the overall process of casting a confusing fog over events, Detective. I added the question mark at the last moment. Something told me that detail would infuriate the police the most. Then the pigs. Did you like that? Any reference to Manson is sure to complicate matters."

"And the multiple samples of semen?"

"I had acquired some of my father's semen long before. The same private detective who found him also discovered that he had given sperm samples. We live in a society in which any hint of sexual impropriety is a death sentence for a career – and all I had to do was wait to deposit it in a damning situation. I carried it around with me just in case. I had a little device made for me."

He reached into his pocket and brought out what appeared to be a cigarette lighter.

"This is not what it appears to be," Ben went on. "In fact, this outer casing is hermetically sealed – with an inner chamber of liquid nitrogen. And in that – a capsule with the semen."

He put the device down.

"When I discovered that Caroline Ramirez had been following me – had seen me dispose of him – the idea came to me. Of course, it was complete luck that Mark had already had sex with her that night."

"How did you kill her?"

"A massive insulin overdose when she was asleep. She never woke in fact. Never suffered."

"Then you decided that this was the time that you had been waiting for. The moment to implicate Dr. Shaffer in a sexual crime."

"Exactly. And wasn't it perfect? A moment of serendipity worthy of a Greek Tragedy. I could mix his semen with that of his son's – and, for good measure, could add some of my own. The stabbing, the message written in blood …. All part of the effect."

McMannis watched the two men uneasily. It was as if they were colleagues discussing their profession as equals. *But then, one cannot exist without the other. And Ben, while not meeting most of the criteria for a psychopathic murderer, at least wants the world to know about what he has done. He is speaking as if he is talking of someone else. Remote. Detached. As if he is already dead.*

"And the planting of his semen on the towel? The allegation that he masturbated to his baby collection?"

"Again – even though you now know he never did such a thing, those images will remain with you, Detective. The thought is so disgusting, so degrading. So powerful. Just the allegation makes it partially true – in your imaginations at least."

"Like a play," McMannis said.

"Exactly, Professor, like a play."

"And Ruth's death? And Ophelia's?"

"They were part of the process. Just after I killed Caroline, I decided that each member of the family must die separately. Physical death. Emotional death. I planned to kill Alan and Hermia before the others, but the plan was interrupted. The final moment though, the actual end – that has been set for several months. How we were to get there became a little unsure at times. But eventually the fog cleared."

"And Tony?"

Toledo had been wanting to ask this for some time.

"Tony?"

"Did he find out about what you were doing?"

"Oh no, not that at all. It was just . . . when the plans were set . . . I realized how terrible it would be for him when it all came out. If he had anything, my dear Tony had class – and all of this is so – classless, don't you think?"

Toledo just looked at him.

"I thought so anyway. He would be utterly humiliated when he was the only one left. Like the character at the end of a Shakespeare tragedy who is left alive, left to explain what has happened. But Tony was no Horatio. He deserved to be in the spotlight. There on the stage. Central."

Toledo sensed the man was coming to an end. *And what happens next?*

"I have left my blocking for *The Homecoming* in the upper drawer of my desk. Maybe the production will be canceled. Or maybe it will run for months as a sellout. You can never tell with theatre. Now gentlemen I think … you know, I have been half-expecting one of your girls to come flying through a window, or least the door. Wasn't it a female student who saved you all before?"

"One had a big part to play in that. Yes."

"But no girl this time. I'm kind of disappointed. Anyway, I would love to carry on with our little chat, but time passes, time passes …"

Just as Ben glanced at his watch the door at the back of the room burst open and three uniformed officers ran in, guns raised. They were led by Carlisle.

"How sad. No girl at all!" And with that Ben disappeared out the other door so fast that McMannis barely saw him move. Suddenly he was looking at an empty chair and Toledo was standing up, picking up his gun and pointing at the empty doorway through which Ben had vanished.

"You took your time," complained Toledo.

"Someone – a detective that will go unnamed – said that it was a joke," the oldest officer said.

"How did you know?" McMannis asked.

"I have a panic code on my phone," Toledo replied. "It does open the phone, but also sends for the police."

"So, where did he go?" McMannis asked.

None of the other men answered, but they soon heard the whir of helicopter blades turning faster and faster until the vehicle soared into the sky.

"He can fly a helicopter?" McMannis said.

"Apparently," said Toledo, holstering his weapon.

"Did he say anything?" Carlisle asked.

"He said plenty, but most importantly I think the rest of the family are somewhere at the coast."

"There is … a lot of coast near here." McMannis replied.

"Thank you for that information," Toledo said, then smiled as Amanda walked into the room.

"Any ideas?" the detective asked. Silence, and then Amanda ran into the room.

"You are late for the party," Toledo said. "If you had arrived on time Mr. Ben Shaffer would have been a little happier."

"Ben Shaffer?"

"I'll explain later. So – any idea where he might have gone?"

"Actually, I do. Remember those grains of sand that I found underneath Caroline's toenail and on Ruth?"

"Dimly."

"Several weeks ago, I received an e-mail from the lab saying they come from a very specific type of material that was dumped on the beaches about forty years ago. The beaches in only one town. Half Moon Bay."

"And you just tell us now!"

"I only just read it – somehow it made it into my Junk folder."

"The wonders of modern technology!" McMannis said.

Toledo took out his radio.

"Is anyone tracking the helicopter that just took off from here?"

There was static, then a voice said, "yes, and it seems to be heading south."

"Any chance of a ride?" Toledo asked.

"We'll be there in two minutes."

Forty

"Where exactly is he going?" Toledo asked, frowning as he looked out at the lights about a mile away from them.

"He is certainly taking the scenic route," McMannis replied.

Ben had flown all the way to Half Moon Bay but then had mysteriously tracked inland before coming back toward the coast.

"Perhaps he is just wasting our time," McMannis continued.

"But he knows we are following him. And he is going where we know the family must be. He probably knows that we identified the sand found on the bodies. Maybe he deliberately put it there."

"Detective, aren't you crediting him with a little too much intelligence?" Amanda asked.

"Try talking with him. He's frighteningly intelligent," McMannis said.

"If I get a chance, I will."

Ahead of them, the helicopter started to descend toward a makeshift helipad on one of the multimillion-dollar estates below them. It was one with direct access to the ocean.

"He's going in," Toledo said.

"Thank God for that!" Amanda replied.

As their helicopter started to lower, McMannis nudged Toledo gently.

"I don't want to piss on your parade on anything, but where are *we* going to land if he lands there?"

Toledo looked at Amanda and the uniformed officer that had accompanied them.

"Pilot, did you hear that?" he asked.

"Certainly, I can get you down right be the roof of the house. There is a fire escape you can go down. Look – right there!"

The three of them looked. All were doubtful.

"You want us to jump out of this thing onto that roof, then down that ladder, then tackle Ben?" McMannis asked.

"Something like that," Toledo replied.

Ben's helicopter landed.

"We have to get down fast!" Toledo shouted. A comment that he soon regretted as the pilot made a steep bank and appeared to be diving straight into the house. But the helicopter ended up hovering about six feet above the roof.

"I can't go any further down!" shouted the pilot.

Toledo, McMannis and Amanda all looked at one another, then away.

"I'll go first then," Amanda said and jumped out, landing as if she had just taken a single step down a staircase. McMannis was next. He landed awkwardly, twisting his ankle. Toledo was last, and soon he and Amanda had sprinted to the ladder and made their way down to ground level. Toledo rushed to the helicopter. Strangely, the rotors were still running fast, and Ben had not got out. The detective hesitated for a moment then opened the door.

"Hi there!"

A stranger. Not Ben.

"Where is Ben!?" Toledo shouted.

The pilot shrugged,

"Where are the children?"

"I don't know – no bullshitting you – I don't know. I just fly him when he wants me to."

"Do you have keys to the house?"

"Yeah, that I do have."

Toledo led him to the house, talking fast.

"I need you to listen to me. This could be the most important minute in your life, so concentrate. Your employer is a mass murderer. He has called four people in the last three months. He has kidnapped three others and put them somewhere either in or around this house. He says they are going to die unless we find them before the tide comes in. If you don't tell me everything that you know, you will probably spend the rest of your life in prison. I will make sure that your life is hell while you are in there. Do you understand?"

The man just nodded, looking shell-shocked.

"I know he spends a lot of time in the cellar and doesn't allow anyone else down there. Really, that's all I know."

The detective took the keys from the pilot and opened the door. The pilot man showed them the door to the basement. Within seconds Toledo saw that a large crate and the rug on which it stood were the only things regularly moved. The box was empty and easily moved. Toledo pulled the rug away. A small trap door was underneath.

"There it is," the detective said. He opened the door and peered down into the darkness below. McMannis had now joined him, closely followed by Amanda. The pilot was last.

"I can't go down there," Toledo said flatly. "I'm claustrophobic."

"I would, but …" McMannis said, lifting his injured ankle as explanation.

"I'll go," sighed Amanda, and lowered herself through the door, down the crude and rusted ladder that led the way down to a small tunnel.

"I'll join her," the pilot said. "Just in case."

"Thanks, my friend," replied Toledo quietly. "I know that you didn't know."

"Just makes me sick to … but that can wait."

The pilot levered himself down the ladder and joined Amanda. The coroner looked up and Toledo tossed down the flashlight that was sitting neatly on a bench a few feet away from the trapdoor. Amanda and the pilot crawled their way along the tunnel. It seemed like miles but was only about a hundred yards. Seawater was dripping down from the ceiling as they reached the end. Another door, latched from the outside but otherwise unlocked. Amanda opened it.

"No!" Hermia screamed as her younger brother started crying.

"Where have you been all my life?" Teddy said with a twisted smile.

Within a few minutes, they were all out of the house and making their way back to the helicopter. The police copter was still hovering above the roof.

"I'll take mine back, so he can land and take you off safely," said the pilot. He got into the helicopter and soon it was a small shape moving east.

Once airborne Toledo radioed back to the Shaffer residence, trying to tell them that Ben was surely hiding somewhere on the grounds. There was no reply except for static.

"Do you copy? Do you copy?"

Apparently not. It took about twenty minutes to get back to Hillsborough. All the passengers were silent, lost in the deep fatigue that comes with a crisis averted. Toledo slapped his own face a couple of times as they approached the house.

"Time to roll."

The helicopter descended onto the now deserted residence that Ben and his lover had so carefully maintained. The blades soon stopped and as Toledo opened the door an eerie silence enveloped them. *Somewhere he is watching us*, the detective thought, but a glance around revealed just the brightly lit lawns stretching away to the still, dark shapes of the trees in the Shaffer yard.

All was quiet.

Forty-One

Amanda led Hermia, Teddy, and Alan to an emergency fire vehicle. They were in remarkably good spirits, and physically unharmed. The coroner returned slowly to the helicopter, where McMannis and Toledo were standing, a little way apart and not talking.

"So, what now?" she asked.

"Once we find Ben – and that will be soon enough I should think - the case will be over. Or as over as something like this ever is." Toledo said.

"Do you want to go over there?" McMannis said, gesturing toward the Shaffers.

"Not really. But I suppose we must."

They went up the driveway and onto the road. Each was a little more attentive than normal but would not admit it to the others. Their usual banter in such situations had vanished and they were isolated within their own, lonely thoughts.

If anything, the police presence up on the road and at the Shaffers had increased. Several different departments, the sheriffs, the FBI and emergency vehicles of every type were crowded onto a road that could barely take two cars passing one another. Somehow even the Coast Guard and Homeland Security had joined the part.

"If we can't solve the case with logic and intelligence," Toledo said, "perhaps sheer numbers of cars and uniforms will work."

They received nods of recognition and an occasional smile as they walked along the road, before trailing in and out of the cars that ran all the way down to the Shaffer house. Some of the Shaffer cars were there in their usual positions, forlorn reminders of a family life now irretrievably vanished.

The surviving Shaffers were waiting in the lounge, sitting in facing chairs and silent.

"Well, let's hear what the happy couple have to say," mumbled Toledo, receiving a slight smile in acknowledgment from McMannis. Amanda either did not hear the comment or ignored it.

"Dr. Shaffer," Toledo said, extending his hand.

A clumsy gesture, but well meant, McMannis thought.

Dr. Shaffer regarded the hand ironically.

"I am still charged with allowing incest to occur, Detective. I am not quite *clean* yet."

"Under the circumstances, I very much doubt whether those charges will still be brought."

Shaffer paused for a moment, before shaking the offered hand and saying, "a small relief. Have you found Ben yet?"

Toledo shook his head.

"Your uniformed officer was most informative on the basic outline of what happened – that he is being charged with the murders. And that I am not. But the rest was totally confused."

Toledo smiled.

"Who was Ben?" Mrs. Shaffer asked, her voice much louder than her husband's.

"You mean you don't know?" Toledo said.

"If I did, I wouldn't be asking."

"Ben . . . Ben was your husband's son. His *other* son."

"His son?" she turned to her husband. "Is this possible?"

Toledo, McMannis and Amanda exchanged glances that suggested – *God, she really didn't know!*

Momentarily, Dr. Shaffer was totally at a loss. Then a glint of recognition came into his eyes, and he lowered his head, shaking it.

"But it can't be, it can't be ..." he said.

271

"Can't be what?! Can't be who?!"

"About the time we met – there was a girl – I don't even remember her name. A girl at a party. A few months later she came to me and said that she was pregnant. Dad paid her off, bought her a vacation in Mexico. She promised that she would deal with it."

"That's not the way Ben told it," Toledo said.

"Well, that's the way it was. I did receive a phone call about two years later from a woman claiming to be her. Claiming to have had my son and wanting to know what I was going to do about it. I put the phone down. I assumed it was an attempt at extortion or a joke. I had just qualified."

"And he would be the right age?" Toledo asked.

"Yes."

Silence for a few seconds.

"This still does not explain why your long-lost child decided to come here, and start murdering us," Mrs. Shaffer said, her voice barely disguising her anger.

"He felt abandoned. He didn't have much of a childhood," McMannis said.

"The professor understates as ever," Toledo said. "Your son was sexually abused by his stepfather for many years. He told us – just before he ran out – that his father had disappeared when he was fourteen. Wouldn't say whether he made him disappear."

"Would you blame him?" Dr. Shaffer said.

"Not really."

"Did he come here looking for me, or did he just accidentally come across us?" Dr. Shaffer asked.

"He claims it was a complete accident. He was looking for his birth parents but had no idea they were his neighbors."

"Now Mark is dead. And Ophelia is dead. And that poor, stupid woman Ruth is dead." Dr. Shaffer sounded almost sad. Almost.

"And Caroline Ramirez," McMannis added.

"Yes, the Ramirez girl. I almost forgot … "

But his sentence faded away, and he looked at the floor.

"Dr. Shaffer, why were you prepared to take the rap? To take the fall and go to prison when you knew that you were not responsible?" asked Toledo.

Dr. Shaffer smiled at them in a melancholy, wistful way.

"I thought that perhaps it was justice. I knew – when I discovered, when we discovered …", this was said to his wife, who looked away, "when we discovered that Mark and Ophelia were more than brother and sister – I knew that we should stop it. Separate them immediately. Make sure that they never saw one another again."

"Why didn't you?"

"Mark guessed what we were trying to do, and threatened to run away…"

Mrs. Shaffer laughed slightly at this.

"Which did not worry us too much. But then Ophelia came to me one evening. Late at night in fact. She came to me and said that if I tried to separate them, she would let everything out. Make their relationship public. Suggest that the incest went beyond … just the two of them."

McMannis remembered the incident with the apple and the blood. Toledo and Amanda, neither of whom knew Ophelia as well, doubted Shaffer's story.

"I knew that something terrible would happen if I let it continue. Had to happen. We cannot go against our nature that much and get away with it. I knew that it would fall on all of us, not just the two of them."

"You knew who Hermia's father was?"

"I did."

Mrs. Shaffer, who had been staring at her husband with increasing disbelief and anger, leapt up and left the room

273

crying, cursing under her breath. Amanda was about to follow but Dr. Shaffer put up his hand.

"Don't. She'll be all right. I think it is mostly for show. She knew as well as I did. She just never admitted it, either to herself or me. But she knew."

"And it carried on year after year?"

"Yes."

"In the date room?"

"Yes. Mostly."

"But Dr. Shaffer, was there nothing you could do? You are a successful man. Virtually unlimited resources. You have influence."

"I am a successful man whose children have sex. Whose children love one another. Whose children have their own children. I remember drinking down there one night, drinking a lot, I remember thinking that it was unfair to their children because they only had one set of grandparents…"

"What?" McMannis interjected.

"Think about it, Professor. I was both their paternal and maternal grandfather. A kind of sick two-for-one special!"

"Jesus!" McMannis said under his breath.

"I hoped they would grow out of it. That when they met other people, they would tire of one another. But that didn't happen. Well, they *did* meet other people, but those relationships just confirmed how much they felt for one another. That story about the night that Alex was conceived…"

"You know about that?" Toledo asked.

"My daughter remained a teenager in many ways until the day she died. She wrote a journal and put everything – and by that, I mean *everything* - in it."

"Which you read," McMannis said, bizarrely aggrieved at such a comparatively mild betrayal of trust.

"Which I read, yes Professor."

"I still don't see how this …?" Toledo went on.

"When Caroline died, and then Mark had his crash, and … it all fell apart – I didn't know how it had happened. But I *did* know why. It was the evil returning. The evil that I allowed to happen. It was the serpent slithering out of the dust, scraping its way along the ground toward me. Toward us. Toward the whole family. And I knew that if I could take the rap, as you put it, then I should do so. How it happened did not really matter to me."

"But to spend the rest of your life in prison?"

"Detective, I have at the most a year to live. Didn't you know that? I'd prefer to spend it here – but if it was in a prison, so be it. I am trapped in the hardest prison of all – one that no-one can escape – the prison of time. And only death holds the keys."

They were silent. McMannis broke it.

"One thing has been worrying me. Why did your German maid attack us?"

Dr. Shaffer laughed for a second.

"That was part of the overall trick I had invented. In my youth – yes, I was once young once – I wanted to be a magician. In the end, I used my hands in other ways – the magic of saving lives. But that desire always remained. Magicians work through diversion – they catch your eye with one hand, while doing the trick with the other. Ruth had been told to act in as bizarre a way as possible if any official presence made itself known in the house. Our secrecy could be explained by the fact that we are so eccentric. That we had a screaming German madwoman in our employment. She had done it once before, when a code inspection officer came to complain about the trees. She ran him off too, while naked, I believe. We never heard anything else about it. He was probably too embarrassed to tell anyone. And who would have believed it?"

275

"Your daughter once said the same thing to me," McMannis said quietly.

"What?"

"About no-one ever believing it."

"Didn't you suspect something about Ben when you met him? About his interest in your family?" Toledo asked.

"He never showed that much interest, beyond the normal comments about how we don't really maintain this place the way everyone expects."

"Didn't you take him to small claims court once, accusing them of throwing grass cuttings into your yard?" McMannis asked.

"Yes. But that was more Mark's doing. He liked playing games with people in that way. Stupid really. But I think he gets bored." He paused. "Got bored."

Dr. Shaffer looked over at some family pictures on coffee table by the couch. One of the whole family, then one of Mark and Ophelia as mid-teens, their arms draped around one another. McMannis glanced at the photograph. Without knowing what they were to one another it was an innocent picture, but the truth imbued the photograph with darker tones. *But was there ever an innocent moment between them after that first kiss? Were they ever really brother and sister?*

Dr. Shaffer stifled a yawn and looked back to Toledo.

"Detective, I am very tired. Could we continue this conversation tomorrow?"

"By all means."

"You are welcome to stay if you want. We have many spare rooms now." And with this last comment he laughed. It was a sound that all three would long remember. One utterly sad and knowledgeable. Full of pain softened by irony.

"Well…" the doctor said, but his voice petered out. He turned, looked out the window and smiled again. "Good night to you all." He shuffled toward the doorway, then turned, and raised his hand slightly in farewell. He left the room.

"That was strange," McMannis said. "He's aged about twenty years in the last few months."

"I almost feel sorry for him," Amanda said.

"Yes," Toledo replied. "But we must remember what he allowed to happen."

"Do you think that Ben was right?" McMannis asked.

"About what?"

"About those images burned into our mind. About what he supposedly did down in the date room. What he is meant to have done to Caroline. Does the very accusation in some sense make it real?"

"God, I hope not," Toledo said. "But you are right in one way. He *is* a very strange man. If you saw him on the street, you would think he was a little crazy. Dangerous even."

"Oh Toledo, you see everyone as dangerous!" Amanda interrupted. "It is in your nature!"

"And a good nature to have for a detective."

They were silent for a few seconds.

"Where do you think Ben is?" McMannis asked.

"Somewhere out there," Toledo answered, gesturing toward the total darkness outside the large windows the ringed the room. "No use looking for him till morning."

"Dogs?" McMannis suggested.

"Somehow, I think he'll have that covered. So – obviously we can't stay here to sleep – but perhaps we do need to in order to …"

"What?" Amanda said.

"Protect them?" Toledo answered quietly.

"Every uniformed police officer – and all emergency personnel of any sort - within a thirty-mile radius is somewhere on this property. Hell – even Homeland

Security got in the act. Half of them are sitting in their cars on the road right now."

"That's what I mean." Toledo said.

"What is?"

"If you were Ben, wouldn't that be a challenge? To get at this house and the people inside it even when it is completely surrounded by police?"

"I assume the house itself has been totally searched?" asked McMannis.

"Naturally."

"But how well could someone really search this place? Have you noticed how people just appear and disappear without warning?" the professor continued.

"What are you saying – hidden passages? Secret rooms?" Amanda asked ironically.

"I don't know," replied McMannis, sighing deeply.

"So, you said we couldn't sleep here. But what can we do?"

"We can ..."

But Toledo never finished his sentence as it was interrupted by a massive explosion outside. They ran to the window and looked out just as another one occurred. The two police cars at the very top of the driveway were on fire and the previously almost sleepy and tranquil atmosphere was transformed into one of chaos, rapid movement, and fear. Police officers, sheriff's deputies, firemen and paramedics ran frantically here and there, some toward the burning vehicles and others away. McMannis watched in horror as one man ran to the top of the stairs that led down to the date-room, tripped on one of the loose planks, grabbed hold of the banisters and then plummeted the twenty feet to the ground as they gave way. *I always said that would happen to someone*, the professor thought momentarily, then inwardly cursed.

Another explosion, this time deep in the vegetation that spread toward Ben's property.

A car near the house now burst into flames. One of the Shaffer luxury vehicles. *What a waste of money*, McMannis thought. He watched as an officer who had been standing by the car ran away from it, his shirt on fire. Strangely, so strangely, he seemed to be moving in slow motion. *He should put that out.* Then he saw who it was – Carlisle. And then the professor turned toward Toledo, who was violently tugging at his sleeve.

"Ian! Ian! You've been hit! We've got to get out of here!"

It was only now that McMannis noticed the taste of blood in the corner of his mouth and reached up to find a massive gash that ran from his forehead to his chin.

"The glass got you!" Toledo shouted, as he half-pulled, half-dragged the virtually non-responsive man toward the stairs that led down to the front door.

The glass got me. What glass? One of Ben's glasses?

"Let's get the hell out of here!" Toledo said, taking McMannis by the shoulder and helping him down the stairs. When they were halfway an explosion occurred within the house. Somewhere so close that they felt the percussion of air, focused, and intensified by the narrow walls as it knocked them down. Both Toledo and McMannis gained consciousness to find themselves being pulled unceremoniously by the legs – and by Amanda - down the pathway, away from the house. Soon they got to their feet and staggered toward the welcoming darkness of the trees, as the conflagration spread rapidly behind them.

As they crawled away, and sat at the edge of the densest vegetation, two people passed them by, inexplicably heading into the house. McMannis recognized them as Teddy and Hermia, still dressed in the muddy clothes they had been wearing when imprisoned by Ben.

279

Teddy was rushing, but Hermia seemed more reluctant. Teddy was saying, "Got to save them! Got to save them!" A mantra that pushed them forward toward what must surely be death.

McMannis looked toward Toledo helplessly.

"Aren't you going to stop them?"

Toledo turned and made as if to go after them, then hesitated. The flames were starting to fly out of the house, and areas previously untouched were now infernos. The detective got to his feet, and was about to return to the house, when he felt Amanda's hand gently but certainly on his shoulder.

"Cassius. There's nothing we can do. Nothing we can do."

The flames grew and ripped through vegetation made tinder-dry by the summer drought. Windows exploded, and the shattered glass melted.

Suddenly, high in one of the rooms, a figure appeared against the flames. A woman. Mrs. Shaffer. She raised her arm as if to attract attention, as if about to cry for help. She was joined by a much larger figure that Toledo guessed to be Dr. Shaffer. Behind them stood Ben, a gun raised toward their heads. As Toledo watched he saw another person leap from behind Ben, but the man simply stepped lightly to one side and the figure, now revealed to be Teddy, fell to the floor.

The fire started to lick around their legs and their clothes spontaneously burst into flames. The family disappeared, and Toledo realized that the floor must have given way below them. Ben looked as though he would fall backwards but raised his arms in triumph as the flames gathered up on his body. Finally, he toppled forward, doing a slow somersault as he plummeted into the burning timbers of the first floor.

He was gone.

Epilogue

Toledo left the details to others.

After a couple of weeks' vacation, he went back to Hillsborough, and to the ruins of the house on the hill. Nearly all the vegetation had burned in the fire, and the structure itself had vanished save for the ghostly remnants of the outside walls. There was a hint of rain in the air as Toledo walked carefully among the earth, burned wood and occasional household items.

As he made his way slowly, something glinting caught his eye. It was under a large timber that had fallen at a strange angle across some bricks. Toledo tried to lift the timber but failed and in frustration kicked at it. The beam disintegrated, and after removing a few bricks, he discovered what had been shining so brightly in the general gloom of this wasteland.

One of the bottles.

One of the babies.

Toledo crouched and looked carefully at it.

Something was very wrong.

The head had two eyes, a nose, a mouth and two ears. Two arms and two legs. Even the umbilical cord was attached.

A perfectly formed, perfectly normal baby.

"I'll be damned," he said, and lifted the bottle up from the ground.

"If I didn't know better, I'd think it had a little smile on its face." McMannis said, as ever closely following his friend, "

"We never did find out where they all came from. Some from Japan – but the others?"

Toledo turned and looked at the professor, shook his head slightly and gestured toward the driveway that led up to the road and their car. McMannis glanced up toward his car, where his wife and the little boy Alan were waiting. He put down the bottle carefully, almost reverentially.

"Fostering that boy was the best thing you have done," the detective said.

They walked further through the ruins of the house.

"We never found Hermia's body." Toledo said.

"You didn't?"

"Nope."

"Could it have just disappeared in the flames? Burned up?" McMannis asked.

"Perhaps. But all the other bodies were found. The bones hadn't even started to melt. I have heard of other cases like that. Sometimes fires are far hotter than physics suggests they should be. Bodies burn to dust as if cremated."

"You are a font of strange information, Cassius."

They stopped and surveyed the wreckage for a little longer.

"Did you hear the strangest thing about all of this?" asked Toledo.

"What?"

"There were other human bones found here. Not belonging to any in the family ... or to any of the babies."

"You mean ... others were killed here?"

"I do. I guess we will never know who. The Shaffers took their secrets with them. Their serpents in the dust."

"Their what?" asked McMannis.

"Their serpents in the dust. It's a Bible verse that Dr. Shaffer quoted when we visited him the first time. Then he said it again, on that last night."

"Now I remember. He didn't look the type to read the Bible."

"No, he didn't." Toledo replied quietly. "And in the end Officer Carlisle was the only one … only one outside of all this … to die."

"Yes."

"Did he have family?"

"Not that I know of."

McMannis looked at Toledo and from the sheepish look guessed that the detective had not even inquired. The loss of Officer Carlisle, who would now be alive had he not run across Toledo on that first day, was something that had barely registered with his friend. But the professor was wrong.

"No – no family. Not here anyway. A grandmother in Scotland was all he had left. I took her the ashes last week. She didn't seem to care that we weren't sure … they were his. I suppose some of it may have been."

McMannis was about to say that this was unlikely because of the sheer volume of things, and people, who had burned that night.

But he didn't.

The two men stood among the silent ruins. McMannis felt vaguely annoyed that he had not been told about the unidentified bones before. More so that Toledo had taken Carlisle's ashes to Scotland. But he was used to it. After a case like this closed, Toledo disappeared into more conventional homicide investigations, leaving McMannis out in the cold. Sometimes, sitting in his university office, the professor felt that his whole involvement in the case was merely a particularly vivid dream - one that he had woken from, and which had then vanished like the bay mist on a summer's morning.

"Doesn't your wife want you to take a break?" Toledo asked. "With your … new situation?"

"She has mentioned it. But wasn't serious. I think."

"Good. I couldn't imagine a better partner."

McMannis smiled, then said quietly, "you know what the worst part of this case was?"

"What?" Toledo asked after a little pause.

"Amanda is never going to let us forget that she saved our lives that night."

Both men laughed and then the silence descended again.

McMannis sighed, frowning at the bottled baby.

"What should we do with it?"

"With what?" Toledo replied, although he obviously knew what was being talked about.

"That." McMannis repeated, gesturing toward the bottle.

Reluctantly, Toledo looked over toward it.

"We can't just leave it here," McMannis said quietly.

"I know. But we can't take it up there like this."

McMannis looked around and saw a piece of clothing. A mere rag, but it served his purpose. He picked it up, then looked at it more carefully. It was a dress.

"I think this is what Ophelia was wearing to Caroline's funeral."

"It is? You have an eye for such things."

McMannis went to the bottle, carefully picked it up and wrapped the skirt around it. He held it slightly awkwardly, like a man unused to cradling an infant.

"Come on," he said. "Let's get out of this terrible place."

And they did.

The End

About the Author
Graham Dixon lives in Honolulu, Hawaii with his wife, a chihuahua and a small parrot. When not working on the Berkeley Mysteries series, he works as a fulltime psychotherapist. He was raised in England but has lived most of his life in America.

www.ingramcontent.com/pod-product-compliance
Lightning Source LLC
Chambersburg PA
CBHW051940220626
47052CB00004B/733